ABOUT THE AUTHOR AND THE NOVEL

Hi and welcome to my first ever novel, The Man Who Kept Dying. I am Vincent Ollivier and ever since I was a teenager, I had the idea that one day I would write a book that would take inspiration from all the stories that happened in my life. My younger self was adamant that I would put pen to paper when I am retired and have lived many experiences to recount, an autobiography of sort, if you like. If this sounds strange and perhaps even preposterous to you, you are not alone: even though I was aware that I had already been through more experiences than the average person my age, I was wondering if the whole idea wasn't a tad narcissistic. But just like a young child is adamant that they want to play the violin or become a doctor, some ideas just won't go away. It might actually be a wise thing to pay attention to them: the soul loves whispering ideas to the mind.

Although the idea was to wait until an older and wiser age to start this project, life remains full of surprises (some good and some less good) and in early 2018 I had an unplanned encounter with death – but do we ever plan such encounter anyway? Later in 2019, reflecting upon this event and my experience of it, I decided it was time to start writing not an autobiography, but a novel inspired by this very experience. Why the change of genre, you may wonder? Well, a fiction leaves room for more creativity, especially when one steps into the big unknown. The aim of this novel simply is to explore the 'What if?' of the continuity of our journey once we depart this world; I hope you enjoy the story and that I have done a good enough job of entertaining you for a moment.

As for the autobiography? Who knows, maybe I'll get to write it one day!

If you want to know more about me, connect with me on:
YouTube: www.youtube.com/@themanwhokeptdying
Instagram: @themanwhokeptdying

To Maura & Tim,

Thank you for being part of this journey.

I hope you enjoy the final product.

Love.

V. Olfivia

The Man Who Kept Dying

Vincent Ollivier

Copyright © 2023 Vincent Ollivier

ISBN 979-10-415-1094-8

First published 2023 © Vincent Ollivier

This publication must not be copied in full or in part, replicated to any degree or transferred to any third party without the explicit written consent of Vincent Ollivier.

YouTube: @themanwhokeptdying
Instagram: @themanwhokeptdying

Acknowledgements

Victoria O'Dowd	www.proofandcopyedit.co.uk
Tania Charles	www.taniacharlesproofreader.co.uk
Alexandra Thuillier	@alexandra_thuillier (Instagram)

All rights reserved.

We live our lives to the best of our ability, but in reality we are put on Earth to fulfil a mission; we have simply forgotten what this mission is because its resolution takes place on a different plane or in another realm. For reasons unknown to us, we live our lives unaware of this mission or of how to solve it. We believe we are awake, but truly we exist in a dream within another dream. The illusion is pretty real, though!

Chapter 1 – A sudden death

England, winter 2018

5.44 am

Darkness still enveloped the sleepy suburban district; the flashing light of the ambulance a faint blue hue on the living room walls as the crisp January air seeped through the front door which was standing ajar. Despite his extreme tiredness, Mika noticed the hairs on his arms rise. He had barely managed to sleep since first experiencing an unbearable stabbing sensation near his stomach three nights ago during dinner.

He was lying on his right side on the living room sofa, plush white cushions supporting his body which was stiffened by levels of pain he had never felt before. For the past two and a half days, he had endured cycles of ever-increasing convulsions, each wave bringing him closer to physical and mental exhaustion. His logic could not comprehend what was happening to him.

His wife had taken him to A&E within hours of the first symptoms appearing and he had simply been diagnosed with indigestion. He had argued with the doctor that there had to be a more serious underlying issue; to him, mere indigestion could not generate such levels of agony, could it? In spite of his protestations, the doctor had sent him home, certain of the diagnosis, advising him to call 999 should his condition fail to improve.

Forty-eight excruciating hours had since passed and his wife had resorted to calling the emergency services after another sleepless, pain-filled night. Something was amiss ... He could feel it ... Deep down, he knew he needed urgent medical assistance ... Now! Thankfully, the 999 operator had sent an ambulance to his home without delay.

The paramedic was now here, but for Mika the relief was mental more than physical. Having gone through the usual health questionnaire, the man in the dark-green uniform had just inserted a canula and started administering pain relief via a drip, then collected blood samples. He was now walking around the living room, taking additional notes on a large notepad. A heavy veil of silence had descended upon the minimalist decor, broken only by intermittent bursts of conversation overheard on the paramedic's radio.

Mika caught sight of his wife: she was standing next to the sofa, her body language giving away the alarm she was feeling. He could tell she too had not slept well over the past few hours. How could her world be turned upside down in an instant? How could her husband – early thirties, fit and active, no chronic health issues, follows a clean diet – be suffering so terribly, his health deteriorating rapidly from an unknown condition? He had never had any sort of indigestion in the twelve years they had been together. She was also struggling to make sense of what was happening.

At long last, he felt the painkillers coursing through his blood, the unpleasant heat they generated inside his veins spreading from his left wrist to the rest of his pain-stricken body. To supplement the injection, the paramedic placed a mask over his nose and mouth and briefed him on how to draw down the oxygen. As instructed, he took a few deep breaths and for the first time in many, many hours, he managed to relax his muscles, which had started to cramp under the stress of the repeated involuntary spasms. From his prone position, his focus adjusted to the tilted view of the coffee table and the plants decorating it: they all looked so peaceful and calm; he could almost sense an unspoken communication with them. It was a strange thought, perhaps, yet somehow it seemed natural that plants could talk too. A tingling sensation emerged from his core and with unrelenting pace spread across every fibre of his body, every remnant of strength progressively abandoning his usually resilient frame. His right hand, which had been holding the mask against his mouth, dropped away from his face in slow motion; his vision blurred, his eyes locked on to a point ahead but were seemingly lifeless; his muscular tension dissipated like a weightless cloud landing on the ground, his body loosening so softly, so subtly, that his wife and the paramedic did not notice it.

He did not realize it – but he had just died.

Chapter 2 – The meeting

Unknown location, unknown time

In a place where time is of no consequence, three beings convened and saluted each other.

'Hakuk, Adonnaï, please be prepared. Mika is fast approaching,' Askayah's calm male voice announced, getting straight to the point of the impromptu gathering.

'We will have to intercept him swiftly and apply a specific strategy. He has lost touch with his true identity in recent months,' said Hakuk, her tone at once assertive and feminine.

'Will he recall his relationship to us more quickly this time?' asked a second female voice. This time it was the cheerful Adonnaï who had spoken.

'As you are new to this, please follow my lead,' Askayah continued softly. 'I have handled this situation multiple times with him and on the last occasion he was relatively quick to recognize me and reconnect with our reality. You are nonetheless correct, Hakuk. This is a novel set of circumstances. Adonnaï, it will be down to him. We can only be gentle, indicate the correct direction and progress one step at a time. Just remember that he is not your average guest.'

'That, we have noticed!' the other two beings agreed with a firm nod.

Chapter 3 – Apprehension

Unknown location, unknown time

At first, there was nothing. It felt like he was waking up from a very long sleep: his mind was numb. He tried to recollect where he had fallen asleep, but his memories escaped him, as if he was suffering a brain fog. Opening his eyes, he discovered it was pitch black all around. He strained to hear: nothing but absolute silence. Where was he? He couldn't remember nor feel anything; was he standing or was he lying down? He couldn't tell. The sensation was akin to floating in space, in a dark void.

Was he alone? Despite the absence of light, he detected a presence close by. No, actually, there were multiple presences ... there appeared to be at least three subjects by his side. Funny how darkness can sharpen your other senses and make you realize that sight is only one of the five, he thought. But hang on ... *Which sense enables you to feel a presence or an energy?*

Without knowing how, he could tell that one of the presences was facing him and the other two were standing further back to his right. Were they observers? Could they see him? Perhaps they were in the same predicament. Or were they here specifically for him? Whatever his situation, being outnumbered, he felt vulnerable. He tried to move but his body remained unresponsive.

'Hello, Mika.' A male voice broke the silence, its tone solemn. 'Glad to have you here with us. We have a lot to catch up on since our last meeting.' The voice came from ahead, its deep resonance betraying an older man.

'Who are you?' said Mika, surprised by the enigmatic comment. As he spoke, he noticed the absence of an echo. The room must be well soundproofed. Had he been kidnapped and drugged? His numbness seemed to support this possibility. Once more, he tried to recall his last memory, but to no avail. If only he could remember how he had arrived here ... even a small detail ... anything ...

'I am afraid this is not information we can reveal to you just now,' said a female voice to his right.

Despite the negative response, the tone wasn't forceful. A nagging thought entered his head: he had heard these voices before but could not place when or where.

The voice on his right continued. 'We understand you are eager to find out who we are, as well as where you are, and we can assure you that both questions will be fully addressed as we progress. In the meantime, however, please understand that we wish you no harm. If you will, we would like to take you through a procedure that will facilitate your ... your recall, shall we say. This method involves us asking you a series of questions which you must answer. So, shall we proceed?'

Mika tried to relax his mind. Although he was unable to move his body, his thought processes were very much active and computing the information he had just received. Unfortunately, they failed to provide any clues as to where he was ... Why couldn't he remember anything? He strained to look back through the black void, incredulous at his situation. If only he could recall what had happened before finding himself in darkness with these strangers, strangers who not only appeared to know him, but who had been expecting him.

His thoughts were interrupted by the softer female voice of the third presence. 'Do you not remember anything, Mika?'

Mika found the query rather vague, which further irritated him. 'About what?' he snapped.

'Who we are?' said the old man. 'Your location? What happened to you before you arrived here with us? Who you *really* are?' His tone was tranquil, almost soothing. A long silence followed.

No, he had no answers to any of these questions. He scanned his mind for any recollection, anything that would help connect the dots together and fire up even the most trivial of memories. Not a single dot. Nothing. All he remembered was his name and his physical appearance: early thirties, tall with a slender and fit body, brown hair, hazel-green eyes ... Anything else about his life was as blank as an erased blackboard, at least to him.

But then, as the sequence of rapidly fired questions continued to ricochet around his mind, a sense of familiarity rose within him. Yes, he had been through a similar questioning before. A vague image surfaced, fuzzy, undefined. Was it the same procedure? The visualization was blurred, yet its contours started to take shape, like a camera lens adjusting to the correct focus. The hazy scene in his mind's eye had taken place when he was in his late teens ... the blue sky ... feeling upside down ... trying to place where he was ... yes, this was when he had last gone through a similar process, faced the same questions ... where? ... what? ... how? The memory sharpened and well-known surroundings took shape around him: that hot summer in Burgundy, the barn, his grandparents' car ...

But something was amiss ... He was not Mika – he was the *car!*

Chapter 4 – The car

Burgundy, France, summer 2001

The barn in which I was parked was adjacent to an old stone house. The thickness of the wall's soft yellow stones kept the inside temperature cool during the scorching Burgundy summer, which could reach temperatures of close to forty degrees Celsius under a cloudless sky. Thankfully, the evenings would more often than not experience a cooling storm, with blinding lightning bolts illuminating the passing clouds – not that I always had the opportunity to witness them. The barn's tall, solid wooden doors had been built and installed long before I was ever assembled in a factory far away. All around me were bales of hay as well as a ladder to access the mezzanine floor, on which more hay was stored. The lofty barn ceiling, which ran level with the attached house, was composed of a timber frame that supported rows of large burnt-orange slates. This construction was typical of the region, and I much preferred it to the small cement garage in which I spent autumn and winter, on the other side of France.

The owners of my summer home, and its adjacent house, had inherited it from their family, and the residence saw much activity during the summer months, when their children, grandchildren, cousins and other relatives came and went for a few weeks. Some family members even travelled from other continents. Through the years, I had seen the youngest generation grow up into strong, boisterous teenagers. Not that long ago, they were three young boys – Leo, Fred and Mika – sitting and bouncing on the grey velvet fabric of my seats, happy to be driven by their grandfather to the nearest bakery to buy French delicacies or to collect comics and books from the library a couple of villages away.

Ah, those villages. I loved being driven through them: the properties similar with their distinctive stonework and wooden shutters, yet different. Everything about them felt authentic and they were an ode to an era when taking your time was the way to enjoy life. Country roads flanked by vast sunflower fields, and vineyards higher up in the hills, linked the hamlets and completed the scenery. For me, this countryside held more appeal than the city where I spent the cooler months.

During the warmer months, activities tended to quieten around lunchtime. Such was the heat that people retreated to the coolness of their homes or to the shade of their gardens when the sun neared its zenith. Only during the evening would they dine under the bright-blue sky. The sizzling weather did not pose a problem for my driver and passengers, though: thankfully for them, I was equipped with air conditioning.

As the years passed by, my owners continued to make the trip across France, but as they got older they started to share the long drive with the eldest of their grandchildren, Leo, who now had his driving licence. The unintended consequence of this was that, once we arrived in Burgundy, I was involved in more activities than during my earlier years. The younger generation was eager to explore the area, and the freedom a car offered was unrivalled in comparison with the bicycles they used to ride in their childhood. Their appetite for exercise meant that they still rode them on occasion, but it was fair to say that I could transport the three young men from one place to another much faster and with much less effort on their part. With them, I explored places I had previously never had the chance to venture to. They loved to listen to the radio or to cassettes, the volume knob turned up high, and would drive me to locations where they could go bathing or play sports, especially basketball, on a regular basis. Interestingly, it was after one of those basketball sessions that my life took a turn for the worse – if I may put it this way.

Leo, the eldest of the three cousins, was followed in age by his brother, Fred, and their cousin Mika. They had siblings, but as the three boys were all born within two years of each other, they formed a strong bond over time and enjoyed spending their summers together. Besides, there was the ever-present competition within the trio, as would be expected among boys on the verge of adulthood. Leo would always sit behind my steering wheel and I would respond according to his handling. Mika, being the tallest of the three, would sit on the passenger seat, while Fred would sit on my back seats.

The three of them also displayed contrasting characters: Leo, the impulsive, fiery, dominant one; Fred, timid yet extremely intelligent, whose preference was to take a back seat in every situation; and Mika, the perfect middle ground between his two cousins. I always suspected that Mika possessed a different sensibility to all my other passengers: he saw life not with his eyes but through his feelings; he could perceive additional layers that most remained unaware of. I could tell by how considerate and gentle he was when he opened or closed my doors, sat on my seats or reached for my seat belts. Before stepping inside my cabin, he would always stop and take in the distinct smell of the barn: a blend of wood, hay and rich soil mixed with the oil and petrol fumes that my engine emitted. He also liked the smell of my upholstery and trim as it reminded him of his childhood and the anticipation of eating those tasty French pastries with his grandfather. Albeit as just a passenger, Mika became synonymous with me, with how I functioned. Few people are aware of the links between a vehicle's components, yet I could tell he had an innate connection with all of my elements, and he had long recognized that a car adapts to its main driver over time. The result of his finely tuned sensory perception was a profound dislike of the way his elder cousin drove me.

'You don't even let the fluids warm up before revving the engine!' he complained to Leo once again as we set off to the basketball courts, five villages away.

'Why bother?' the oldest of the trio replied with disdain, applying more pressure on my throttle to prove his point. 'Be happy that I can drive you around, *Mr Sensitive*. Without me, there'd be no basketball today, and you'd have to cycle to the lake to meet that girl you fancy. By the way, when are you making a move on her? If you could find the courage to talk to her, you might discover if she fancies you as well,' he added with a smirk.

Deep down Leo knew that Mika was right in regard to his handling of me. However, he felt compelled to show he was the alpha male. On the other hand, Mika knew that his elder cousin had a point about his being shy, but it was not that easy to approach a girl whose parents were always around – a challenge Leo would tackle without hesitation, most certainly charming the parents at the same time. During these exchanges Fred often chose to remain silent, lost in deep thought, staring at the outside world as it passed by.

From my point of view, it was true that Leo drove me too fast and I was not used to coping with such aggressive handling from a cold start. Although he took me nowhere near my limits, he did without doubt test those of the road, often demonstrating impatience when following a slower driver. The more he pushed, the more his confidence grew. Mika felt it and he did not approve of it. Should Leo continue in this manner, it would not be long before the three of them had an accident. As for me? I just responded to the input from my driver. Life was that simple.

Pulling up at a concrete car park, Leo parked me close to a large building which housed a public outdoor swimming pool, a fire station and four open sports courts. It was the middle of the afternoon and the sun was still high in the sky, my dark-grey metallic paint absorbing its heat. To avoid the temperature soaring inside my cabin, Leo left a gap between the tops of the windows and the door frames before locking the doors.

While I waited for my next trip, the boys played basketball. They practised their favourite players' moves until fully mastered. To analyse their balance and coordination, they brought a small camera with them. Although the young men would have preferred to scrimmage against other opponents, they were the only ones willing to show up in the middle of an August afternoon and endure the scorching heat radiating from the tarmac court. After a good hour of play, they rested in the shade of the basketball backboard and rehydrated, impatient to see the footage they had captured. But the viewing would have to wait until they could connect the camera to a computer.

With a bounce in their step, and full of banter, they walked back to me, changed their clothes – the car park was quiet and no one could see them stripped to their underwear – and threw their sweaty, smelly sports kit into my boot. Sitting down behind the wheel, Leo turned my ignition key and drove off, leaving the windows open for a few seconds before closing them and switching on the air conditioning.

'It's a wee bit stinky in here, isn't it?' he chuckled, catching the gaze of his younger brother in the rear-view mirror. 'When we arrive at the lake, I suggest we dive in right away, otherwise no girl will let us near her,' he added with more seriousness, his eyes back on the road ahead.

'Don't underestimate the effect of pheromones in the physical attraction between two people,' Fred replied, his tone matter-of-fact, for once breaking his usual silence to highlight a scientific fact oh-so evident to himself.

Leo rolled his eyes. 'First, you would have to get close to a girl to assert that, and I have yet to see that happen!' he countered, laughing hard – he possessed a natural talent for verbal jousting.

'Unfair,' Fred argued. 'Not everyone is as self-assured as you are. Try to put yourself in my head for a second and you will see it's not that easy.' He sounded defeated before they had even arrived.

'Do you know what drives me mad with you?' Leo asked, glancing in the rear-view mirror. Fred already knew he needed not answer the question; his brother would do that for him. 'You drive chicks away just by believing you're inferior to other guys. If you want to be confident with girls, then show confidence, even if deep down you're scared.' Leo continued, this time with the encouraging tone of an older sibling. 'Do you think I'm always that sure of myself? I might surprise you. Anyway, let's go to the lake and put my words into practice.'

Mika had only been half-listening to the conversation. Although he knew that brotherly love was often expressed by fighting or rivalry, an uneasy feeling he could not shake enveloped him: their group would never make it to the lake ... and his feeling was heightened when he sensed my chassis's response to Leo's reckless driving. 'Leo, slow down, please. I swear we're going to have an accident if you continue driving like an idiot. There's no need for it. We've all the time in the world.'

'He's right,' said Fred, leaning forward. 'You don't need to speed. It's dangerous and unnecessary.'

But their comments only strengthened Leo's determination to prove them wrong. As my metal frame exited a village, his right foot became twitchy on my throttle. We were following a small white car which was being driven by other youngsters, albeit at a slightly slower pace than legally permitted. An *apprenti* plate was displayed on its boot, which explained its leisurely progress. As soon as the road straightened, Leo floored my throttle, and my automatic gearbox dropped down a couple of gears to provide the required amount of torque to overtake.

'See what I mean? Why the need to overtake? They weren't driving that slowly,' Mika said with a sigh, glaring at his cousin.

Leo remained silent. His eyes narrowed on the road and his jaw clenched, his concentration rising.

Having overtaken the other car, the four of us arrived at a sharp right-hand bend carrying great speed. Up ahead, recent roadworks had left a thin layer of gravel across the otherwise impeccable tarmac. It would have been impossible for Leo to spot the danger before reaching the bend. As I started to slide on the loose debris, I discovered that the laws of physics were somewhat limiting: my tyres lost grip with the road surface and my wheels started to spin, sending my metallic frame and its occupants sideways across the road, like a bobsleigh gaining speed on slick ice.

Leo's reflex was undeniably human: he slammed on my brakes and turned the steering wheel in the opposite direction of where I was pointing. This sudden and extreme action caused my weight load to shift from one side to the other. With my brakes fully locked, my tyres burned across the tarmac, screeching in protest, and I flew over the road, heading straight for a bordering grassy bank.

Leo snapped the steering wheel left and right in a desperate attempt to regain control, his right foot still jammed on the brakes, but it was too late: there was insufficient friction to slow down my mass, or to alter my trajectory; nothing could stop the laws of physics now. I was relieved that I was not heading for a concrete barrier and hoped that the grassy bank would absorb some of the impact. Nonetheless, I knew the collision was going to be brutal, for me as well as for my passengers. Cars my age do not have airbags, ABS, traction control or any other security features that my modern counterparts now possess ...

Moments before the crash, Mika screamed, 'Leo! No!' His hunch that the three of them would never get to the lake had become a reality. Everything happened so fast. One instant he was trying to reason with his cousin, the next he heard the sickening sound of gravel spewing up from underneath my tyres and slamming into my undercarriage. Time slowed as he realized he was the only one sitting in the spot which would withstand the impact. His mind evaluated my speed and he estimated that the chances of survival were slim – he was about to be crushed, flattened even, his life ending in a car crash he had tried to prevent. With the grassy bank a blink of an eye away, the young man had the strangest of reflexes: he crossed his arms in front of his chest, just as a racing driver would when caught in an accident. The last image he remembers before passing out was the straw-coloured grass I was about to hit.

I hit the hummock at quite a speed. As predicted, the earth absorbed some of the shock, but the sound of hundreds of metallic parts being crushed in the collision was deafening. Impact absorption often generates a bounce back, and this was no exception: I flew back towards the road, flipping onto my roof in the process. My metal body screeched across the gravel-covered tarmac, the panel above my front passenger seat completely flattened. Beneath it, Mika's unconscious body was held firmly by the seat belt he never forgot to fasten.

His limbs, however, dangled like a dancing marionette, countering every impact I endured. Fred, on the other hand, remained semi-conscious, aware of their critical situation as the car slammed into the verge. Leo was still gripping the steering wheel and applying pressure on my brake pedal, which was clearly pointless, but I understood why he kept doing it: he was desperate for me to come to a stop. From the initial loss of control to my sliding on my roof, no more than two ticks on a clock had passed.

Leo turned his now upside-down head on one side and gasped at the sight of an approaching vehicle. I was not about to be hit by it, however: I was still travelling at some speed and crossed the road, where I ultimately came to a standstill on the opposite verge, away from oncoming traffic.

An old woman living in a house with a prime view of the road heard and witnessed the collision from her garden. The poor lady passed out at the sight of my crushed, upside-down self. Thankfully, she was not on her own and her husband ran to the telephone to call the emergency services; there were bound to be casualties ...

'Everyone ok?' Leo asked tentatively, finally letting go of my steering wheel. His right foot persisted in applying tremendous pressure on my brake pedal. He checked his limbs were still responsive and automatically pulled on the handbrake, finally lifting his foot off the brake pedal and turning off my ignition. With my four tyres now pointing towards the sky, he had the common sense to turn off the engine in case there had been any fuel spillage.

No reply came from inside my cabin. Leo held his breath, clearly panicked that his brother or his cousin might have suffered an injury as a result of the accident … especially after they had both warned him so vehemently about his dangerous driving.

'Hmm, think so …' Fred mumbled after a while, struggling to move.

'Mika, are you ok?' Leo asked, poking one of his cousin's arms.

Mika's tall frame was contorted at awkward angles beneath the compressed roof panel. A look of panic spread across Leo's face. He had to release his cousin from his distorted position and quickly, but my windows and windscreen had been shattered in many places, and small fragments of glass had sprayed everywhere. Would my doors even open to allow the trio to escape from the metallic cage in which they were now trapped?

The driver of the oncoming car that Leo feared would hit me stopped at a safe spot and sprinted towards my shattered frame. After failing to make any of my doors budge, he shouted inaudible instructions to my trapped passengers.

'I'm fine,' said Mika, exhaling heavily after what seemed an eternity but which in reality had been no more than a few seconds. 'What happened?' he asked, dazed and confused.

'Can you two move?' Leo asked, giving an 'ok' sign to the man outside, who was now assessing how to release my three occupants.

The eldest sibling breathed a sigh of relief that both Fred and Mika were alive. Yet I'm sure he knew he would still have to call both sets of parents and explain what had just happened, a call that would hopefully not include any mention of serious injuries.

'Yes,' Fred replied, as calm as ever, still processing what had just unfolded. 'I seem to be able to.'

'I can't really tell,' said Mika in a low voice. 'I barely have any space to shift position.'

'Fine,' Leo said with a reassured tone. 'Let's unfasten our seat belts and try to get out. Let me know if it's possible or not?' Undoubtedly, the emergency services were already on their way, but being a trained first aider, Leo took it upon himself to assess his brother and cousin for any injuries.

The three young men simultaneously unfastened their seat belts and all fell in different fashions from the effects of gravity. Although they were conscious, they were in a state of shock and as such had forgotten that they had been hanging upside down for the past thirty seconds or so. Miraculously, my driver's door opened before Leo could reach for its handle. Someone outside had managed to unlock it. Not without difficulties, the three cousins managed to crawl out but in doing so, Fred and Mika suffered cuts from the scattered shards of glass from my shattered windows.

As the attention shifted to the physical condition of my three passengers, I lay on the verge of this countryside road on a warm, sunny summer afternoon in a region I loved. I knew that my driving days were over … I would be dismantled and my parts surely reused. In that sense, I would still serve to a lesser degree, and I took comfort in knowing that.

* * *

Mika opened his eyes to the bright hue of a cloudless sky,

feeling numb and clueless about his current location. He was lying on his back. He tried to move but his body felt leaden. His vision was blurry and his hearing muffled. Disorientated, he wondered for a brief moment why he was glued to the ground instead of plummeting towards the infinity of the sky, which was pulling him in as if gravity had been inverted. It was akin to waking up from a deep sleep and struggling to regain full consciousness – an unspoken heaviness drawing him back into a sleepy state.

But where was he? Certainly not in the bunk bed in the bedroom he was sharing with his cousins and younger siblings in the summer house. No, that one had a ceiling above it. How had he fallen asleep outdoors, and where exactly?

He rolled his eyes upwards and caught a glimpse of a car wheel; it too was facing up towards the sky. *Since when do cars drive upside down? Why does my head hurt so much?* It took him a while to register that the vehicle was not in its customary shape. People were milling around nearby, talking, yet their voices remained distant. The smell of warm tar and dry grass reached his nostrils, suggesting that he was most likely lying on a grass verge. Sight, hearing, smell. One by one, he reconnected with his basic senses.

That was it! It was all coming back to him: the why, the where. 'We've just had a car accident,' he muttered to himself. The upside-down car was simply resting on its roof, and not set to navigate into the endless sky, and he too was not at risk of dropping into the bottomless azure.

No, hang on a second. This isn't possible. I can't believe it happened … I understand we've been involved in a crash, but I can't remember anything about it … How did I get out of the car? He frowned and tried to recall what had happened. Taking a few deep breaths, he visualized his last moment of consciousness: *the grassy bank … then it all went blank …*

He gasped and his eyes widened. *Am I injured?*

He wiggled his fingers. All moved without any pain and he could feel delicate blades of grass beneath them. He repeated the test with his toes. Thankfully, they all responded – however, his right foot was shoeless. Unable to detect any tenderness, relief washed over him as physical sensations continued to permeate his body.

'Ah, you're back with us,' said a loud voice from behind. A man in his mid-twenties knelt down beside him. 'Do not move!' he ordered, keeping his eyes locked on Mika, his tone firm but gentle. 'We lost you a couple of times already and you need to undergo some basic checks.'

Mika recognized the unmistakable polo shirt of a firefighter. He managed a weak smile. 'We had a car accident, didn't we?'

'Yes, you did. Quite a serious one at that, judging by the state of the vehicle. Were you sitting in the front passenger seat? It's amazing that you're still in one piece,' said the man. 'My name is Sylvain. I'm a firefighter. You're in a state of shock and I need to ask you some questions to evaluate your condition. Are you OK with that?'

'Where are Leo and Fred?' said Mika with some difficulty, ignoring Sylvain's question.

'The two boys who were with you? They're fine,' the firefighter replied with a nod towards the road. 'What's your name?'

'Mika,' he said with a sigh.

'Good. Mika, what day is it?'

'Wednesday.' He was clueless about what day it was, so it came as a surprise that he had blurted out an answer, and the correct one at that.

'Correct. And do you know where you are?' Sylvain continued.

'Burgundy, not far from the lake.' He didn't understand how he could provide such straightforward answers when only a moment ago he had had no idea where he was.

The firefighter smiled. 'Good. What happened to you and your friends?'

'We lost control of the car and it crashed, but what happened after that is a blur.' The procedure was effective. The chronology of the events was now seeping back into Mika's mind. However, parts were missing, from when he had blacked out – several times. He had no recollection of those.

'Any pain anywhere?'

'Not that I can feel.'

'How's your neck?'

'Fine,' Mika said, rotating it in the gentlest possible manner.

'Without sitting up, let me know if you can move all your limbs and if you feel any pain.'

He moved a leg with extreme caution, followed by the other, and then his arms. 'Yes, I can. No pain.'

The young firefighter continued writing each response on a thin notepad.

'Where's my shoe?' Mika asked him with a puzzled look.

'What shoe?' said the man kneeling by his side.

Mika lifted his right leg again and pointed at his sock. He noticed that the white fabric was bloodstained.

Despite his professional manner, Sylvain laughed, sounding relieved. 'You are well and truly back with us now if you are worrying about this sort of thing. I don't know where it is but we will try to find it for you,' he said, standing up and disappearing from view.

As Mika lay there not moving, as instructed, Leo hove into view.

'Hey, Mick, how are you?'

Mika looked up and groaned.

Before he could reply another firefighter appeared next to Leo. 'Right, young man,' he said, taking Leo gently by the arm, 'we need to get you checked out at hospital. Don't worry, we'll be back for your friend,' he added, smiling kindly at Mika as he led Leo away.

Mika closed his eyes. All of the information and the sensory overload were taking their toll. His consciousness started to drift. He wished it was just a bad dream from which he would shortly wake up to find himself in his bunk bed, a few miles away. Two strong hands shook his shoulders and his eyes flew open. Sylvain's face was right up against his.

'Stay awake! You have already passed out twice. You need to stay with us,' the firefighter commanded.

It took Mika an incommensurable effort to resist succumbing to the heaviness of his eyelids, but he knew he had to fight the urge. If he drifted off once more, he had no idea what might happen – could it endanger his life?

Chapter 5 – Confusion

Unknown location, unknown time

Without warning, Mika found himself back in the dark, silent room. He felt weightless once again and could sense the proximity of the three unknown presences who had questioned him previously. He now knew with certainty when he had last encountered this questioning.

Despite the clarity of the unfortunate incident, something remained off. At the time of the crash, the firefighter's questions had helped him re-establish a notion of time and place. In the present moment, however, the queries of his three invisible interrogators had failed to prompt any explanation as to how he had ended up in this dark place. More astonishingly, reliving an episode of his life – this one especially – had only raised more questions: why had he seen the accident unfold from the car's perspective and not solely his? This didn't make sense. It was simply *not* possible, and yet, by a mechanism he was unaware of, he had been able to recall and feel every moment, every emotion, and from two different viewpoints. Had he just dreamt all this?

Mika sighed. 'I'm sorry, I still can't recall anything. This is all very ... confusing.' Was the absence of any memories a positive or a negative thing? If only his interrogators would show their faces. This might help, he thought.

'Please, do not be sorry, Mika,' said the serene male voice. 'You are not the first subject to find themselves in this situation. It is only a matter of time before all your memories flood back to you. If it helps, please know you have been here with us multiple times before, and on each occasion you were able to recollect all the necessary information. Fear not, for we are here to guide you through this process. Then, you will understand our procedure and the importance of allowing you to progress at your own pace, however puzzling this may seem to you at this current moment.'

Mika felt the remarks were genuine and unthreatening, yet many questions flashed through his mind. He had been here before? On numerous occasions? Surely, he would remember. Having said that, forgetfulness appeared to be a common thread ... Did he want to start pulling at it? Facing an increasingly complex situation he was struggling to comprehend, he had no alternative. *Calm your mind, you are a logical person.*

'... I'm at a loss,' said Mika, breaking the silence. He tried to organize the structure of his next sentence in his mind's eye, visualizing a string of words falling next to one another. 'I'm at a loss about all of this. I can speak but can't feel my lips moving. How is that even possible? And your questions ...'

'Yes ...?' the male voice replied, encouraging him to continue.

'They brought back the memory of a car accident I was involved in when I was seventeen. I didn't know where I was when I regained consciousness after the crash. A firefighter asked me a similar set of questions to those you have asked me and I managed to recall within seconds the precise events that led me to lose consciousness ...' He paused again. *Why had it not resulted in a similar outcome right here, right now?* 'At the moment, though, I am clueless about my location and your identities. Your voices are familiar, but I can't establish where or when I would have heard them. Besides, what is the connection between you and the car accident? Were you even there?'

'These are legitimate questions indeed.' The man's voice remained sincere. 'You have always had many questions about life, and now is no different. We told you earlier that the process would be easier if you could simply answer our questions, but your lack of ability to situate yourself in this present time and space implies that we need to provide you with some answers. This is to help you, of course.'

'Perhaps it would be useful for you to know,' said one of the female voices in the background, 'that some of us were present during the car accident and followed you closely. We have been watching you for a very long time, from the moment you were born into this world ... Does this piece of information help you to remember who we are?'

The last comment was spoken in such a matter-of-fact manner that it froze Mika's mind. Like a giant wave slapping against a lighthouse, panic swept over his mind. His suspicions had been correct then: he had been kidnapped. He had been under surveillance his entire life and had probably failed a mission. And now it was judgement time! The sympathetic tones of his captors were simply a mind game to obtain information from him, and they had used the advantage of darkness to protect their identities.

But … no … Mika's alarmed train of thought was stopped short by logic. If his reasoning was sound, it didn't explain why he had experienced a past event from a car's viewpoint. How could that be? Was he under the influence of some powerful psychedelic drugs? *Um …* Perhaps this would explain his feeling of disembodiment, why he couldn't feel his heart pounding in his chest despite his agitation …

'The reason you witnessed the car accident from the point of view of the car is to offer you a different perspective on this event,' said the man warmly. He didn't sound like a captor, did he? 'It is common to be taken aback when you first re-experience an event in your life in such a manner,' he added.

Mika's horror escalated. His question had been answered before he had even asked it. Were his detainers able to read every single one of his thoughts? Was he an open book? How could they do that? Had he no privacy? Nothing, no nothing made sense anymore. 'What kind of dark magic is this? How many times have I been here before?' he demanded of his hidden inquisitors.

'As Mika? This is our fifth meeting,' the male voice continued, as calm as ever.

Really? As Mika? What did they mean? Did he have more than one identity? For all he knew, the three invisible figures could be leading him up the garden path, but he was desperate to understand his predicament. 'Is five times the average for someone my age? Or am I the record holder?' he said, his tone sarcastic.

'We will get to the specifics in a moment,' the male

voice continued, brushing away Mika's bitter comment. 'But before we do so, let's reacquaint you with a different perspective from one of your childhood memories in Africa. It might help you make sense of what is happening to you.'

Before he could protest, Mika found himself in what was once a very familiar place ... And again, his physical form morphed.

No, not again!

Chapter 6 – The snake

Africa, on the Atlantic coast, 1993

The lime-coloured scales covering my long, thin body made me almost invisible in the high grass surrounding the humans' dwelling. I had spent the past few days skulking in its vast green expanse, which stretched over two different levels, each separated by a low cement wall and stairs that connected the front and back gardens. I had enjoyed the tranquillity of the lower level, away from the house, lurking in a large wood stack or under the lush vegetation, taking in the diversity of the surrounding flora. It was the continuous search for a meal that had prompted my arrival in the quiet back garden. Getting in had been effortless – I had simply slithered through a large hole in the chicken-wire fence, like snakes do. The front garden was a busier affair in comparison: situated by a dirt track, it saw much activity during the day as it offered access to several other houses as well as a shortcut to a nearby school.

A few days later, my hunger satiated, and having explored every corner of the gardens, I began to wonder about the inside of the human dwelling. My knowledge of it was non-existent, save for the fact that four humans – two tall ones and two smaller but livelier ones – inhabited it, and my curiosity encouraged me to discover more about their home. My interest was further piqued when I spotted the distinctive grey bodies and orange heads of a couple of agama lizards that had casually invited themselves into the habitation over the last few days. On each occasion, they had ended up running out at full speed, fuelled by panic. Despite being fearful creatures, they had plucked up the courage to pay a visit. However, my exploration of the human space did not seem like a good idea, for humans dislike snakes. I was, nonetheless, inquisitive – if the agama lizards had done it, why couldn't I? After all, if I were to stumble across a human, I would simply hiss at them, scaring them, and escape into the garden. Besides, I am a green mamba and just like my cousin, the black mamba, my reputation as one of the deadliest serpents on the continent precedes me. Humans would not dare mess with me, would they?

As confident as I was, I nonetheless remembered that I had once been beaten out of a human home with sticks. It remained an unpleasant memory, so this new adventure would require careful preparation. During my time in the lush gardens, the habitation's front and back doors had been left open all day, whereas the windows were often shut. I decided my safest option would be to stay close to the glazing on the side of the house, just above the sumptuous red and yellow hibiscus bushes, which had grown tall enough to provide me with a way up, so I headed straight towards them.

Approaching the large, colourful blooms, I further appraised the building: the uncomplicated structure was made out of painted wood and covered by an angled roof composed of a succession of corrugated iron sheets. Supported by wooden pillars, they extended beyond the exterior walls on both sides of the building, creating a front and rear canopy which offered protection from the infrequent tropical rain. The doors, window frames and shutters, in contrast with the white exterior walls, were painted aquamarine.

Once at the hibiscus bush, I coiled around the main branch and climbed it without effort, the ascent not taking long. Stabilizing my weight on top of the main branch, I stretched the front of my body with caution and rested it on one of the open shutters. I extended my neck and peered through the glass: it offered a view of a dinner table set with plates and cutlery, indicating that the midday meal was in preparation. My hunch was confirmed by the aroma of cooked food emanating from the open front door nearby. Maintaining my finely balanced position, I assessed the rest of the interior. My inspection helped me devise a plan: once the four humans had gathered to enjoy their feast, I would enter via the main door and explore all of the rooms except the one they were gathered in, thus remaining undetected.

But without notice, a human silhouette grew in size as it approached the window. I recoiled with a swift movement, banging my head against the shutter in the process, and the branch I was balancing on swung slightly. The figure raised a hand, turned a handle and opened the window a few inches before retreating. The human – a she – who had thankfully not noticed me, left an opening large enough for me to snake in. What luck! The temptation to accept the unintended invitation, instead of having to descend the branch and enter through the front door, was strong ... The open window proved impossible to resist and I slithered over the windowsill in one swift movement. Balance secured, I slid down towards a white-tiled floor, making regular stops to stick out my tongue and scan for vibrations: they were faint; the threat of danger was low.

I let myself fall onto the cool porcelain floor. Its smooth surface reduced the friction noise from my undulating movements, but I had failed to anticipate its lack of camouflage opportunities as well as its slippery texture, which made it harder to move with stealth. As I neared the dinner table, I could feel reverberations, the hard floor propagating successive waves in my direction ... human steps ...

I was trapped: beyond the dinner table was a sofa where two humans were sitting and to its right was a room from which I detected additional activity. I had entered the room too soon and my chances of remaining undetected were becoming increasingly small. Mercifully, I noticed a tall potted plant to my right, in a nearby corner of the room. *Excellent!* The large green leaves would create the most perfect camouflage while I waited for a more opportune time to resume my visit.

Once at the pot, however, another challenge awaited: it proved too high and smooth for me to drag myself up. Meanwhile, the reverberations were becoming stronger and stronger, and the humans who had been sitting on the sofa were now standing up. Instinctively, I sneaked towards the nearest chair, coiled around one of its legs and remained immobile. Bright green on black wood was far from the ideal camouflage, but I remained still and waited for the next opportunity to make my move.

The unrelenting rhythm surrounded me, its powerful percussion vibrating through the chair leg, wave after wave coursing through my alert body. Though we snakes may not have good hearing – well, not like humans at least – we are much more sensitive to vibrations.

In the next instant, three chairs around me danced in unison as three humans sat down around the table. What a strange situation I found myself in. I would probably have to keep still on the chair leg for a while. At least, I had remained out of sight and the vibrations had quietened.

Um ... What was that? ...

A slight tremor grew and I watched in horror as the fourth human, one of the smaller ones, grabbed the chair I was using as a hiding place and moved it before sitting on it. My predicament was becoming a rather complex one. I ever so slightly tilted my head backwards, only to check what the small boy was up to ...

He must have sensed my gaze upon him as the next instant, he turned his head and looked downwards, his curious eyes meeting mine.

Please stay calm, young human, I mean no harm.

* * *

As a very young Mika grabbed a chair to sit on, ready to enjoy lunch with his younger sister and parents, he couldn't help but feel observed by an invisible presence.

What's that green shape?

Instinctively, he turned to his right and looked down at a long, thin green form coiled around the leg of the chair he was sitting on. A pair of black eyes met his hazel ones.

A snake! Mika froze.

Although he did not detect any aggression in the

serpent's stance, he knew full well a green snake could only be a green mamba and the reptile was too close for comfort. As a burst of adrenaline rushed through his veins, Mika abandoned his chair with an impressive leap before running to the other side of the room, screaming in a terrorized voice, 'Snake! Snake! Snake!'

* * *

It is said that wild animals react in three ways when encountering a human: they run in fear; they remain indifferent; or they defend themselves, the encounter sometimes being lethal. I concluded that the exact same logic applies to humans when I saw the young boy jump out of the chair and run wild, gesticulating in a rather agitated manner.

I, on the other hand, remained as still as a statue: bright green on black – an elegant contrast that would prove fatal.

A fleeting moment of confusion occurred, until another human moved the chair and stared into my inscrutable dark eyes. A cacophony of vibrations followed when all the other humans ran from the table, some disappearing into other rooms.

By now, it had become apparent to me that I would not be exploring this house any further and that I needed to escape. A retreat to the window not being an option, I figured out that my best hope of escaping was to slide along the base of a wall until I found a doorway, hopefully one leading to the gardens, where, unlike on this slippery floor, I would be able to slither at speed. Abandoning the chair leg, I had just started to build momentum when another set of heavy steps ricocheted through me. I stopped for an instant and looked up at a tall human holding a long, thin item in his hand, which was closing in on me. I hissed, my sharp fangs clearly visible, informing the human that I would not endure being chased away with a stick once more.

But the human hit me with a blistering move.

Pain.

Blood.

Rage swirled inside me.

The tall human was holding a machete in his hand, a palpable tension keeping his body on high alert as he swung the long, sharp blade, slicing it through my skin.

I hissed once more, ready to bite this time, but the long cutting tool slashed my body a second time, and again. The strength to fight back deserted me as rapidly as my physical self lost all sensation, slipping in its own blood as it convulsed one last time. Although brutal and violent, it was a swift death. Taking my final breath, I wondered if the emotion I was feeling was similar to that felt by my prey after I inject my deadly venom into their terrorized and shaking bodies.

As I looked upon my dead body, my last thought was one of absolute certainty: that humans can also react in three ways when facing a wild animal: they run in fear; they remain indifferent; or they defend themselves, the encounter sometimes being lethal.

I, for once, had chosen to remain indifferent. Unfortunately, my curiosity had got the better of me …

Chapter 7 – First revelation

Unknown location, unknown time

Mika's consciousness drifted away from the memory presented to him. Leaving the scene behind, he had hoped he would wake up in a familiar place, but to his dismay he re-emerged in the unknown and peculiar place where darkness reigned and physical sensations were absent.

Although experiencing another slice of his life through a different perspective than his own had proven easier this time, the sensation had remained a disturbing one. Not to mention that being decapitated by the keen edge of a machete had left him with an uneasy feeling – it was his dad who had expertly, and coldly, delivered the blows. Nonetheless, the scene had triggered the memory of his leap of fright at the sight of the snake. But surely, the selection of this particular scene wasn't random; there had to be a reason behind it … Whatever the connection, he remained perplexed.

'Do you see the common thread between the two episodes of your life we have reviewed this far?' asked the male – the leader of the three-strong group, once again reading Mika's thoughts like an open book.

'Let me guess. Some of you witnessed the full scene?' he replied with a sneer.

The sarcastic comment was met with an unimpressed silence.

Mika sighed. '... Sadly not. I'm afraid I'm still trying to comprehend how it's possible to experience a life event from another's viewpoint, to feel all the sensations and emotions linked to it.'

'We thought the similarities would be more obvious to you, but please do not be alarmed if they are not resonating with you as we had hoped. As for the recollections, they show you that your own perspective is always limited,' the male voice continued. 'Only when your actions are reviewed through the lens and emotions of another's consciousness can you truly grasp their impact.'

In what way are my actions connected to the snake's curiosity?

How was he meant to solve the jigsaw puzzle he had been presented with? He had been under observation since his birth ... and questioned by his mysterious hosts no less than five times ... Well, five occasions under his current identity, since the leader had hinted at others, whatever that meant ... What more? By some mechanism that defied logic, he had relived two scenes from his life and each time not just from his own viewpoint. Had his parents hidden a secret from him? However far-fetched, a hypothesis sprang to his mind: were his parents taking part in a secret programme in which he had been enrolled, unbeknown to him? *Um* ... even though they tended to remain secretive about many trivial life events, the probability was low.

'I never meant for that snake to die in our house, if that's what you're implying. What is the link with my actions?'

The leader answered coolly. 'Do you not find it odd that of all the chairs, the snake picked yours?'

Mika remained silent, anticipating that the unseen speaker would provide the answer.

'It was your fear of snakes that drew it to the very chair you ended up sitting on. Your ophidiophobia, combined with its interest in humans, created two vibrations which attracted each other like magnets. This is one of the great principles of life, one that we once taught you, which in human terms is labelled as "energy alignment". Does this term ring a bell with you?'

Ophidiowhat? Human terms? He sensed he was being given a hint, but he was still utterly clueless. 'No, it does not ring any bell at all ... Besides, snakes in that part of the world are deadly. And you do realize that every single comment you make only raises more questions for me? The only thing I'm currently aligning with is more confusion!' he replied, his frustration nearing tipping point.

'We do realize this, Mika,' the leader replied, remaining composed despite Mika's provocation. 'However, we do so in the hope that one of our comments will unlock the doors to full remembrance. So, let us continue and put aside energy alignment for now. How was life in Africa for you?'

Mika's patience eroded. *What is this game?* 'I wonder why you even bother to ask. Since you claim to have been following me since the day I was born, you should know that I was happy back then. Life was simple. My connection with nature was ever present and the sun shone most days. I lived close to a decade in this simple environment; there was beauty in it and for a very long time after we returned to Europe with my family, I looked back on it with much nostalgia. I missed the rich aroma and taste of the local food, the bustling street markets, the vibrant colours and soft fabric of the clothes, the deep reds and oranges of the soil, the lush vegetation and the warmth of the ocean. Having said that, I was only a child back then, growing up without any thoughts about the continent's socio-economics; social and political instability was above my head.' He paused as more images from the first decade of his life flashed in his mind's eye: coconuts and mangos falling from trees, playing barefoot in the garden, observing exotic animals and insects … 'Every day was an adventure and for that reason I had a privileged childhood. Is that the answer you were expecting?'

Unperturbed by Mika's rising exasperation, the male voice ignored his question. 'You love nature, Mika. Have you ever wondered where your connection with Mother Earth originated?'

'Oddly, I can recall a few memories from the first months of my life and they are of tall concrete buildings and very little greenery. So, I guess the connection stems from my parents' move to Africa, when I was about a year old.'

The male observer didn't reply. The two female voices had been silent for a long time – and with nothing but darkness surrounding him, Mika had forgotten about their presence. Was their withdrawal deliberate? Was their limiting of the conversation to only one interrogator a shrewd psychological technique to gain his trust? Not that he cared anymore. His patience was at an end and he wanted answers – real ones … not evasive, misleading ones. He shouted, 'Why are you hiding in the dark? Why are you not showing your faces? Do you think I can't see through your futile mind games?'

'Since you ask, perhaps it is time for us to show our faces,' said one of the female voices in the background. Her playful tone suggested she had been anticipating this moment and was even relishing it.

The cheerful tone took Mika by surprise. Every time he had attempted to gain clarity on his situation, his questions had been countered with expertise, prompting even more questions. These people were playing chess with his mind and they were masterfully executing their game plan.

The male voice took back the lead. 'For reasons you will understand in a moment, our trio cannot reveal our identities before you reach a further understanding of your current location, otherwise you would most probably ... panic. However, we can now tell that you are starting to access *certain* elements of your consciousness, elements which mean the timing could not be more appropriate for me to at least re-introduce myself. I have dearly missed you, Mika, and it is a delight to once again be in your presence.'

The warm words left Mika cold: what trickery would his captors now use to further confuse him?

In the black void enveloping him, a white and gold shape, so small it had been imperceptible at first, started to glow before him, like a growing luminescent cloud of smoke. Mika stared in awe as the form expanded and gained more definition. Within a few moments, a clear and unmistakable figure materialized against the pitch-dark background ...

Mika's eyes grew wider.

In a heartbeat, he recognized the figure standing in front of him. That's why *he* had questioned him with insistence about his innate connection to Mother Earth.

'Askayah!' he said with a gasp.

Chapter 8 – Askayah

Projected physical reality, North America, unknown time

Milashakham spotted the waterfall in the distance: continuous white torrents rushed down from its top plateau, ricocheting against the grey rocks and spraying a dense mist over the evergreens scattered along the banks of its majestic downward trajectory. Its low rumble added to the breathtaking scenery.

Every element looked as real as in the physical world.

Having landed in the simulated reality, Milashakham surmised from his body and temporary attire that he had taken on the form of a young Native American man. *Hardly surprising considering Askayah's background.* Indeed, the elder spirit had fond memories of his time as a shaman in a tribe on planet Earth, and he had devised an immersive experience, an effective method for communicating one last teaching. 'Once you open your eyes, you will find yourself in a location unknown to you. It is no different to previous exercises. As usual, follow your heart to discover the purpose of the exercise,' the wise spirit had told his mentee.

Although readily available and adaptable to every imaginable scenario, the projected physical realities were seldom used, for there was no greater experience than that of physical life itself. Nonetheless, such simulations were a useful tool: one was able to arrive at a point in time, perform the desired exercise and return to spirit form thereafter. And despite being aware that their surroundings were simulated, the spirits were fully immersed in their temporary personas, as if they had lived their whole lives in this form.

Standing tall, Milashakham focused on the energy in the centre of his chest. His intuition told him that the top of the imposing waterfall was his destination for this exercise. Having decided on the best route, he set off, picking up the pace as he jumped over boulders, easing the prickly vegetation out of the way with a wooden stick as he progressed.

Reaching the bottom of the cascade, he was deafened by the roar of water crashing into the plunge pool as it continued its course towards nearby rivers and lakes. He peered up through the clouds of refreshing mist at the towering, slippery rock above him. His intuition hinted that his borrowed body had climbed the waterfall on many occasions. Closing his eyes, he tapped into the Native Americans' unparalleled understanding of nature, which had taught him that each ascent required a novel approach. The wind direction, the humidity level, the amount of precipitation, all would determine his route to the calmer plateau one hundred and fifty metres above him, where the water plunged over the edge. The weather was humid and overcast, so the effort required would be moderate, or so he reckoned, the only difficulty lying in the first steps through the spray, where the vegetation was dense and the surfaces wet and slippery.

Picking up his stick, he opened up a path in the surrounding vegetation, opting for a narrow upward track that skirted the right-hand side of the cascade. His bare feet left shallow imprints in the soft, damp soil, which provided reassuring support underneath his swift steps. The track soon veered away from the waterfall and the ground under his feet became dryer. He stopped by a sharp stone sticking out of an otherwise flat and stratified wall that skirted the narrow path. He dropped the stick and smiled as he looked up; with nature providing a shortcut, the rest of the journey would be easier.

Relying on the powerful grip of his fingers and the strength of his arms, he hauled himself up on top of the stone protuberance without even breaking a sweat. Looking up, he jumped to his left and grabbed hold of a thick tree branch. With his feet dangling in the air, he began to swing his hips and legs to generate momentum and pulled himself up in one swift movement. He steadied himself, moved along the sturdy branch towards the trunk and continued to climb, reaching a position where he could leap onto another track a few metres above. His pace unabated, he scanned his surroundings for his next hold or step – boulders, trees, anything, as long as he could keep going.

The rest of the journey followed the same routine: fast-paced but with regular stops to consider the most appropriate path to follow; Milashakham executed his plan with a focused mind and an agile body. There was no room for mistakes. The young Native American channelled the bare hand-and-feet climbing technique that his tribe had learnt at an early age. To them, a fear of heights was non-existent. Nonetheless, slippery surfaces or precipitous drops from tree branches were not the only dangers he had to consider: many animals lived in the mountains; he could encounter a wildcat or a snake at any time. However, the tribesmen had instilled in him the importance of ensuring his steps and actions were loud enough to alert the animal kingdom of his peaceful presence, offering them ample time to decamp or hide before he entered their vicinity.

Finally, Milashakham reached the top of the waterfall, blood pumping in his solid arms and legs as he took his time to pull himself up the last few metres. Despite his muscles tensing from the effort, he was barely out of breath or even sweating – focus and composure were the prerequisites for such a performance. The exertion helped him to attune to all the elements that formed his ephemeral physical body, enabling him to keep strong and push forward. His efficient breathing technique, along with the multiple short pauses which had punctuated his ascent, had helped to cool his robust frame. 'Mind, body and soul' was the tribe's philosophy. Closing his eyes for a moment, he sensed that the latter was the reason he found himself on this journey on this warm, cloudy day.

As he stood on the calm plateau above the tumbling cascade, feet firmly planted on the rough ground, Milashakham took a deep breath and looked all around, enjoying the perspective that the vantage point provided. A gentle wind brushed his dark, callused skin and ruffled the long, black hair that fell on his shoulders. This was an ideal moment, he thought, to pause and listen to the tweeting birds, although their vocal performances were somewhat muted by the deluge of water rushing down the flume. Standing there alone, taking in the spectacular scenery, he felt a deep bond with nature – so tranquil and immense.

The Man Who Kept Dying

Emerging from his meditative lull, Milashakham walked away from the waterfall towards a large, rugged formation of rocks of different shapes and sizes, above and beyond which the first trees of a dense pine forest rose towards the sky. He stood there and waited, as his heart dictated, allowing the distinct smell of the fir cones to fill his nostrils: of all the floral perfumes nature had to offer, this one was his favourite.

How long would he have to wait? He didn't have the answer, but this didn't bother him – he would be as patient as was necessary. As he focused on the trees ahead, his intuition told him that only a few moments would elapse before the purpose of the exercise would crystallize.

A few heartbeats later, and as predicted, a small, stocky figure emerged from the forest. As it approached, the young Native American recognized his mentor's distinctive features. Askayah's relaxed, composed gait was unmistakable. Besides, the elder had changed little in appearance from his spirit form for the purpose of the exercise: long, grey hair and dark, wrinkled skin; he wore a distinguishing headdress and clothing made from animal hides. Despite the distance between the two men, Askayah's piercing gaze revealed an undiminished vivacity.

Under the dimming late afternoon light, the Native American elder walked straight towards his mentee and both men stared at each other for a long moment, not uttering a single word. Milashakham was taller than his elder, but Askayah's presence and spiritual energy remained dominant. Several heartbeats passed before both smiled and allowed their foreheads and noses to make contact: a calming and soothing practice which replaced the need for words and forged bonds between members of the tribe, generation after generation. Their faces touching, they gripped each other's shoulders and an invisible flow of energy circulated between the two men. Askayah delivered a revitalizing life force to Milashakham's body, and in return the young Native American transmitted the feelings and emotions he had experienced during the climb. Much love and respect flowed between the two men before they gently stepped back from their particular embrace and sat down on the ground, legs crossed and facing each other. Milashakham bowed his head towards the elder and closed his eyes.

The Native American elder placed his palms together and he too closed his eyes. 'Today is a significant day and I honour your courage in facing it, for it is no small task that awaits you,' he said solemnly. 'Milashakham, as I am sure you are aware, a similar environment was once part of my journey on planet Earth, when I lived as a shaman. My tribe's connection to nature and the animal kingdom was a core learning I took from this specific physical life,' his mentor continued. 'My ancestors disseminated their knowledge through every generation. They understood that the animals, trees, fruits, plants, the sun, the moon, the wind, the rain … every single element of their environment, including themselves, was all a part of a greater whole. In other words, if a single link is removed from the chain, the chain ceases to exist. And this is the greatest wisdom that can ever be imparted: we are all but one part of *a greater whole*. Yet, mankind has forgotten this most important wisdom, and they are mindlessly destroying their natural habitat, removing flora and fauna from the planet at an alarming rate in the name of a belief system they call 'the economy'. Their true nature is a long-forgotten fact, and the reality they now operate in is only experienced through their physical senses and their minds. Sadly, ignorance of the soul has come to be the norm for most humans.' Askayah's voice remained neutral as he imparted his knowledge, removed from the sadness his words conveyed. 'Milashakham, the event you are about to experience will transform you tremendously. I deem you ready for this advancement.'

The younger of the two men opened his eyes. His elder was holding his arms out wide, although his eyelids remained firmly shut. The old man murmured a sequence of words and Milashakham stared in awe as animals approached from all corners of the forest and lined up, side by side, behind his mentor in complete silence: a reindeer, a black bear, a wolf, a wildcat, a rattlesnake, rodents, insects, birds, an eagle and an owl. The wildlife assembly formed a long wall, obscuring the view into the woods behind the old man. With perfect symmetry, the old man raised his arms to the sky, as if they were a folding fan, and all the animals disappeared at once.

Although Milashakham saw through the illusion, it remained a performance to marvel at.

The elder opened his eyes and smiled with pride, his eyes glinting, knowing the trick never lost its charm. 'As you know, what you saw were not real animals. I called upon their spirit energy, and their physical form manifested before your eyes. In their current state of consciousness, humans would not be able to make sense of such a sight, for they no longer remember they can. Yet, there was a time when they too would have seen through this particular illusion.' His smile faded, indicating for the first time a degree of despair in the state of the human condition.

Milashakham looked on in silence. He had sensed the combined energy of the animals – it had formed an empowering force.

His mentor turned and reached behind his back for a small bag made of animal skin, which was tied with a plant stem. Opening it with great ceremony, he withdrew with delicacy a necklace. Secured in the centre of the ornament were several animal teeth, and what appeared to be small crystals were dotted at regular intervals on the dark leather cord. Askayah held it up in front of his mentee. 'This gift represents all the forces and energies of nature and all the animals on planet Earth; it will give you strength and resilience and create a powerful bond between you and every living thing on the planet.'

Milashakham bowed his head and the elder fastened the leather cord around his neck, moving the young man's long, black hair to one side. The ornament sat just below his clavicle.

Askayah placed his hand on the pendant, pushing lightly against his mentee's skin. 'The power of all those forces now resides in you. You have elected to depart to planet Earth and identify as Mika for a lifetime. Once in Mika's physical body, you will no longer see the gift I have bestowed on you, but whenever you bring your fingers to your collarbone, you will instantly and always draw spiritual balance and energy from the forces it contains.'

Milashakham's eyes shone. Clasping his hands over his heart, he tapped the top of his strong chest. 'Askayah, I will honour your gift and remember to make good use of it.'

The ceremony now over, both men stood and looked up into the sky; the sun had sunk below the horizon. Placing their arms on each other's forearms, they locked their deep, dark eyes as a combination of profound respect and pride passed between them – so much could be expressed without uttering a single word. Releasing their grip, they walked back in silence to the entrance of the forest, taking in the magnificent scenery around them as day transitioned into evening.

They stopped. Milashakham knew it was time they left one another. He would take on a new identity as a human, and his next encounter with Askayah would take place on the day he will take his last breath as Mika. The rite he had undergone had simply been an exercise to provide the soon-to-be-born Mika with additional knowledge about humankind's relationship with its habitat. Nevertheless, he was conscious that both his future physical form and environment would be quite different from the one he had experienced for the purpose of the ceremony. Yet, he relished the prospect.

The old Native American put one hand on his mentee's shoulder, gripping it tightly. His eyes were gleaming. 'I have one last disclosure to make: I have chosen to serve as your guardian angel for the lifetime you are about to embark on. As you know, once you identify as Mika, you will forget your spirit name, Milashakham, as well as your spirit nature; such are the parameters of physical life on planet Earth. Yet, I will always be watching over you, even though you will not see me as you do now. To call upon me, look from within, for the truth always lies in your heart. I will communicate with you through signs, synchronicities and emotions. Pay attention to those and you will never fail to identify my invisible support.'

Milashakham's mouth curved into a smile and he gave a thankful nod. No words were needed to convey his emotions. Both men brought their foreheads and noses together again, this time to say goodbye, before Milashakham watched the old Native American walk back into the coolness of the green canopy with assured steps. The mentor did not turn once.

The human-to-be placed his hand on his chest, just below his clavicle, and felt a deep sense of gratitude for the gift he had just received. He was equally thankful to be in very capable hands. Askayah was a wise spirit and would prove to be an exemplary guardian angel for his life on planet Earth as Mika.

Chapter 9 – Reunited

Unknown location, unknown time

'Askayah?' Mika murmured, losing himself in the depths of the eyes of the being he now recognized as his guardian angel; they displayed even more wisdom and compassion than he remembered. He could not have mistaken the identity of the presence before him. The old Native American looked younger than he recalled: his skin had fewer wrinkles and his hair was darker. But the most noticeable difference between the man standing before him and the one who had conducted the ceremony near the waterfall was the white glow surrounding his body ... which signified that ...

'Askayah ... Have ... Have I—?' Mika stuttered, grasping the horror of the situation.

'Not quite, not quite,' said the elder in a soothing tone, before finishing Mika's sentence. 'Have I died?' The Native American smiled. 'That is your question, isn't it?'

Mika gasped. '...Yes.'

'Fear not. Despite your being in my presence, your life has not ended.' Askayah gazed steadily at him, conveying his reassurance. 'Otherwise, I would have said earlier "It is a delight to welcome you back with us", instead of "It is a delight to once again be in your presence". You are, for the time being, hovering between life and death and remain attached to your physical body, which is why you are still identifying as Mika. Nonetheless, you have left your physical shell and are currently reviewing specific moments of your life. This is an essential process and it will lead you to make a decision of the utmost importance once completed.'

Despite feeling disorientated by the unsettling news, Mika heaved a huge sigh of relief. Ignorant though he was about the ins and outs of the process Askayah had spoken of, being in the presence of the wise elder put his mind at ease – wherever he was, he knew he was in a safe place. There was nothing to fear; he hadn't been kidnapped. He had simply left his body, which explained why he was unable to feel anything. Most unexpected was the inner peace he felt, despite the announcement of such grim news. He took a deep breath and exhaled heavily. At long last, he could afford to let his guard down. As he allowed himself to relax, a new sensation took hold of him: it was as if his heart was still beating, but instead of blood it was pure energy that was flowing through him.

Is death always such a tranquil process? Maybe we fear life ending because we have no idea about how peaceful it actually is once on the other side? We are familiar with the pain caused by the departure of our loved ones, but what if they all transition into this wondrous state with serenity? So many questions remained, though.

'So, life *really* continues once we pass away?' Instinctively, Mika already knew the answer to that question, but he felt compelled to ask.

The dark eyes of the Native American brightened. 'Of course it does. It always has and always will. Have you forgotten all that you truly are?' he asked with a broad smile. 'It seems that the more time you spend on Earth, the more removed from your true nature you have become.' His relaxed tone shifted to a contemplative one. 'Sadly, this is the case for many departing this planet.'

'Askayah, how did I ... arrive here?' Mika said, unsure if deep down he really wanted to hear the response to his question – he knew the physical body he remained energetically attached to was far from being old.

'We will review this very soon,' Askayah said, his eyes softening. 'First, we need to continue with the reactivation of your memories as Mika. There is a lot more for you to reacquaint yourself with.'

More questions flooded into Mika's mind. He interrupted his guardian angel. 'Why don't I seem to have a body like you have, Askayah? Is it because I am in what you call "the process"?'

The elder's eyes narrowed. 'Yes and no is the answer. The place you presently find yourself in is what you want it to be, the result of your own creation, if you like. When people leave their physical shells, each individual experiences a reality that matches their own belief system. In recent times, you have stopped believing in the afterlife, and this is precisely why you awoke in a void and continue to be confused about your change of reality and everything it implies. But we digress ... you will soon understand more about this. The review of important life events, however, is part of a process over which you have less control but which allows you to assess how satisfied you are with the life you have led up to this point. Hence you are given the opportunity to review it from different perspectives instead of solely yours. You came to Earth with a purpose, which you kept close to your heart at all times, and your one true desire was to fulfil that purpose.'

Mika's mind buzzed with activity – now that he felt safer, and better understood his predicament, his appetite to remember was growing fast. 'This sounds enigmatic to one who doesn't recall the process. What was my purpose?'

'One step at a time. First, we shall continue with more life reviews to help you restore some memories. Through those you will be able to reconnect with more specific aspects of your life as Mika,' Askayah replied. The guardian angel then raised his eyes.

Mika followed his gaze. Much to his surprise, millions of stars appeared all around them in clusters of thousands of galaxies, the celestial bodies flickering in hues of green, red and white. Mika stared in awe at the immensity of the heavenly backdrop surrounding them. Hovering in space created a sensation of calm – quite the opposite of the agitation of everyday human life.

'Coming back to your initial question,' Askayah continued, as composed as ever, 'a physical body is not required in our current state because we are now in spirit form. I have chosen to display myself in the form you once knew so you can recognize me, but I could have taken on many other appearances. At this moment, I see you as Mika, the tall, young man whose body you have just left yet remain connected to, and not the young Native American who climbed a cliff to perform the rituals of the ceremony near the waterfall. As I explained earlier, this is because you still identify as Mika.'

Askayah's words, combined with the peaceful silence of the distant constellations, invited a moment of self-reflection, yet Mika's mind bubbled with even more queries. 'Askayah, how are we communicating if we no longer possess a physical body? I can see your lips moving but the sound of your voice seems to be received via what I perceive to be my mind instead of my eardrums. How is this possible?'

The guardian angel smiled. 'We communicate using telepathy, with concepts conveyed in energy forms that you, as Mika, subsequently translate into your language. This occurs because your mind is still computing those energy forms as words, which are the main medium for human communication.'

Askayah's tone was suffused with patience. Beyond the younger physical shell, Mika recognized the wise nature of the elder. He fell silent as he absorbed the information. Albeit incomplete, a picture was taking shape. 'We are in spirit form but I am not dead,' he summarized.

How is this even possible? The concept of the afterlife had fascinated him since his childhood. He had read many seductive – and also horrific – stories about the possible existence of a spiritual plane, yet the facts he was now facing were so indisputable they needed no logical explanation. He surrendered to the evidence before him without the hint of a doubt in his mind. The existence of the afterlife was a perfectly coherent concept once bereft of a physical human body. This thought brought to mind a memory of an experience he had had as a young teenager, when shortly after the passing of one of his grandfathers, he had spoken with him in a dream state. Wrapped in a vibrant white glow in front of a pitch-black backdrop, radiating love and happiness, his grandfather had saluted him with a broad grin and explained to him that he had wished to impart some knowledge about the mystery of the afterlife – essentially that one's life continued after one's passing. In his grandfather's words, death was only a passage and one should not fear it, for life was eternal. Gold roman numerals had materialized beside his grandfather's luminous body, and he had indicated that there were several levels of evolution one's consciousness could attain. The levels depended on the actions you had taken during your life, the way you had lived your life, among other criteria. Before his grandfather left him, he told Mika which level he was on and that he had already attained a similar level to that of his grandfather … hence he had felt it important to communicate with his grandson, to provide him with this information lest he should forget his innate connection with the spirit world. During his later teenage years and early twenties, Mika had often wished he had had the chance to spend more bonding time with his grandfather, confident in the knowledge the two of them would have had fascinating conversations about the mysteries of life.

Askayah, who had been observing the man who had once been his disciple with rapt attention, nodded. 'It is common for deceased ones to visit their relatives following their passing. The message your grandfather felt compelled to deliver to you had a tremendous impact on you. It made you acknowledge the possibility of a different realm and your own level of existence within it. It is only in recent times that you have started to doubt it. Speaking of acknowledgement, how often have you felt my presence next to you on Earth?'

Mika could not help but laugh out loud, the first time he had done so since emerging into this alternate reality. 'Well, I have always claimed that I have a lucky star watching over me, without ever being certain it was real or ever recalling that its actual name was Askayah!' He laughed again as occasions when Lady Luck had assuredly been on his side popped into his mind. The gate to his memories was slowly opening ... 'Is it a difficult task, being my guardian angel?' he asked, looking back at the Native American's spirit form.

Askayah could not suppress his smile. 'It most certainly is at times! Although my role is to guide you, not protect you. You are responsible for the latter. Is there a particular moment you wish to revisit?' the guardian angel asked, extending an open hand towards Mika.

Mika looked thoughtful. 'Perhaps not an individual moment but rather a string of events,' he said, becoming serious once more. 'I used to dub these events "the doppelgänger effect" and have never understood why life seemed to be taunting me in such a manner.'

'Excellent choice. I see you are starting to remember your life on planet Earth without us three needing to prompt you. Please entertain us from your perspective, this time.'

Us three? Of course! He had forgotten that Askayah wasn't the only presence who had welcomed him. He had no doubt the other two would reveal their identities at the most appropriate moment. Surely, this was part of the plan to help him remember more of his 'true nature'? But for now, he needed to focus. An episode from a series of events that at the time had seemed surreal filtered into his mind. He let himself become submerged in the memory, frame by frame, ready to relive it once more.

Chapter 10 – The doppelgänger effect

South of France, winter 2008

It was already late in the evening when the two men pushed open the imposing, heavy metal doors of the sports centre. The youngest of the pair held the door open and let his elder step out first. Once outside, the cold air wrapped around them and the smell of dried sweat permeated Mika's nostrils: not the most pleasant scent, but in fifteen minutes he would be home and enjoying a warm shower before grabbing a late dinner and counting his bruises.

The others from the self-defence class had already left the building; they were the last to leave. Mika stopped next to his sparring partner on the concrete concourse in front of the sports centre. Both were still wearing their combat kit: a pair of trainers, black trousers, a black T-shirt and a coloured belt that determined the experience level of each participant.

'I really enjoyed tonight's class,' Mika said, absentmindedly, searching for his car keys in the side pocket of his bag.

The man in front of him nodded. 'I can see you're progressing quite fast. That was an impressive move you performed on that guy, considering he's had more training than you. Poor fella, he didn't see that coming!'

The Man Who Kept Dying

His sparring partner was wearing a black belt, so Mika was truly flattered by the compliment, especially as he was only in his second year of training. It was brutal at times, fun at others and frustrating when he was defeated by more experienced students. For once, the roles had been reversed.

'Ah, I saw that move in a video the other day and decided that if the opportunity presented itself, I would try to pull it off. The chance arose tonight and although it looked impressive, it really was quite simple,' Mika said, almost embarrassed for his opponent who was probably still trying to figure out how he had been forced to tap out.

'You'll have to show me next time,' said the man with the black belt, curiosity twinkling in his eyes. 'I have to go, though. See you later this week,' he added, grabbing his motorcycle keys from his pocket and walking away.

'Sure thing,' Mika replied. He gazed up at the clear, navy-blue sky above him and shivered. Important though it was to cool down, the crisp evening air reminded him he should press on and get home before he got cold. As he walked back to his car, which was parked a good fifty metres away in the poorly lit car park, he heard the distinct rumble of the motorcycle of his fellow student already fading in the distance.

He had walked no more than a dozen steps when an uneasy sensation took hold of him. Maintaining his pace, he looked over his shoulder: nobody was around. Straining his eyes, he scoured his surroundings and spotted the potential cause of his sudden uneasiness: under a large tree nearby there was a black car. Inside, someone was waiting with the backrest in such a reclined position that his or her face was obscured.

As Mika walked briskly past the vehicle, he smiled to himself. *These self-defence classes are making me paranoid. It's probably someone waiting to collect their kid from another class ...*

Feeling reassured, he strolled towards his own car and pressed the round button on the key that was supposed to open the boot. Unfortunately, the car was showing its age, as was the key whose buttons had been pressed so many times they barely functioned anymore. The boot remained shut. Mika sighed, slid the key into the lock and turned it, releasing the boot. He dropped his bag in the back of the car before shutting it in slow motion – his arms were already aching. Opening the driver's door manually, he lowered his tall frame into the driver's seat and peered over at the dark vehicle parked under the evergreen. The unidentified driver had adjusted their seat to a more natural driving position.

Coincidence?

Fastening his seat belt, he turned the ignition and selected some music, only to mute it the next instant. With his head pressed against the headrest, he discreetly angled the wing mirror towards the mysterious car: there was no movement within, but its engine roared into life.

'Must be someone who knows the exact time the person they're collecting will arrive at,' he reasoned aloud. 'After all, there are quite a few classes on at the same time.'

Although he knew the underlying reason for his excessive nervousness – the exact same reason that had convinced him to take self-defence classes in the first place – he refused to acknowledge it. 'When did it last happen?' he asked himself, unable to remember the exact date.

The engine emitted a gentle thrum as he reversed with caution over the bumpy gravel of the car park's uneven surface, before he powered it towards the exit.

A dark mass materialized in the rear-view mirror.

Mika paled. The mysterious car was tailing him.

He stopped at the exit to check for traffic before pulling out onto the main road. His heart rate surged. Resisting the urge to use his indicators, which would have offered a clue on the direction he was about to take, he turned right. The vehicle behind him followed. A layer of moisture formed on his palms as he gripped the steering wheel tighter.

His feeling of unease had been confirmed: he was being followed. The person in the car behind him hadn't been there to collect someone from a class; they had been patiently waiting to track him down.

He exhaled heavily. *Be reasonable, you're imagining all this*, his logic told him. But deep down he knew better.

About one hundred yards up ahead was a roundabout. Taking the first exit, he could drive his usual route home. But he could also use the second exit, a slightly longer route. Taking advantage of the lamp posts that dotted each side of the road, he strained to see the face of the driver behind him, but all he could make out was a dark, shadowy oval. The driver appeared to be male, though. He changed down gear on the approach to the roundabout and slowed his breathing, but his heart rate kept rising. *Take the first exit or the second one? You need to make a snap decision!* With the enigmatic car still on his tail, he indicated for the first exit, changing direction at the last minute and opting for the second one. He glanced in the rear-view mirror as the black car disappeared via the first exit.

Phew! I really thought it was going to happen again!

He exhaled heavily, let his muscles relax and dried his palms on the fabric of his T-shirt. Finally, he could unmute the radio and let the tunes fill the car. But with his nerves still jangling, he turned it off again. He drove down the long main street of a quiet residential area. All these events were rather irritating and only resulted in unnecessary paranoia. It was the unpredictability and the variety of characters involved in what he dubbed the 'doppelgänger effect' that was frustrating.

He turned onto a wide, straight avenue that ran parallel to a tramway line. A series of street lights cast their soft light over the palm trees planted alongside the tramlines. Coupled with the sparse traffic at that time of the evening, they created a peaceful atmosphere. Driving on autopilot, he cast his mind back to the first time the doppelgänger effect had occurred ... The absolute rage pouring from the eyes of the stranger in the changing room at the swimming pool ... his barely controlled agitation, as if Mika had committed atrocities against his family ... Yet, the man had kept himself at a reasonable distance from him ...

Simply recalling the episode made him tense up again, his hands clutching the steering wheel. He loosened his grip and allowed himself to smile at the scare he had experienced a moment ago. His paranoia had tangible roots, but thankfully on this occasion it had just been a coincidence.

Following the long avenue, Mika drove past a couple of traffic lights and reached another roundabout, one he would have otherwise arrived at sooner had he taken the first exit earlier on. The large ring-shaped stretch of tarmac was protected by a concrete wall that blocked the view of incoming traffic, forcing every car to come to almost a standstill before entering it. A dark shadow took shape in the corner of his eye. Instinctively, he stopped to give way to the oncoming car – except something was off: the vehicle to his left was actually stationary and almost blocking the exit!

Like a volcano erupting, adrenaline rushed through his blood. In front of him was the black car and its anonymous driver, whose identity was obscured by a black beanie and a scarf that covered his mouth and nose.

Once again, he had been waiting for him!

And if the man had been expecting to meet his target there, it meant that whoever was behind the wheel knew Mika's route home and had anticipated his move at the first roundabout.

'Again, this has to be a coincidence,' Mika murmured to himself, trying his best to regain some composure.

Not wanting to appear suspicious of the other vehicle, he slowly pulled away. Any remnant of uncertainty dissipated faster than a cheetah pouncing on its prey when the black car appeared in his rear-view mirror …

Thinking on his feet was not his forte, even less so after two hours of physical exertion and on an empty stomach craving calories; his preference was to weigh up the data and listen to his instinct before reaching a logical decision. Yet, the adrenaline rush had slowed down time, and his brain was mapping possibilities at an impressive rate as the roundabout unfolded in slow motion ahead of him.

In a split second, he made his decision, completing a full loop of the roundabout to confirm his follower's intentions as well as to let him know he had seen him. He glanced into the rear-view mirror at frequent intervals, trying to catch the eye of his pursuer. But the driver never took his eyes off Mika's car, like a missile locked on its target.

'Ok,' Mika reasoned aloud, 'you probably know where I live so there's no point in taking a long detour back home. Let's drive and see if you decide to chase me.' Not entirely convinced it was the smartest decision, he nonetheless exited the roundabout on a long avenue which a few miles ahead intersected with the street on which he lived.

'And naturally I have left my mobile phone and keys to my flat in my bag, which is now locked in the boot!' he said, slapping his hand on the steering wheel. Nevertheless, his escape plan was simple: if the car continued to shadow him, he would drive to the nearest police station, which was conveniently located a few streets from his flat. It was a back-up plan he hoped he wouldn't have to use.

The wide avenue once again ran alongside the tramline and was dotted by a series of traffic lights. Mika maintained the car at a normal speed as he neared the first set of lights. His mind was still racing. Tonight, the doppelgänger effect was promising to reach new heights … He would have easily dismissed the behaviour of the man at the swimming pool if the young male had been the only person displaying such hatred for him … but it had turned out that this had just been the start of a series of encounters that had all borne the same pattern: a stranger, or a group of strangers, would notice him and become agitated. He couldn't fail to notice them, for they often became loud, and although he didn't always pick up the comments directed at him, the strangers rarely hesitated to point him out. From there, one of them would, with caution but no subtlety, attempt to get a closer look at him. Usually, they would realize he was not the man they were after; nevertheless, there were occasions when some had followed him for a little while; and there were the times when one of his 'aggressors' had stood right in front of him and locked eyes with him, not saying a word. They were looking for something in him. Something they never managed to find. Puzzled, they usually gave up and walked away. The disconcerting element for Mika was that he had no idea who these people were nor what he represented to them. Having noticed that his potential assailants were always prudent when approaching him, he had always opted for the most neutral of responses: remaining steady, silent and unflappable. Somehow, this had proven effective. Yet he could not help but feel vulnerable in the face of the astonishment, fear and finally anger he witnessed in the body language of the people that came up to him.

He had crossed paths with the man at the swimming pool multiple times and although he had never addressed Mika directly, the fierce stares had never subsided. A friend of the young man had once asked if he knew Mika because he never stopped staring at him: 'Oh yes ... I know him *very well*.' the man had said with barely concealed anger. Much to Mika's bewilderment, who was on that occasion catching his breath between two sets of strokes, the irate man had emphasized the last two words of his sentence.

Perhaps I look like someone who left long ago, or worse, someone who is now dead and these people can't believe he's still around. Perhaps they believe I faked my death and are incredulous that I dare to show up and pretend I don't even recognize them? This had been his theory at the beginning. Besides, all the encounters had involved shady characters, so the likelihood was that his lookalike was perhaps not the most socially acceptable person. His assumptions had been proven right the day he had walked past a group of men sitting on the bonnet of a car and one of them had sniggered: 'Oh, a living dead!'

Seeing the traffic lights move swiftly towards him, Mika stepped on the brakes, his mind lurching back to the present moment. The incognito man behind him followed suit and a third car joined them, coming to a stop next to Mika. He turned and glanced at the driver to his right: a middle-aged, blonde woman was sitting behind the wheel of a red convertible.

You're unlikely to be teaming up with the black car …

A couple of vehicles emerged from a street to their left and drove past the waiting trio. A lightbulb flashed in Mika's mind. He assessed his surroundings: no police cars, no incoming trams, no reason for any other vehicle to arrive from the left; just a traffic light about to turn green any moment, the street lights of the city, a deserted avenue, him, his pursuer and a random person unaware of the situation about to unfold.

Putting road safety to the back of his mind, Mika thew the car into first gear and hammered the throttle. The sound of screeching tyres was followed by an abrupt right turn that led him out of the main avenue and into a residential neighbourhood whose streets were akin to a complex labyrinth. He had walked in the area on many occasions, so he knew the street layout quite well. However, negotiating them by car and at night was another thing altogether.

His impulsive manoeuvre must have taken his pursuer by surprise because the black car was nowhere to be seen. But maybe running a red light had been a pointless exercise after all; maybe the mysterious driver knew his home address and would meet him again in a few minutes, unimpressed or perhaps amused by his quarry's futile attempt to escape him. Still uncertain of whether or not he was engaged in a high-speed pursuit with a now invisible chaser, he continued to drive at some speed through the residential streets, taking arbitrary right and left turns. One safe option would have been to find a parking space, turn off the engine and the lights and wait, but none was available and he felt compelled to press on. After a few minutes, he emerged from the other side of the residential area onto a wider street. He stopped and looked around: the street was deserted.

His jaw still clenched, Mika reasoned that he could now drive at a more inconspicuous and law-abiding speed. Over the past few minutes, he had been so intensely focused on every element of his driving that his senses were still on high alert, his heart thumping in his chest, refusing to calm down despite the sudden quietness. *The makings of this doppelgänger episode are straight out of an action film … But aren't films often inspired by real events?*

Knowing that his energy levels would drop following the adrenaline rush, he drew his attention back to the unnerving possibility of finding the black car waiting for him outside his flat, which he would arrive at in a matter of seconds.

'Let's approach slowly and if I am met by him, I will simply drive past, park the car elsewhere and find another way to reach the entrance of the building. Worst case scenario I'll drive to the police station, but that doesn't solve the initial problem and could even aggravate it …' he said aloud as he drummed his fingers against the gear stick. Somehow, talking to himself made him feel less alone in the midst of this alarming situation.

One left turn. One last right turn. He drove slowly down his street expecting to be met by the lights of the black car in front of the gates of the block of flats. Instead, he was welcomed by an eerily empty street.

All of the cars were parked.

Immobile in the middle of the road, his engine still running, he shook his head slowly. If his mysterious pursuer had known he would encounter Mika on the roundabout, how could he not know his address? Had he already parked up? Was he lying in wait by the main door of the building, a smile on his hidden face?

Heart pounding in his chest and sweat once more forming on his palms, he scanned the street ahead. The black car was nowhere to be seen. There was a possibility he had parked elsewhere, but many cars were lined up along the street in front of the flats, and the night did not allow for optimal visibility. He was very close to the safety of his home now, and although difficult to imagine, maybe his stalker was after all clueless about his actual address and still looking for him in the residential labyrinth he had emerged from just moments earlier?

The Man Who Kept Dying

Opening the glove box, he reached inside with a trembling hand for the remote control that opened the gates to the car park and tentatively pressed the button. The rectangular, grey metal gate engaged with a loud crashing noise and slid open in slow motion. His senses remaining on high alert, he entered and parked the car in its designated spot. He turned off the engine and switched off the lights. After unfastening his seat belt, he sat still for a solid minute, monitoring the elements around him.

Everything was quiet. Perhaps too quiet.

I can't stay here forever.

He opened the door with one swift move and unfolded his tall frame like a spring whose tension is suddenly released.

There was no one around.

The car park, which occupied the ground floor of the building, provided plenty of concrete pillars for someone to hide behind. Vigilant, Mika darted towards the boot. Thankfully, this time, the key cooperated. Looking over his shoulder, he grabbed his bag and pulled the keys to his flat from inside the side pocket.

Absolute silence.

After closing and locking the car, he slung his bag over one shoulder and stepped furtively onto the path that led to the building's one entrance. He flicked his eyes from left to right, expecting someone to run towards him, but nothing happened. Reaching the door, he hastily punched in the code on the keypad. A metallic buzz indicated the gate was unlocked. He pushed it open, stepped into the hallway, which was half-open to the elements, and securely closed it behind him.

A quick look to the left and to the right ... The hallway was deserted.

Ordinarily, one might have breathed a huge sigh of relief or broken into a fit of nervous laughter, but Mika was adamant he still couldn't afford to relax. What if someone malicious had obtained the code from one of the residents? What if the mysterious driver had an accomplice waiting for him right by the door to his flat. What if they were already inside it? The thought sent a chill down his spine. As he eased opened the door leading to the stairwell, his paranoia was reaching its pinnacle. Just like the character in an action film, he crept onto the concrete staircase and paused for a moment, listening for any potential sound that might give away the presence of another being.

He was met by absolute silence.

He moved on, making sure his steps were as quiet as a predator stalking its prey – except he was the prey this time.

Funny how staircases always make for great fighting scenes in films ... but landing badly on solid concrete or an iron handrail must really hurt!

He pushed the thought away – how did his brain have the audacity to generate such random thoughts in a situation like this?

Arriving on the first floor, he refocused on his surroundings and edged open the door leading into the hallway with extreme caution, making sure it didn't make any sound that would betray his presence.

Blood was pumping ever faster in his heart. This was the penultimate step.

He stood still.

The Man Who Kept Dying

Again, no sound.

He slid his head around the door frame and peered left and right down the hallway.

Not a soul in sight.

He moved towards the door of his flat. Next to the main door, was a very small window onto the kitchenette. He peered through the glass: it was dark inside. He looked back down the hallway. Above the cement rail he could see the line of trees that separated his residence from the next building. He couldn't sense anyone's presence.

As he turned back towards the door of his flat, his intuition told him he was safe now. Logic, however, dictated he should remain observant until he had reached the absolute safety of the small flat. As calmly as possible, he inserted his key, turned it and then burst through the door.

He was met by sounds emanating from the darkness at the end of the hallway. Sounds that made him sigh with relief: his fiancée was singing in the shower, which was why the rest of the flat was in darkness.

Tension drained from his muscles as he locked the door, dropped his bag on the floor and virtually ran to the sofa and sunk down into it. He was breathless and physically and emotionally drained, yet he couldn't suppress his nervous laughter. It had been his secret agent moment, the strange events just like those you would see in a film. But thankfully, unlike a film, the episode hadn't resulted in any casualties from a car crash or a fight.

'She will never believe me when I tell her my story,' he said with a chuckle, his heart rate returning to a healthy rhythm as his body continued to relax. But in the next instant he sat bolt upright, anxiety returning all too soon as an illogical element of the evening's events occurred to him: the absence of his mysterious pursuer at his flat. Had the man taken a gamble that had paid off at the roundabout yet he had been clueless about his target's home address? Or had it just been another yet more serious misplaced act of intimidation? Either way, Mika knew what he needed to do next: shave his head. He didn't really like his hair short, but he never seemed to encounter any trouble this way. It was only when he let it grow into curls that he attracted the wrong attention. Nevertheless, this would only be a temporary solution. Mika and his fiancée would probably have to leave the city before his situation became more dangerous.

Chapter 11 – Stargazing

Between life and death, unknown time

Mika relaxed as the scene of the car chase disappeared before his eyes – reliving a slice of his life solely from his own perspective had proven to be a much easier process this time.

At the time of the incident, after his mind had assimilated it, he had reasoned that it had all just been a coincidence. However, when he had recounted his incredible story to his fiancée and his friends, they had all agreed that Mika had been chased. A coincidence it wasn't. Concerned for his safety, they had encouraged him to exercise extra caution when attending his self-defence classes, even suggesting he should skip them for a week or two. Eventually, convinced that the incident had not been a mere coincidence, he had agreed in principle. But if someone already knew the time and location of his classes, skipping them was a pointless attempt at avoiding a situation that sooner or later would reoccur. If anything, the incident had served as a reminder that the self-defence classes were a necessary investment.

Naturally, other encounters had ensued after this episode. Nevertheless, the mysterious car had never shown up again and the car chase, thankfully, had remained the pinnacle of the doppelgänger effect. A few months later, the opportunity to move to a different country had presented itself and he had taken it, leaving the disturbing incidents behind.

Bringing his focus back to his immediate environment, he gazed at the starry heavens surrounding him, enjoying the unusual sensation of floating in space: there was no up or down, no left or right, no north or south. His eyes drifted back to his guardian angel, who was sitting with his legs crossed. Instinctively, he tried to imitate him but remembered he didn't possess a physical shell. Instead, he mentally projected himself in a sitting pose. His efforts proved effective as in the next instant he found himself sitting on the same level as Askayah. The elder gave a nod of approval, acknowledging Mika's burgeoning reconnection with his spirit identity.

'Askayah,' the young man said. 'I now understand that we're seeing chosen moments of my life and that it forms part of a procedure, but can you please shed some light on the doppelgänger effect? Why did I face these incidents at that time? It was like being the bad guy in some dark film … yet, despite the rising tension, nothing dramatic ever happened?'

The Native American stayed silent for a moment, looking deep into Mika's eyes. Mika sensed the elder spirit was expecting him to access the answer from within.

Holding Mika's gaze, Askayah folded his arms and, as calm as ever, replied, 'The answer is two-fold, Mika. Firstly, you always managed to remain neutral when your assailants were provoking you. They expected you to run in fear, or at least to show remorse … But it never happened and deep down it troubled them. They no longer felt familiar with the man they had once known or hung out with, and that man didn't recognize them either. Only when they got close and looked you in the eye did they realize that they had mistaken you for someone else. They then abandoned the idea of causing trouble and were left feeling like they had seen a ghost. Believe me, that is a disturbing sensation for a human. Secondly, I was always here, compelling you to remain neutral, to not engage in an argument, to not let your sometimes impulsive nature take over your emotions. And you did listen to your inner voice on those occasions.'

Mika smiled. That unwavering sensation of an invisible presence guiding him to the best resolutions had been real. Askayah had been effective in suggesting, in his subtle manner, the best course of action to defuse or escape those difficult episodes. 'Did I really have an evil twin?' he asked.

'What is an "evil twin", Mika?' said Askayah, frowning.

Mika hadn't anticipated the Native American spirit's response.

'Isn't it something I once queried when, one day, weary at having evaded yet another would-be assailant, you looked to the sky for answers? You did hear my question on that particular occasion, but like many humans, your brain interpreted it as a result of your logical reasoning rather than an element of guidance originating from beyond the visible reality of physical life on Earth. So, I am asking you again. What is an "evil twin"?'

Humbled by the comment, Mika nodded and conceded that the notion of an evil twin was a product of the imagination. 'It is true that during my teenage years I started to entertain the idea that somewhere in the world, the polar opposite of one exists. Like the yin and the yang, matter and antimatter ... a real person who is malevolent if one is benevolent, and vice versa, yet who shares an uncannily close physical resemblance to their other. Of course, the concept of an evil twin was not a new one, but I also concluded that if the twins were ever to meet, only one of them would survive the encounter. Was this idea accurate then?'

'The truth is slightly more complex, but one key element of life on any plane is that you create your own reality,' said Askayah, his eyes still locked on Mika's. 'You do remember I made a reference to energy alignment earlier, don't you?'

The piercing irises of the Native American made Mika feel uneasy. 'Yes, I do remember this comment, but the concept remains somewhat unclear.' He had difficulty connecting energy alignment with the creation of one's own reality, especially if it had the potential to bring unwelcome events like the doppelgänger effect.

Askayah relaxed his stare. 'It is quite simple,' he said, using his hands to illustrate his point. 'Everything you think of or believe in will eventually manifest into reality when you are aligned long enough with the energetic vibration of that thought or belief. Let's put this into context. You believed in the concept of an "evil twin" living somewhere on this planet, right? As you had no resistance to this concept, it became a reality and you experienced it. The reason you never faced your "evil twin" is because, contrary to the latter part of your theory, you were adamant that it was pointless to bump into him and have a deadly reunion. Consequently, you created a resistance and the meeting you imagined could simply never occur. Had you truly believed it, or feared it, because fear also brings on events faster than anything else, the energies would have been aligned for the dangerous encounter to take place. In fact, the two of you almost crossed paths in the same geographical location … But the person you refer to as your "evil twin" had already moved on when you turned up. Hence your arrival, not long after his departure, caused his nemeses a lot of confusion.'

Mika listened with rapt attention as Askayah finished his explanation.

'And in this example I have just described to you the principle of aligning with energy in all its simplicity. What you believe in will happen to you. What you fear will also happen to you. But what you have a resistance to, even subconsciously, will never materialize until you have lifted that resistance.'

Mika reflected on Askayah's words. As fascinating as his guardian angel's explanation was, he found it unconvincing for one simple reason: all he had ever wanted in his life was peace and tranquillity, not having to constantly be on the qui vive for when the next dangerous situation should arise. 'You say I created all this, but why would I do such a thing to myself? This makes no sense, Askayah. I certainly didn't want any of this to happen to me.'

'Really, Mika?' Askayah replied in a loud voice, once more pinning Mika with his eyes. His tone was caring but the unexpected volume surprised Mika. The Native American gently shook his head. 'Didn't it make for some entertaining stories with your friends and allow you to command their attention, pleasing your ego by the same token? Although the rush of adrenaline induced by these encounters was far from enjoyable, the incidents did make you feel special and it was a feeling you nurtured. In doing so, you brought more of these episodes upon yourself.' Askayah lessened the intensity of his gaze and the corners of his mouth turned up by a fraction.

Mika looked down. His guardian angel had a point. 'Touché! I must admit that, yes, a part of me enjoyed feeling on edge and recounting these tense situations afterwards. It made me feel special indeed.'

Curiously, admitting his subconscious motivation in facing the unpleasant string of incidents did not generate any particular emotion in him, no shame, guilt or even pride, and he perceived no judgement from Askayah either. The confession was akin to stating a fact and being at peace with it in the next instant. Clearly, there was no hiding from life's mistakes in this process, but it actually felt liberating to be able to reflect on the events without attempting to justify them. However, it remained astonishing to him that he had, albeit in a subconscious way, brought upon himself situations, which at face value, he would have had much preferred to avoid.

'But to think I created all this, Askayah? This is such a strange concept to comprehend. As bizarre as it may seem, I'm starting to appreciate this whole process. I'm starting to see the complexities of experiences I have regularly questioned.'

The glowing spirit in front of him chuckled. 'Undoubtedly, every experience in life brings wisdom when you experience it through your non-physical eyes and with a full understanding of the role played by every element. I am glad you are beginning to settle into this procedure and are starting to reconnect with your spirit nature.' Askayah smiled at his mentee. 'I believe you are comfortable enough with the procedure for us to progress to the next phase – one I think you will thoroughly enjoy.'

Having remained sitting with his legs crossed for the whole conversation, Mika noticed the absence of the itch to move, which would normally happen after sitting for a long time in one position. *Interesting, the absence of a physical body further highlights its limitations.*

His guardian angel pointed at the myriad of twinkling stars around them before returning to look at Mika. 'Do you believe in extraterrestrial life, Mika?' he asked with a degree of playfulness in his tone.

Mika looked up, perplexed. As interested as he was to delve into a topic that polarized humanity, why would the Native American spirit want to know his opinion? 'I suppose I always have,' he replied matter-of-factly.

'Do you remember those warm, cloudless summer nights in Burgundy when you stargazed as a teenager, eagerly anticipating the passing of a shooting star so you could make a wish?' As he asked the question, he pointed a finger downwards and the sky below their crossed legs illuminated with a shower of yellow and orange meteors.

The swooshing sound they emitted reminded Mika of a meteor that had passed so close to Earth it had sundered the darkness of the night. Its trail had remained visible for a few seconds and Mika and his cousins had danced with joy in the garden, marvelling at the astrophysical phenomenon and conscious of having witnessed an event they would perhaps never experience again during their lifetime.

'Yes, I do,' said Mika looking wistful. 'Those are fond memories you're bringing up. We used to reinvent the world, me and my two cousins. We would imagine how we could make it a better place, and we would discuss all the life goals we had and the exciting lives we would lead. We also often debated the possibility of there being life out there. There are so many stars and galaxies that you would have to be extremely narrow-minded not to at least consider the possibility …' His gaze remained fixated on the location where the shooting stars had just passed. The memories evoked a deep sense of serenity in him. Immersing oneself in the infinity of a starry sky in the quietness of the countryside was a calming experience he had never taken the time to replicate once he had reached adulthood.

'Are we alone in the universe and does life continue after we die are two of the most important questions humanity has asked itself for aeons. If humankind could only remember the answers to these questions, any petty argument arising from them – often enough to start a war between two groups – would be irrelevant, for of course, the answer to both questions is an emphatic yes!' said Askayah, laughing and throwing his hands up. The Native American spirit looked radiant, his eyes twinkling.

Mika looked pensive as more meteors zipped around the sitting pair. In recent months he had begun to doubt the possibility of an afterlife: none of the literature or videos he had stumbled across had managed to convince him of the reality they described, for too often they were contradictory. He had given up searching and had concluded that whether you were a life form on Earth or elsewhere, you were born, lived, died, and then ceased to exist. End of story. What is the meaning of life? He had no idea but at times he believed it was all just total nonsense.

'I suppose recently I have believed more in extraterrestrial life than in the afterlife or even in life itself,' Mika said.

Askayah looked at Mika with understanding. 'When you looked up at the stars back in those days, did you ever feel drawn to a particular location in the sky?'

Mika sighed. 'I sometimes sensed that I belonged more with the stars than I did on Earth. It always brought a painful realization and I would often question, if other life forms did exist, why hadn't they visited us?'

'One has to remember that when looking at the stars, one is looking at the past. But those realizations were simply the manifestation of the connection you had with other galaxies and universes and with the spirit world. You were also able to sense the distant origin of some of your spirit guides, although you could not pinpoint it to a specific planet or galaxy. So many answers transpire when you listen to the inner voice in your heart, yet many humans refuse to do so, afraid that the truth they find there will forever shatter their world. They prefer to remain ignorant and their heart cries. You see, the sole purpose of life is to listen to your inner voice, for this is how the spirit world communicates with you and directs you to the path on which you can achieve your potential.'

Mika was taken aback by Askayah's profound words. *The concepts made perfect sense. But if they were so obvious, why was humanity so incapable of grasping them?*

Without notice, Askayah stood up, interlocked his

fingers in a solemn manner and briefly motioned his head to his right, as if checking something behind him.

The sudden movement broke through Mika's thoughts, sweeping them away. Understanding he too should stand up, he ordered his invisible body to rise to his invisible feet, rapidly bringing himself half a head above Askayah's eye level – after all, he was quite tall on Earth so why wouldn't he replicate it in the spirit world?

'I believe the moment has now come to introduce you to your spirit guides …' the elder announced, his tone conveying much pride.

Mika had been so engrossed in his discussion with Askayah that he had once again forgotten about the other two presences who had been assisting the Native American spirit since he'd arrived on the other side. The new label puzzled him, however. 'My "spirit guides"?' he asked.

'Do you not remember the concept of a guide?' his guardian angel replied with a chuckle.

'Well, isn't a guardian angel a guide by definition?'

'Yes, but there are subtle yet important differences.'

'Well, please enlighten me,' said Mika, still sounding a little confused.

Askayah's eyes twinkled. 'You could not have chosen a better word.'

Standing opposite his mentor, Mika couldn't fail to see the spark in his eyes. Askayah was clearly thrilled to have reached this part of the so-called *procedure*.

'A guardian angel follows you from birth to the moment of your very last breath. It only supervises one physical being at a time. A guide, on the other hand, provides temporary assistance when required. Some guides have expertise in specific domains, and sometimes this expertise is required to navigate a difficult passage in your life. You might have one or several guides, this number varies for the aforenamed reasons. There are also rare occasions where a guide will remain with someone for their entire lifetime. Lastly, whereas a guardian angel is dedicated to one incarnated life form, a guide can look after several beings at once.'

Instinctively, Mika raised an unseeable hand and imagined his head tilting to one side. 'Hold on! I have to stop you there because you're starting new threads. You referred to a guardian angel as an "it" instead of a "he" or "she", and you used the words "incarnated life form"?'

Just like a parent about to confide a secret to their offspring, Askayah exhibited a knowing smile. 'As stated before, rest assured that all your questions will be answered, Mika. Every single one of them. Besides, your guides are best placed to shed some light on your queries. I believe it is high time for you to meet them, for they have refrained from showing their true forms for quite some time now.'

For the first time since awaking in this non-physical place, Mika felt himself bubbling with excitement. His initial suspicions were now long forgotten. At long last, all the presences around him would be revealed and he would be able to put faces to the familiar voices. *No more mystery!*

'However, before they reveal themselves, I would like for us to revisit a not-so-distant dream of yours. Please do not be disconcerted by this delay. Revisiting this dream will be most helpful for the rest of our journey.'

Not just a life moment … A dream. How was it even possible?

Intrigued to find out which dream the Native American spirit was referring to and why he had deemed it necessary to revisit it prior to the reunion with his guides, Mika let himself relax, now accustomed to the process of emerging into a visualization. Frame after frame, the memory selected by Askayah took him back to the back seat of a moving bus …

Chapter 12 – A lucid dream

South of France, summer 2017

The air-conditioned bus trundled along a semi-deserted road of the north-east suburb of the city. Full of daily commuters in the late afternoon, it headed towards its next stop, which was between two car parks where many of the passengers had left their cars for the day. Most were looking at their mobile phones or listening to music, but sitting at the back of the bus were two commuters engaged in deep conversation.

'My worry is that mankind is creating something over which we will soon have no control, and we will become subject to *its* decisions. That's what troubles me about artificial intelligence,' said a petite woman with shoulder-length, curly, blonde hair. Her last two words made a few nearby passengers turn and give the pair an inquisitive look.

This topic tended to make people feel uneasy, Mika thought, looking at his fellow passengers. Most were hunched over their mobile phones, out of touch with their environment, which is why he always preferred to watch the world go by through the bus window, when he was not chatting with a colleague, of course. 'I'm fully with you, Ewa,' he replied, offering his colleague some reassurance 'This is why I come back to the necessity for safeguards and regulations. With those in place, AI can and will change the world. It will support humanity in terms of the logistics and distribution of resources in ways our brains cannot imagine because they have been biased for too long by our political, financial and education systems. It has the power to ultimately create economic equality in this imbalanced world.'

'But it can also lead to state-controlled societies in which your every action, word and even thought is analyzed and controlled. The unbridled appetite of some magnate or dictator might be too strong for ethics to even stand a chance …'

Mika paused for thought. He enjoyed debating issues with Ewa as she was an insightful person whose opinions often differed from his own. They would always respectfully listen to one another and never try to impose their own ideas on each other; rather, they would use the other's perception to enrich their own logic and feelings about a specific topic. However, he sensed that this debate could go on and on, and the next stop was nearing. They would have to resume it tomorrow, perhaps.

'I believe that as humans we are inherently free and creative beings. I doubt we will ever subject ourselves to such control without at some point wanting to destroy the machines. And remember, the algorithms are soulless and, despite appearances, emotionless. So, when you turn them off, they cease to exist the next instant. Much more difficult to do with billions of humans …' he said in conclusion, rising from the seat, careful not to hit his head on the metal handrail above. 'I'm getting off here. Have a good evening, Ewa, and try not to have nightmares about robots trying to end humanity.'

'Have a good evening too, Mr Idealist,' she teased, her blue eyes sparkling with merriment.

As Mika moved past the commuters who had earlier caught part of their conversation, he wondered if they had eavesdropped on the rest of it.

The bus stopped and the doors opened, drawing in a pocket of dry, warm air, an unpleasant mix of hot tarmac and freshly cut hay, into its cool interior. As he was about to step outside, a woman appeared in front of him and, ever the gentleman, he stopped to let her get off first.

'Hello, Mika,' she said with a broad smile as she walked past him.

'Hey, hi, Emilie,' he replied, caught off guard. He stepped down off the bus after her, noting they were the only two getting off at the usually busy stop. 'I'm surprised to see you here. I didn't notice you earlier. How are things with you?'

The full heat of the early evening weighed him down, heat not so much from the sun but from the ground progressively releasing the high temperatures it had absorbed during the day. Even night-time didn't offer much respite from the heat in that part of the world, yet somehow the human body managed to adapt, probably thanks to the lack of humidity.

'Well, I usually drive into town but today I decided to give the suburban transport scheme a go,' she said, pointing at the multi-storey car park across the road. 'Otherwise, all is well with the kids, husband, etc. What about you?' Emilie asked, adjusting her sunglasses and running her fingers through her thick, auburn hair.

She had been working in the same company as Mika

up until a few years ago when she left to lead a new start-up business that created robotic equipment which assisted in surgical procedures. Despite her executive position, she had always maintained a laid-back attitude that translated into her appearance: her elegant black dress was covered by a fine, beige, linen jacket and she wore flashy, red, leather trainers with thick, white soles, complemented by a red flannel handbag. Mika had always admired her attitude: intellectual prowess was not measured by the way one looked, therefore being true to oneself had no impact on how effectively one functioned.

'I'm good, thanks. Has the bus ride convinced you?' he replied, keen to keep the conversation formal. A fleeting awkwardness passed between them. Was it because he had been under her direct management in the past? Perhaps it was better to let her introduce more informality into their conversation. Besides, he was as introvert as she was extrovert; she was not likely to judge his quiet demeanour.

Beneath her dark sunglasses, her eyes twinkled, humour dancing in them. 'I will have to try it for a few consecutive days before deciding,' she said, laughing, grabbing her car keys from her bag. They continued to walk side by side for a few metres, as Emilie asked after some of her ex-colleagues.

Reaching a crossing next to a building under construction, Mika turned to his former colleague. 'I'm not using the multi-storey car park. I've parked in the other one behind the building site.' He nodded towards the far end of an earth track that skirted the half-built structure. 'It's certainly dirtier, but it is much cheaper.'

'Hmm, I'd be too scared to walk over there on my

own,' said Emilie. 'Well, have a good evening, Mika, and say hello to the team from me, especially Ewa.'

Mika nodded. 'Will do. See you tomorrow, maybe.'

'Maybe,' she said and waved her hand as she stepped onto the pedestrian crossing.

Mika turned and headed off down the untarmacked track. He was pleased that Emilie seemed happy in her new role, which appeared to be a rather demanding one. Looking up, he slowed his pace, as if by instinct. Further down the path, there was an old lady dressed in black with a shawl covering her face. She was leaning against the wall, fixated on an invisible point on the horizon. 'Since when did old ladies make you uneasy?' he asked himself as he almost came to a standstill. Two large dogs emerged from behind her, roaming along the path, a good twenty steps away. 'Well, this is a bit odd ... Something's off,' he muttered. Tuning into his intuition, he stopped and made a U-turn, walking around the construction site instead of continuing along his usual shortcut. It will only take a few extra minutes to reach the car park, he thought.

As he emerged from the track, and his feet met the solid pavement again, he turned right and walked alongside the half-erected building. The foundations had been laid down and a few assembled blocks of cement formed tall walls, but although the project had only started a few months ago, it appeared to have come to a standstill. *Perhaps a lack of funds is the cause of the lack of progress?*

A furtive movement in Mika's field of vision drew him from his thoughts. Was that Emilie sneaking through one of the metallic fences that concealed the building's doorframes?

What's she doing? Wasn't she heading back to her car?

Nothing seemed normal this evening. He quickened his pace and slid through the metallic fences by easing one of the panels aside. He found himself in an open room with bare cement walls all around him. The concrete floor of the room was half covered in dust with piles of brown sand in places. Dark metallic rods indicated where future walls would be elevated, and despite the visible frame of the stairs on one side, there was no ceiling and the early evening sun's golden rays reflected on the otherwise grey walls. A moving shadow caught his attention: his former colleague was walking into another room at a decided pace.

Had she noticed his presence? Was he supposed to follow her?

He stepped cautiously into the next room. Apart from less light, and consequently a cooler temperature, the room was a replica of the one he had just left. Once again movement caught his attention. He turned in time to see Emilie's silhouette passing through yet another doorway. Assessing his surroundings, he moved swiftly towards the next doorway, coming to an abrupt stop when he was met by a most unusual scene. Instead of another room, he found himself stepping into a large area bathed in sunlight, an earthy, compacted soil beneath his feet. But it was not the open space that made him gasp, rather it was the presence of at least fifty people, all of them men, whose menacing eyes moved between him and Emilie, who was now just a couple of steps ahead of him.

Tension prickled in the air around him. These people must have set up camp in the unoccupied site, which explained the presence of the old lady and the dogs he had seen earlier. As Emilie continued to make her way through the camp, the men, some standing and others sitting, remained immobile. Walking behind her at a brisk pace, he leaned forward and murmured, 'Emilie, what are you doing here?'

She ignored his comment and instead opened her handbag calmly, reached into it and pulled out an object that Mika couldn't make out. Bending her knees, she placed the unknown object down on the ground with extreme care. The men who were sitting rose to their feet and the group of fifty or so collectively took a few steps forward. Mika felt as though the walls were literally closing in upon him on every side, yet all the men stopped at a safe distance from the new arrivals. As Emilie rose with elegance, he was finally able to identify the object next to her colourful sneakers: a thick stack of five-hundred-euro notes.

Am I dreaming? This cannot be really happening.

'Emilie, what are you doing?'

Oblivious of his presence, she resumed her march towards the other end of the open room.

There was no point staying among the strangers, and turning back didn't seem like a viable option either, so, without saying another word, he followed on her heels, moving through another door frame into yet another room, this time one bereft of living beings.

Jeez, this building is a labyrinth. And it's much bigger than it seems on the outside.

The duo arrived at a tall double metal door with reflective glass panels. It was the only part of the building that seemed to have been completed. Although he didn't see any motion-detecting sensors, the imposing panels slid open as they approached.

'Is this a dream?' Mika murmured as he followed a still silent Emilie through the doors and into the reception area of an imposing office building. His jaw dropped as he stopped to take in his new surroundings, which stood in stark contrast with the abandoned, half-finished construction site he'd just left behind. The polished, black tiles beneath his feet stretched towards the stainless-steel doors of a lift, while just to the right of the lift a single escalator was moving people perpetually upward. *Where did they all come from?*

Alarmed, he spun around and the towering sliding doors reopened onto a busy street overshadowed by tall buildings and, judging by the clothes they were wearing, office workers who were walking past in a hurry. Mika took in the unbelievable scene unfolding ahead of him: it looked like the heart of a major city's business district.

As he stood still for a moment, trying to comprehend how on earth he had travelled many miles by simply stepping through an automated door, Emilie popped back into his mind. He spun back round but she was nowhere to be seen.

'Damn it!' he fumed. 'She tricked me.'

Acting on instinct, he ran to the escalator and shoved his way past a couple of people who were standing on the steps passively. Seeing red, he ran up the metal stairway to a door that led to a covered car park. He thrust open the door and sprinted into the car park, scanning the parked cars. A woman with auburn hair and a beige jacket was standing in front of a distant pay station.

There she is! He raced towards the woman and grabbed

her by the shoulders. 'Emilie, what do you think you're doing?' he yelled as the woman turned around to face him with a horrified stare. It wasn't her. Her clothes were a similar colour but from a distance he hadn't noticed that they were different from Emilie's. 'I'm ... I'm so sorry ...' he spluttered, leaving the confused lady behind him and dashing back to the door that led into the car park.

From the top of the one-way escalator, he looked down on the floor below. He had lost her for good. It was difficult to accept, for he was now trapped in this other world. His only logical option was to attempt to exit by the main entrance of the building and hope that the next time the doors slid open, it would be to offer a way back to the sunny south of France. But first, he had to reach them.

Mika slammed his fist down on the moving rail. 'How do I get down this escalator?' Strangers passing by like absent-minded robots turned to look at him with mild curiosity, yet none stopped to enquire about the cause of his agitation.

Restless and heart pumping fast, he felt an all-consuming urge to run towards the escalator and jump as far ahead as he possibly could. The landing would be brutal, but he dismissed this thought out of hand. He was now adamant that this wasn't reality; he was experiencing a lucid dream. They occasionally happened to him and he could control these dreams to an extent. Within them, new possibilities came aplenty and flying was one of them. The nonsensical string of events that had led him to this exact moment indicated that the risk of his falling was non-existent.

As anticipated, he found himself floating in a

horizontal, forward motion, and no one below him seemed to care or even notice. It was as if they were simply present to inject more authenticity into the imaginary backdrop. With effortless focus, he stopped in the middle of the air, revelling in the sheer enjoyment of feeling weightless – flying was at once exhilarating and liberating. Concentrating his mind, he made a controlled, vertical descent and softly touched down on the polished, black tiles as passers-by remained oblivious to his seemingly out-of-the-ordinary actions. As immensely satisfying as defying the laws of physics was, Mika knew that lucid dreams often included unpredictable components, not all of which he could control. He still had to figure a way out of this place. Exiting the building via the main entrance could be fruitless. Counter-intuitively, he turned his back on the exit and walked towards the lift. Alone in front of the brushed stainless-steel panels, he placed an open hand against a small, black, digital screen. A green sign illuminated as it scanned his palm. Seconds later, the tall doors of the lift slid open with a muffled hiss, inviting him to step inside the steel box.

Mika walked inside but before he had a chance to ponder which button to press, he gasped and almost fell backwards at the vision of himself in the floor-to-ceiling mirror opposite. Staring back at him, aghast, was a pea-green being with a square jaw and large shoulders, dressed in what looked like black motorcycle leathers. The fabric clung to his skin, accentuating a surprisingly muscular frame. Mika was tall but his frame was lean and athletic rather than bulky and sinewy ... yet the reflection was definitely him but with a different physique!

The Man Who Kept Dying

What on Earth!

He stepped closer to the mirror, his eyes blinking rapidly in disbelief, and agitation stirring his core, as the being on the other side of the reflective glass mirrored every one of his moves.

With his heart pounding, he leaned in towards the bald, green being. There was no doubt about it – the reflection was his. An inner voice started to scream in horror at the sight of his unexpected incarnation.

It's only a dream, Mika, do not wake up … You can do it. Do not panic, do not wake up … All is well … it is you with a different body, but it is you … Such was the train of thoughts that ran through his mind as he tossed and turned in his bed, his breathing laboured. Allowing the vision of the green man to surround him once more, he slipped away from consciousness, back into his profound dream state.

Now that the fear was gone, he was able to examine his face, running his rectangular green fingers along his new features: white eyes with black pupils, undefined eyebrows, a flat nose with tiny oval-shaped nostrils, barely visible ridges with small holes on each side for ears. His mouth was small and linear and his apparent lips were the same green colour as the rest of his hairless face. He smiled at the vision and small, white teeth beamed back at him. The dark, second-skin suit covered him down to his feet, incorporating integrated boots. Taking his eyes off his reflection, he inspected his exposed hands: green with five chunky fingers. His body had transmuted into a non-human one, one he could move freely in.

What a discovery. What an odd feeling.

He had never doubted the presence of other types of life forms elsewhere in the universe, but experiencing himself as one of them was on a different level. He smiled and nodded with approval at his reflection.

The opportunity to linger was cut short when an imposing frame entered the lift behind him. Having no desire to turn around, Mika looked up at the newcomer. Wearing the same outfit, and standing a good head and a half taller than him, another being with similar physical features was looking down on him. Aside from his height, the main difference was the being's skin colour: it was cobalt blue.

With a stern expression, the blue giant crossed his arms, flexed his colossal biceps and locked eyes with Mika in the mirror. 'What colour are you?' he said in a gruff voice.

'I'm green,' Mika replied flatly, unimpressed by the giant's tone and his attitude. As far as he was concerned, the giant's arrival had just ruined his grand moment.

'Good,' the tall being said with a smirk. 'And what colour am I?' he continued, his tone filled with arrogance.

Mika stared back at the giant. Was he trying to prove a point or was he wanting to find fault with him? 'Easy, you're blue,' he answered, matter-of-fact.

The colossus smiled with contempt. 'And now what colour am I?'

Mika's mouth fell open and his pulse began to race as the skin of the being overshadowing him changed to ruby red before settling on the same shade of green as his own. Was he a chameleon? Did he have the ability to change colour as well?

'Perfect,' said the giant, not even waiting for an answer. 'Now, can *you* do the same?' He lowered his head and pinned Mika with his eyes.

The Man Who Kept Dying

'Well, I'm already green,' Mika quipped, sensing that the Herculean chameleon was after any excuse to catch him. Had Mika done something he was not supposed to? Was the being part of the building security staff sent after him for shoving bystanders out of the way or for flying in the lobby? The doors to the lift closed, intensifying his feeling of dread.

'Precisely what I thought,' the giant stated with a strange calmness as his skin transitioned from green to orange to blue again. 'See, I do not believe you have the ability to change colour, which tells me that you don't belong here. Now let's deal with you, Mr Intruder.'

As he finished his sentence, the enormous being made a grab for Mika's neck with a swift, calculated movement. Mika, who had perfectly anticipated a potentially aggressive reaction, ducked and twisted around as soon as the giant uncrossed his arms. Avoiding the steel grasp of his opponent, Mika launched himself at the giant's legs. But the blue being was quick to react and sidestepping swiftly he threw his other arm around Mika's neck and tightened his grip.

Adrenaline pulsing through his blood, Mika realized that the vision of himself as a green alien was so real and intense that it had made him forget he was dreaming. He needed to neutralize his assailant – now! As he positioned his neck so that he could catch a short but vital breath, memories of his self-defence classes flooded his mind. Perhaps he was no match for his rival's strength, but he was smaller, more agile and certainly smarter.

Twisting his torso as far as he could, and summoning all his strength, he threw a right hook at the giant's backside. The giant's grip around his neck slackened just enough for him to escape the vice-like headlock. In the same motion, he grabbed hold of his challenger's still flexed arm, pivoted his own body upside down and launched his legs towards his combatant's head. The sudden move surprised the giant, who didn't have sufficient time to react when Mika's strong upward kick connected with his jaw. The colossal adversary faltered, sending the pair crashing to the floor of the lift, which shook violently as their bodies connected with it.

As the vibrations subsided, a breathless Mika checked that the being lying next to him was unconscious before easing himself up to sitting. All that self-defence training had been worthwhile, he thought, blood still coursing through his body. Looking at the body lying there, he couldn't have imagined that the improvised uppercut kick could neutralize such a colossus. Mika knelt, not without difficulty, and checked the pulse of the bulky blue being.

'He will wake up soon. Better get moving,' he murmured, still catching his breath.

As the rush of adrenaline subsided and his tunnel vision ceased, Mika got to his feet and took in his surroundings. He was surprised that no one had called the lift during the time the fight had taken place. Standing in front of the digital screen, unsure of how to open the door from the inside, he tentatively swiped one hand in front of it. Right on cue, the doors slid open and he stepped out into the foyer.

Much to his surprise, the reception area was now empty, but a familiar tune was echoing around the vault-like ceiling, its volume rising to the point of becoming deafening. It made him feel like he was physically in two places at the same time …

The Man Who Kept Dying

He awoke with a start to his morning alarm. Turning over, he reached for his mobile phone, which was placed on the bedframe, and tapped the glass screen to stop the music. Rolling back over, he sighed and grumbled about his rude awakening. A vivid green face swam before his eyes and his mouth curved into a smile.

I've had countless weird dreams, but oh my, that was a first.

Still grinning about the dream that had unfolded, he stretched drowsily and placed a loving arm around his wife's shoulder to wake her up.

Hey! I hope you're not dreaming that you're a blue alien at the moment.

Chapter 13 – The guides

Between life and death, unknown time

The visualization faded. Mika was astonished that even dreams could be relived in such vivid detail. But should he be surprised? At this rate, however, the review could take forever but reliving the dream had left him beaming. Unusual dreams were something he had always shared with his siblings and their mother. Some of the adventures they had experienced while asleep had been otherworldly but being an alien life form had been a first for Mika. Usually, the anomalies would be limited to his surroundings: animals he had never encountered before, cars that didn't behave like normal vehicles and even planes that weren't what they appeared to be. Where else can you observe planes landing vertically on water or cars hovering above roads? Despite his brain's half-successful attempts at rationalizing and humanizing his dreamscapes, he had never noticed other non-human beings around him, let alone discovered that he himself had taken on an extraterrestrial form. On the rare occasions he had recounted his dreams to his friends, they had laughed and said he should put together a compilation of the best ones … 'It will be a bestseller,' they had invariably encouraged.

Facing the young man, and looking rather content, Askayah interrupted Mika's thoughts. 'That was quite an unprecedented dream for you, wasn't it?'

Mika chuckled. 'Askayah, believing in alien life forms is one thing. Being one, even if it was in a dream state, is something else! It was such a shock when I saw a different "me" in the mirror. The sensations of having a different body … and my alien alter ego oozed confidence … I still wonder how I didn't wake up in sheer panic at the vision.'

'You handled the situation skilfully. It is not a simple phenomenon to transcend.'

Mika could see pride in his guardian angel's eyes, but he knew that every review served a purpose. What was the intent behind this particular one? 'Askayah, does this species exist? Why was *I* this green alien?'

'Yes, is the straightforward response to your first question, yet it is not for me to reveal the answer to your second one …'

Letting his somewhat mysterious words hang in the air, the Native American spirit pivoted on his bare feet and extended an inviting hand into the empty space next to him.

Two luminescent clouds materialized in front of Mika, but instead of the white and gold glow that had surrounded them previously, an impressive miniature firework display of green and pink lights illuminated their cores. As the two forms took shape, Mika found himself flying backwards as if taking a step back in fright. However, the distance between him and the two creatures facing him remained the same and the motion stopped. Mika glanced at Askayah; he sensed his guardian angel was enjoying the situation. To Askayah's right stood two beings he had never seen before, two beings whose appearances were very different to one another, and very different to that of a human. Mika stared wide-eyed. Even by tapping into the wildest, most creative parts of his imagination, he would never have dreamt up the two forms before him. With alarm, he looked from one to the other.

Directly to the right of Askayah floated a tall, blue, scaly creature with no apparent feet. The being smiled at him. 'Hello, Mika, my name is Adonnaï. It is a pleasure to meet you in full consciousness. We often meet and have discussions in your dream state, but you either forget about me or your brain humanizes me, hence my voice is familiar to you but not my face,' said the blue being in a reassuring tone. As she spoke, she spun around, moving like she was in a slow-motion dance, her fluid movements bewitching. Despite not wearing an outfit, she possessed an extreme elegance, her elongated torso matching her equally long arms that ended with five slim, webbed fingers. Her face struck Mika as being fish-like: it was very thin, but the two black eyes staring at him were positioned at the front of her head rather than on each side. Her mouth was surrounded by thin lips and her ears were replaced by gills. She also had a very flat nose. The shiny scales of her body reflected various shades of turquoise. He couldn't see any muscle definition – her skin appeared extremely smooth and her legs merged into a blurry, pointy end.

Maybe her spirit form doesn't need feet?

The contrast with the other creature standing next to Adonnaï could not have been more dramatic. Dressed in a shiny, high-collared, navy-blue coat, which hung down to her feet, she was smaller than the other two spirits, her skin a brown so dark it was almost black. Just like Askayah and Adonnaï, a white glow surrounded her. Aside from her darker skin, she was the epitome of the little grey alien Mika had seen in many books and videos: she had an elongated head with a disproportionally tall forehead, two tiny nostrils, a thin mouth with no lips and large almond-shaped eyes, which, similar to an owl, possessed several eyelids. The alien crossed her hands, which Mika noticed had four long, pointy fingers each, across the silky fabric of the coat covering her chest and bowed. 'I am Hakuk. It is a pleasure to assist you in your physical life, Mika,' she announced, her energy poised.

Mika's eyes widened; her lips had barely moved as she conveyed those words.

'The species I have chosen to appear as speaks with tones instead of words. Their mouths do not need to move as much as a human's when speaking. Of course, the advantage of being in spirit form is that we can converse telepathically, so communication is not an issue,' she said in answer to Mika's unvoiced question.

Silently, the young man observed the two spirits standing in front of him, searching for a connection that failed to materialize. The shock of seeing two new types of beings had evaporated quickly – after all, had he not just seen himself as a green alien? – yet an uncanny feeling was bothering him. He shook his head. 'Adonnaï, Hakuk, your voices are somehow familiar, yet I don't recognize you … at all! I mean, when Askayah emerged from the darkness, I instantly remembered the ceremony near the waterfall and the agreement we'd both made, but I am sorry to report that this isn't happening with either of you …'

'This is normal,' said Adonnaï, her lower body still twirling in slow motion – standing still did not appear to be a feature of the species she had chosen to embody. 'We both recently stepped in to act as your guides. Your set of circumstances changed and demanded a different type of support, a less-human type of support, shall we say, which is why we chose the forms you see before you. We talk at length during your dream state, hence the familiarity of our voices, but you never remember those conversations when you wake up. Your experience of the green alien dream demonstrates that the human brain has difficulties computing such information and attempts to normalize it to its own reality. It required a concerted effort on your part to cope with seeing yourself as an alien and not wake up.' Adonnaï's eyes sparkled in the face of Mika's perplexity.

'So, you're the reason I had this dream?' Mika asked, looking at both Adonnaï and Hakuk.

'Yes, we are,' replied the smallest of the three spirits with a serene smile.

'So, am I an alien?' Mika said, his eyes flashing with enthusiasm.

The two guides and Askayah chuckled. Mika once again noticed that Hakuk's facial movement was barely perceptible as she laughed.

'We know you are not going to like it, but yes and no is the answer,' Hakuk continued, holding up her right hand in placation. 'Because, Mika, you are a human, yet there are parts of you that are not human. Earlier Askayah mentioned that every life form has connections with other skies, galaxies and even universes. We will explain why in a moment.'

The Man Who Kept Dying

'But before we delve into this most wonderful topic, let's all sit,' Askayah said, turning to Mika. 'Now that you have reached a level of understanding that allows the three of us to appear in our chosen form without unnerving you, we can return to our review with a complete crew.'

Adonnaï twisted her lower body gracefully and sat on it, like a snake would on its coil. Askayah and Hakuk crossed their legs and sat down at each side of her. Having observed the three spirits for a brief moment, Mika visualized himself sitting down, lowering and levelling his spiritual body with the presences around him. Hakuk, whose eyes were difficult to read as they conveyed little emotion, was on his left; Adonnaï, who was smiling, faced him; and Askayah, on his right, completed the circle. The Native American spirit leaned forward and curving his lips, he blew into the middle of the circle. The next instant, the warm, flickering flames of a campfire materialized, complete with loud crackles and bright-orange sparks spitting from its logs. Spellbound, Mika leaned in towards the fire. However, the comforting sensation of sizzling flames emanated more from the memory of sitting near real campfires than the simulated one in front of him.

'So human,' Adonnaï said with a cackle as she patted Askayah's knee. She cupped her webbed hands and a small puff of smoke appeared, which then morphed into a translucent, aquamarine crystal levitating between her palms. With both hands wide open, she directed the shimmering stone towards the burning flames, and the yellow and orange colours turned into shades of blue with hints of emerald. Mika gazed in awe at the cerulean hues.

He had never witnessed such beautiful magic before. Yet, there was hardly any reason to be surprised, he thought. Everything could be created here.

'I see you are in a *high-spirited* state, Adonnaï,' said Askayah, winking at the tallest of the guides.

Adonnaï laughed. 'Humans have such a great sense of humour. The campfire is a great idea, Askayah. Through the ages, humans have gathered around one to meditate and reflect.'

Mika's guardian angel looked up at him and smiled. 'Do you recall why sitting around a campfire has a deep, relaxing effect?'

'No,' Mika replied absentmindedly, reconnecting with his surroundings. Hypnotized by the flames, he had momentarily disconnected from the conversation, his mind still absorbing all the information he had been given: he was somehow half-alive and half-dead at the same time, and in the presence of three spirits whose role it was to look after him and who all looked so different. *Are you not supposed to be greeted by loved ones who have already passed when you die? Maybe this isn't a normal death. It seems I have been in this situation multiple times before. But I never died in the end, did I? Is there a possibility that I can go back to my physical body on Earth – and is that what happened on each occasion?*

For once, none of the guides picked up on his train of thought and Askayah was already explaining the positive physiological effects of sitting by a campfire. '... the oscillations of the flames possess a hypnotic effect: they have a low frequency and moderate brightness which does not blind the human eye. The physical result is a lowering of blood pressure, which is why humans are instinctively mesmerized by fire. Interestingly, in current human society, the glow emitted by digital screens engages the same part of the brain, except they emit too much white light, which has the opposite effect on the body, increasing anxiety.'

'Is that why people are glued to their mobile phones to the point of sleepwalking, unaware that they are walking on the road instead of the pavement?' Mika asked, re-engaging with his guides.

'It can be that addictive, yes,' said the guardian angel, resting his hands on his lap. 'Conversely, when meditating one can light a candle and stare into the flame. It helps one to reach a tranquil state.'

The aquamarine and emerald reflections of the campfire danced on the three figures around Mika. He was surprised by the unforeseen turn his journey was taking. 'I didn't expect the spirit world to be so ... relaxed. You were all so serious when I first ... woke up.'

'Sadly, it is a common human belief ...' said Hakuk, her posture upright and her face expressionless. 'Earthlings tend to imagine that spirits are always serious, that the afterlife is regimented by countless rules, that life itself has to be austere and filled with hardship. They could not be further from the truth. The essence of life is love, self-love. Don't you humans claim you should "Live, Love, Laugh"? Yet you struggle to apply this to your everyday life.'

Mika heaved a sigh and looked back into the dancing flames. 'Well, for mankind I suppose it is as easy to laugh as it is to cry ... Why is humanity so remote from the essence of life?'

With her fingers interlaced and her hands resting on

the delicate fabric covering her lap, Hakuk continued. 'It is a transposition of the life humans lead and the belief systems they currently hold. It is easier for them to imagine that all facets of the afterlife would follow the same pattern as their existence. As a result, the simple fear of dying is sufficient to remove their connection with the essence of life. It's a mental projection that prevents humans from living in the moment because they fear a future possible judgement. In fact, some humans are so adamant that life is limited to planet Earth that they first need to be greeted by loved ones who have passed away when they transition realities. Only then are they ready to meet other spirits who might not be human in appearance. With you it has always been different, that is until you stopped believing in the afterlife. And because you have left your body, though you are not dead, we have elected to follow this procedure designed to help you reconnect step by step to the spirit world and to us.'

Mika absorbed Hakuk's words. Askayah spoke the truth: the older he got, the more impervious to his true nature he had become. 'Well, it's good to be back in your presence, and I understand why you were reluctant to disclose your identity when I awakened. I would have become rather agitated. One question remains, though: how does a guide or a guardian angel operate? I have never seen you before, nor do I recall receiving obvious guidance from you. I'm certain that seeing you would have left its mark on me.'

Adonnaï took over, her affectionate, optimistic tone spreading much love around the quartet. 'We never show up in the physical world because we exist on a different plane or dimension, if you prefer, yet at all times we monitor the persons we look after. In short, we can observe you but you cannot see us. Nevertheless, you can *feel* us and that is precisely how we communicate, by conveying feelings and emotions, by engaging in discussions during dreams. Sometimes we also appear during meditation. There are many avenues for us to communicate with you.'

Although the explanation made sense to him at a conceptual level, he remained unconvinced for he felt the message had failed to reach humanity. For one, he had no memory of ever receiving any clear message from his guides. 'Please don't take this the wrong way but looking at the state of planet Earth, I don't see your guidance as being particularly successful. Unless it consists of recommending ignorance, stupidity and violence?'

The three guides did not wince at the discontentment of their guest.

'It is a far more complex design than you might imagine,' Adonnaï replied, leaning forward, her eyes playful. 'Do you remember ever wanting to turn into a street and suddenly feeling that you should not enter?'

'Yes, I can certainly recall such a feeling,' said Mika nodding, his eyes locked on to those of the tall, blue spirit.

'This is how we communicate with you sometimes. How you act on that feeling is your decision. In your physical form, you possess one crucial element that spirits never tamper with: freedom. Freedom to decide every action you take and every move you make in the wonderful game of life …'

'Crazy game of life!' Mika corrected. His tone was abrupt, betraying some of the uneasiness he was feeling.

'But again, sometimes I have entered a street despite having a negative feeling and nothing bad has happened.'

The corners of Adonnaï's lips curved upwards and she leaned closer to Mika to the point that the tallest flames were almost touching her face, illuminating her unique turquoise features. 'The feelings we convey are not necessarily to inform you about an upcoming danger … they might also be a prompt to make you take another street so you will bump into someone, someone whom it is important you encounter on your journey through life. When responding to this feeling, you might exclaim afterwards, "It was fate that I met this person at that time. Had I not changed direction, we would never have crossed paths." We merely call it guidance. We also talk in your dreams, almost every night, but the human brain filters this information and you usually cannot recall the details of our conversations. However, you might wake up with the impulse to partake in a specific activity on that day. This is a sure sign that our guidance has been received. Whether you act upon our guidance or not is up to you. We make no judgement on your choice.' Adonnaï leant back again as she finished her explanation.

Mika frowned at the serene faces around the campfire. 'Invisible guidance … feelings … emotions … freedom … This is a lot to take in for someone whose memory is failing him. Coming back to freedom, am I correct in saying that the Earth is in a bad shape because humans fail to listen to their inner guidance?'

The Native American spirit nodded. 'Sadly, yes, you are correct.'

'But if the messages are so subtle, how can you expect people to identify them as such?'

The Man Who Kept Dying

Askayah leaned towards his protégé and placed an open hand on the location of the young man's heart. A warm sensation grew inside his invisible chest as the Native American spirit looked straight into his eyes. 'This is why it is important to always listen to your heart, for it is your emotion centre and will always tell you how you *really* feel. Truly knowing how you feel about an event or an emotion will help to guide you in the right direction. When listening to your heart, it is important to stay true to the first emotion that arises, otherwise the brain starts to interfere and impairs your judgement. Should every human follow this most basic principle, dilemmas would disappear and consequently there would be no more war, no more struggles and no more ignorance. Most importantly, there would be no more repression of one's deepest emotions.'

Mika nodded as the guardian angel gently removed his hand from his chest. This discussion was the cornerstone of a potential pivotal change in human behaviour and he sought to fully comprehend the intricacies of the principles that had just been stated. 'But then why have I felt violent or negative emotions in my life? Do you also convey these feelings?'

Askayah raised his eyebrows. 'This is where the complexity lies. A positive emotion can all too easily become a negative one because of various ordeals. For example, a child who is taught to repress the natural emotion of love will often misinterpret possessiveness as love when growing up, which is not a natural emotion. More often than not, this leads to negative actions, with the person often not even realizing it.'

Hakuk smiled at Mika and picked up the thread. 'As

every person possesses inherent freedom, also referred to as "free will" in the human language, the misinterpretation will persist until a resolution occurs. In these situations we do not remain passive. Rather, we attempt to guide the person towards a resolution, which can take various forms. For example, he or she will be drawn to a book or a video on the real meaning of love as opposed to possessiveness. Of course, it remains this person's choice to pick up the book or watch the video, to assimilate their content and make the necessary changes in their life to resolve their internal conflict. Until they do so, and no matter how much distance they put between themselves and people who stimulate this situation, they will notice that life keeps finding a way to confront them with their difficulty. It might take the shape of different occasions and people, but ultimately they will always be drawn back to the same issue ... Throughout this time, we keep offering subtle guidance on how to resolve it, with unabated love.'

Mika held Hakuk's steady, calm gaze. A profound compassion and sincerity infused her words, but Earth had always been such a mess in his view, and although the explanation shed a welcome light on his personal questions, he couldn't shake the feeling that it was beyond the capability of most humans to grasp such concepts and act on them. Growing up, he had pursued studies in science, but he had always maintained a keen interest in psychology. As a young adult, he had performed his own psychoanalysis, and the exercise had been invaluable in uncovering many patterns and some ordeals from his childhood. Despite all this, he remained humble; he knew his knowledge of human psychology was limited. And if he – someone who was interested in the topic – was rediscovering all these long-forgotten concepts only now that he had left his body, what chance did humanity stand?

Adonnaï smiled, grabbing Mika's attention. 'Your interest in psychology is not random, for it certainly helps you to gain a solid understanding of human patterns. Yet, there is no need to study psychology. The simple act of observing other humans in their day-to-day lives naturally brings this understanding to anyone.'

'This is a profound message,' Mika replied, 'but it seems that avoiding ordeals is simply impossible on Earth. Is it the same on other planets?'

'I am pretty certain you can find the answer within you, Mika. What would be your guess?' said the tallest of his guides, resting her chin on her interlaced fingers and looking intently at the young man from across the campfire.

As he stared into the fire, a blurry sequence of images and emotions flooded his mind. 'I ... I sense there are as many possibilities as there are life forms and planets, from recurring difficult or painful experiences to an absolute absence of them, and everything in between?'

He looked back at Adonnaï, hopeful.

Adonnaï smiled gently and bowed her head.

It worked!

Although he now had a better understanding of Earth's situation, he wanted to focus back on his own journey – humanity could wait for the time being. 'I haven't always listened to your guidance, though, have I?'

'In the past? Pretty well, although you did not always comprehend it. Recently? I am afraid not,' said Askayah abruptly.

Despite the sharp delivery, his tone was upbeat and Mika didn't sense any criticism behind the guardian angel's words. 'Is this why I'm now dead?'

'Remember, you are not dead. You are currently in the spirit world but still attached to your physical body. But yes, it is because of this attitude that you find yourself here with us.'

A question hovered in Mika's mind: Askayah had earlier promised he would tell him how he had died, but first he wanted to know more about the connections between human beings and other skies, galaxies and even universes. 'I guess all this leads me to two more questions, the first one being how did I arrive here? But before you answer this question, can we please discuss the ties with other galaxies?'

Of the three guides sitting around the campfire, Hakuk was the first to respond. 'Does Sirius spark any memory in you?' she asked with a motion of her skinny hand towards the surrounding stars.

Mika's expression morphed from curious to astonished. He gasped and turned to Askayah. 'So, it was you?'

Chapter 14 – The multiverse

Between life and death, unknown time

'So, it was you ... the voice telling me to check the Sirius stars?'

The memory was crystal clear for it was one that was difficult to forget. In the middle of the night, Mika had opened his eyes to the complete darkness of his bedroom. Lying still in bed, he had heard an ethereal voice talking to him. The faceless voice was as real as if someone had been sitting next to him, perfectly audible in the otherwise silent bedroom. 'The Sirius stars, Mika. Check the Sirius stars,' the strangely familiar male voice intoned softly. He was certain he had heard this timbre before, but he couldn't remember whom it belonged to. Now fully awake, he looked around his room, helped by the faint light outside seeping through the small opening in the drawn curtains; aside from his wife sound asleep next to him, he was alone. 'What was that?' he whispered, only to be met with a long silence. The calm voice repeated the sentence. 'I don't know anything about Sirius,' Mika murmured, not certain why he was engaging in a conversation with an invisible presence that apparently only *he* could hear. The connection had then gone silent and the response he had been hoping for never came. He then drifted back to sleep, making a mental note to check the Sirius stars in the morning, if he still remembered by that time.

The memory resurfaced over breakfast and later in the day he took the time to research the distant Sirius stars, learning much about them and the mystery surrounding an African tribe, the Dogon, who had been aware of the existence and precise location of the celestial bodies long before scientists discovered them through their telescopes.

Mika discerned an approving look in the eyes of his guardian angel.

'I debated with Adonnaï and Hakuk the best way to reconnect you with your true nature and decided to pique your curiosity with Sirius, knowing it would lead you to the Dogon people. See, you did listen to our guidance. You dedicated some time to research it,' said Askayah.

'It was hard to ignore that message when it was so clearly articulated. If only I'd realized its origin. Can't you communicate like this every time?' Mika said, laughing. 'On a more serious note, though, the theory that a civilization from the Sirius area visited the Dogon people and imparted knowledge of their stellar system is unproven.'

'Regardless of what your scientists think, the Dogon have been passing on accurate astronomical knowledge from generation to generation for aeons, and this remains scientifically unexplained. The idea behind our message was to make you think about the connection between the different types of life forms from other galaxies or even from other universes, and the fact that the ties still exist in present times.'

Mika looked at his guides and narrowed his eyes; they

all wore knowing smiles, as if they were about to share another big revelation. *But what could be bigger than life continuing after death or the existence of alien civilizations?*

The two guides eyed Askayah, who made a nod of approval.

'Let us please hold each other's hands,' the guardian angel said, as he held out his hands, inviting Adonnaï, Hakuk and Mika to do the same.

The young man reached out for the human hand of his guardian angel with his invisible right hand and Hakuk's long, soft, delicate fingers with his left. Although conscious it was not real, he could feel the contrasting textures of both their hands. *It still feels strange not having a body yet being able to feel certain sensations ... as if I have one ...*

Once they were all firmly holding hands, the Native American spirit looked upwards and a section of the heavens, with multiple suns and planets, zoomed into closer focus. They continued to move in closer to one of the suns and then to an at first almost indistinguishable dark-blue vortex which drew ever nearer, engulfing the small group and their aquamarine campfire. A vast, dark tunnel, bounded by long violet filaments that marked its numerous undulations, surrounded them, buckling and twisting as the quartet travelled like a fast-moving, protected bubble through the middle of a covered water slide, or to be more precise, *a space slide!*

After a very short journey, during which they all remained silent, the spirits and their guest emerged in space, floating between planets of various colours. One specific celestial body caught Mika's eye: covered with different shades of yellow, its atmosphere radiated a golden glow and the young man felt an instant and unexplainable yearning. He looked behind him and noticed the point from which they had surfaced was similar to the dark-blue vortex they had first entered. However, the energy of this new place felt distinctly quieter than their previous location: it possessed a softness that reminded Mika of pure cotton.

'We have just crossed into a different universe, Mika,' said Hakuk, releasing her hand from his. 'Everything you can see is real. We are observing the physical world and moving through it from a non-physical standpoint.'

So, we can move at will anywhere we please? That's impressive. 'I didn't know there were many universes. I've always suspected there could be, but we don't have any scientific proof aside from theoretical physics. Are you from a different universe?' Mika asked, scrutinizing Hakuk's difficult-to-read face.

Her eyes ever so slightly brightened. 'People of the species I have chosen to appear as do indeed come from another universe. As you have just gathered, once you leave your physical body, you reconvene in the spirit world, and the barriers between the different universes are no more.'

Mika's gaze moved across the unabated campfire. 'And you, Adonnaï?'

The tall, blue guide appeared flattered by the question. 'Ha! This most beautiful species I have chosen to appear as lives closer to planet Earth that you might think. It actually thrives inside a planet located in the Orion's Belt constellation.'

'Did you just say *inside* a planet?' Mika asked, certain she had meant to say *on* a planet.

'Yes, what is so surprising about that?' said the most

exuberant of his guides, amused by his bewilderment.

'Don't you need the energy of a sun to survive?'

'Need I remind you that there are many animal species on your planet that live underground? Just because you do not see them does not mean they do not exist,' she stated, raising one of her webbed fingers to accentuate her point.

'But do you live in the dark?'

'No. The physics is different on this planet: crystals illuminate our surroundings and feed us their energy. The biology of planet Earth requires most living organisms to feed off organic matter to stay alive. That is not the case with this planet,' Adonnaï replied with her habitual cheerfulness.

Mika was grateful for the insights his guides were sharing with him. He took in the planets around him, noting the differences with those found in the Solar System. Aside from the large yellow sphere, he was drawn to a lush green planet with no apparent water, a gaseous planet whose colour kept transitioning from tangerine orange to sapphire blue as if undecided on its atmosphere, and further afield a sizeable beige one whose surface seemed solely formed of rocks the colour of pale pearls. All the planets were glowing as if they were alive. Perhaps from the spirit plane it was possible to see the energy of physical elements, hence the glow around every object or spirit. And a gigantic sun was shining behind the planets yet somehow he wasn't blinded when observing it.

Clearly another feature of not being embedded in the physical world.

Returning his attention to the yellow planet and the

unexplained attraction he felt, he surmised that this was hardly a coincidence: his guides must have chosen this particular location … but why? 'Is there a link between me and this planet?' he asked, pointing at the solid, yellow sphere rotating slowly to the right of their group.

The spirits once again exchanged knowing looks and silence hung heavily over them. Mika felt tension build within him. What was it? What did they want to say to him? He looked from one guide to the next. Would it be Hakuk with her poised energy that would convey the important message, or perhaps Adonnaï in her vibrant and carefree way? Maybe the honour would go to Askayah, the wise and ever gentle mentor?

Hakuk looked up at the planet, which was partially reflected in her large eyes, and broke the collective silence. 'The attraction you feel for this particular planet is simply because you once lived on it,' she said in a straightforward manner.

'I what?' Mika felt his jaw drop, although he was certain the sensation was just memory and not real. 'No, stop! If I had lived on a different planet, let alone in a different universe, I would definitely remember it!'

Chapter 15 – Infinite lives

Between life and death, unknown time

The words conveyed by Hakuk floated in the air, or whatever it was that filled this space, as if he was refusing to let them in, to absorb their meaning. Indeed, the scenario they brought with them troubled him deeply.

Imagining himself inhaling deeply through his nose, he ran over the teachings he had received from his guides: life continued after death and every moment of one's life could be reviewed from multiple perspectives; there was life on other planets, and other galaxies and even universes existed; reality was created by one's approach to life; and spirits were in continuous communication with physical beings, in their subtle manner.

Nevertheless, the possibility of being reborn in another body and location generated a mild panic inside him. Every concept he had been introduced to he had at some point believed in, or at least entertained the idea of. Reincarnation, on the other hand, was a belief he had never entertained and which he had even rejected. All the texts he had stumbled across limited the possibility to Earth: humans had to repay a debt for faults committed in their previous lives ... It was a disturbing idea that would trap most in an eternal cycle. Living your life without committing any faults was impossible, for an action that might seem positive to one person could be perceived as negative by another.

He stared at each of the three spirits from left to right. Unperturbed by Mika's emotional state, they remained sitting upright and motionless, even the ever-undulating Adonnaï was still. Both she and Hakuk glanced at Askayah. The Native American spirit drew his eyes away from the campfire and back to Mika. A deep wave of serenity emanated from the strong spirit figure and enveloped the young man's invisible body. Relaxing into the sensation, Mika nodded, indicating to his guardian angel that he was ready to continue. The two guides looked on in silence.

Closing his eyes, Askayah took a long, deep breath and raised his hand. 'Mika, I am going to open my eyes. When I do so, please let yourself be absorbed in my gaze.'

Fixing his eyes on Askayah's, Mika watched as the Native American spirit entered into a trance-like state, his body spasming in rapid pulses before his eyes flew open. To his astonishment, his guardian angel's eyes were completely black. As he looked deeper into them, the two black, almond-shaped eyeballs drew him in, occupying all of his vision. A slideshow of flickering images of the lives of different life forms appeared on the black screen. The images seemed to be alive and he had the feeling he was related to them, that he actually *was* them … Or maybe they were him? Or one and the same? He merged into the visualizations: he was an American eagle flying over the Rocky Mountains, preying on rodents; then a gigantic bird made of translucent, orange flames, flying between miniature planets that emitted waves of electromagnetic radiation. It locked its enormous claws onto one of the small planets, trying to fly away with it, but the action only disturbed the magnetic force field and the planet did not move an inch; now he was a small alien similar in appearance to Hakuk. With two other aliens, they visited what looked like planet Earth at the time of the dinosaurs. He was standing in front of a giant grazing triceratops-like animal and the skies were cloudy and orange from volcanic activity. Choking, suffocating air filled his lungs. The small skinny aliens then returned to their planet via an enormous, black, rectangular spaceship in the company of hundreds of lookalike beings.

The next images he absorbed were of a life under the surface of a planet, the spiritual life of a community of short beings with light-grey skin and square bodies and heads. Another set of pictures displayed a desert environment in which he was guarding a tall pyramid plated in gold. He had a large, muscular human body but his head was that of an animal, more precisely that of a black dog with a long snout and pointed ears. Other half-human, half-animal beings were standing guard, chatting with him. More images of lives on other planets flashed by, but the last pictures were those of a very tall, grey, V-shaped being holding an illuminated sceptre in its left hand and slamming it down on a stone floor. The impact created mighty waves of light at its feet and the being shouted incomprehensible words at him.

The reel then stopped and as rapidly as he had entered the visions within Askayah's eyes, Mika found himself back in the circle around the campfire, floating between the planets and their peaceful atmospheres. Adonnaï and Hakuk closely observed the mentor spirit as Askayah's eyes became human-like once more. He exhaled heavily, as if reconnecting with his surroundings. A quiver ran through his body and a broad smile illuminated his facial features as he turned towards Mika.

There is a reason why Askayah was once a shaman.

'This was … quite … a trip, Askayah … I'm not sure I really … understand?' he managed to say, still uncertain of the images he had just seen. 'It felt like I was reviewing episodes of my life … except these episodes were *not* of my life …'

The guardian angel's smile grew larger and he leaned towards his protégé. 'Yet they all were,' he replied in a reassuring tone.

Mika frowned and shook his head.

Askayah patted the young man's invisible knee and continued. 'Mika, this is the answer you have been searching for your whole life, the meaning behind the mechanics of life itself. You only have one life and it is eternal. The secret of this everlasting life resides in the spirit world, where we are right now. However, this perpetual life is made up of multiple experiences in the physical world, in a physical body. In human language, each identity would be labelled as an "incarnation" and you experienced this notion the time you dreamt of having a different body. Although a dream, the moment you saw yourself as a valiant, green alien was nothing more than you semi-consciously re-accessing the body you possessed during this particular lifetime.'

Askayah's words hung in the air as Mika, speechless, looked from Hakuk to Adonnaï, whose facial expressions conveyed deep compassion, in the face of the young man's uncertainty.

Mika turned back to his guardian angel. 'If all these

lives were *me*, does it also mean that Mika is only one life of a larger *Me* that contains all the other lives? This concept is quite confusing but would explain your earlier mention of multiple identities. Please expand, Askayah, your explanation is too conceptual. I need to understand why I can't remember any of these other bodies I have lived in.'

'You are very close to remembering, Mika, very close,' Askayah said, straightening his back, his eyes beaming with enthusiasm. 'You see, humans who believe in an afterlife are mistaken about its true nature. Many believe that they lead a single human life then arrive in the afterlife, where they remain forever, doing nothing. When you think about it, how boring would this be? For others, reincarnation is a continuous cycle, yet it is limited to planet Earth, where they constantly need to repay debts accumulated from actions carried out in previous lives. How limiting when you think about it. Throughout the history of planet Earth, only a handful of humans have remembered their true nature. Once a life in a physical body has been completed, the ultimate *You*, often referred to as the "soul" in human terms, which is neither male nor female and which contains the wisdom of all lives lived, is enriched by the experience and grows. You have endless opportunities to experience growth, and in more places and physical forms than you could ever imagine. This is your true nature and the humans who remember it never look at life in the same way, ever again.'

The explanation was crystal clear: spirits did indeed seem busy in the 'afterlife'. Mika's initial denial was replaced by the sensation of an incommensurable weight being lifted off his shoulders. A sudden joy bubbled over as he burst into uncontrollable laughter. He clapped his invisible hands in front of his chest and looked up. 'You do realize the enormous relief this gives me?'

Hakuk was the first of the three spirits to react to their guest's ecstatic comment: 'Most certainly, Mika. The very notion of reincarnation has always been problematic to you, as you have always found it too limiting if only restricted to planet Earth. See, the answer has resided in your heart all this time,' she acknowledged with a faint smile.

Mika beamed widely. 'This all makes so much more sense now. Askayah, were those all of the lives I have already lived?'

'No, Mika, you have lived many more lives. You have only accessed a sample of your most recent ones,' the guardian angel replied in a soothing tone.

'But if I am now out of my physical body, why I am still identifying as Mika and not as the ultimate *Me*? Why didn't I instantly remember any of this? Why did I have to rely on you peeling away layer after layer of this reality?' His tone transitioned from excited to perplexed.

From across the campfire, Adonnaï smoothly took over the explanation: 'You still identify as Mika primarily because you are not yet dead, so this identity is very much alive. The second reason is because you have arrived from a human life with little recollection of this greater reality. Planet Earth is a planet of extreme focus which limits spirits' perception of who they are to their physical body and mind rather than to the fuller picture of their true *Self*. In summary, spirits forget their true nature once they become embodied as a human. There is a reason for that, but it is true that at the time of leaving their body, many continue to relate to their human identity. Only once the bridge between life and death has been crossed do they reconnect with their spirit nature. This passage takes time because, more often than not, humans fear death and retain emotional attachments to painful experiences they must shed before their human identity can reintegrate into their ultimate *Self*, transforming into spirit form again. They can then choose the next form they desire to embody, or they may wish to remain a spirit and be of service in that form, as we are currently doing with you. Understand that forgetfulness is not limited to planet Earth. Conversely, some civilizations are aware of their true nature from birth, and when they draw the final curtain on their physical life, the transition to spirit is seamless. This is the simple reason behind this procedure, to step by step help you regain full consciousness of your true nature.'

Hearing the blue guide's lengthy monologue, Mika was reminded of the words spoken by Askayah near the waterfall in the simulated reality: 'Their true nature is a long-forgotten fact, and the reality they now operate in is only experienced through their physical senses and their minds. Sadly, ignorance of the soul has come to be the norm for most humans.'

Pensive, he stared into the crackling flames of the campfire and focused his attention on the colour green, visualizing the flames in this colour. Instantaneously, the burning fire abandoned its blue hue for beautiful malachite and emerald tones. Had he done that? His guardian angel and Hakuk clapped their hands in joy while Adonnaï performed a dance and chanted a short melodious chorus. The ever-joyful spirit possessed the most perfect pitch he had ever heard.

'See, you are reconnecting with your true nature.' Hakuk congratulated him with a bow, complete with arms crossed in front of her chest.

'So, to reuse Adonnaï's analogy,' said Mika, 'we're in the middle of the bridge, hence your explanation that I'm hovering between life and death.'

The smaller of the guides confirmed the young man's analysis with a bob of her elongated head.

Mika's eyes darted to the yellow planet, which had now moved below them. Or had they moved above it? He couldn't tell. 'So, I have lived on this planet? Hence my attraction to it?'

'You are correct!' Adonnaï was prompt to respond, clasping her hands in joy.

'And as spirits, you have chosen appearances from one of your previous lifetimes?' he continued, now seeing the ramifications of the concepts his guides had revealed.

'My favourite one, actually,' Adonnaï said, beaming, running her right hand from her head down to her coiled legs, presenting her body with much pride.

The other two spirits nodded in unison.

'I now understand the need for what you refer to as "the procedure" … which would certainly have been unnecessary had I not arrived from a human experience.' Mika looked thoughtful for a moment. 'Is there anything humanity can do to remember this truth? Why, aside from a handful, have the majority of humans long forgotten it?'

'Remember,' Adonnaï continued, 'that from a spirit's perspective there is no right or wrong. These are human constructs. Your ultimate *Self* merely sees opportunities to grow through new experiences. Planet Earth is unique in that it is a planet of extreme contrasts and where possibilities and experiences are far richer than on any other planet for this very reason. Yet, it takes bravery to submit yourself to such opposite potentials. Forgetting your true nature actually helps you: by allowing a deeper engagement in the experience itself, you become fully immersed in the physical form and centred on one identity only. It is because you have experienced many lives on planets with a lesser level of duality than Earth that you find the experience more challenging than the average human does. You could say that planet Earth has more ... *density* than other planets. The energies of life are more condensed, more intense.'

Mika was captivated by her explanation. *Density*. The word brought the undefined contours of a memory to the forefront of his mind.

The tall blue guide must have sensed his mental activity as her small lips curved upwards and a playfulness shone in her eyes. 'Mika, you meticulously planned this life and decided to leave yourself clues to help you remember your true nature. One of these clues was specific to density and you encountered it as a child. You tried to make sense of it but failed because no one around you could find a suitable explanation ... Do you remember what this clue was?'

Mika's eyes grew wider. 'Does it have anything to do with a rock?' He looked at the guides for confirmation.

The three pairs of eyes surrounding him brightened and his vision started to blur ...

Another visualization ...

Now fully at ease with the process, he relaxed into the

environment crystallizing around him.

Chapter 16 – Density

Africa, on the Atlantic coast, 1991

A young Mika woke up with a throbbing head.

It was that dream again.

He could still feel the incredible weight of the miniscule rock.

Simply remembering the scene distressed his brain to the point of generating physical pain, so intense was the recurring dream. And a nightmare it wasn't. No, a nightmare would have awoken him with a start and a pounding heart.

The young boy sighed and pushed himself up to a sitting position, letting his eyes adjust to the darkness of the bedroom. It was still the middle of the night and the surrounding silence was somewhat daunting. Tentatively patting the bed sheet, his hand stumbled across the soft, comforting object he was searching for: his much-loved cuddly toy, which he had named Pito. He grabbed the cotton dog and brought it close to his chest, cuddling it, finding comfort in its silent presence.

Like many other kids, the stuffed toy served as a confidant and Mika immediately divulged his dream to Pito: 'It was the same dream, again. There is this big bouncy rock that is as light as my colourful beach ball … it rolls down a grassy slope and as it does, it becomes smaller and smaller and smaller and also very, very heavy … so heavy that it can hardly move … and then I wake up and my head hurts.' Mika placed his index finger on the middle of his forehead, indicating where the temporary pain was located.

Despite being a wonderful listener, the grey and brown toy never offered any advice. But at least Mika felt better for having told Pito his dream.

He stretched and yawned. Why had he had the exact same dream over the past few nights, each time waking with the same headache? What did it even mean? Why would a small rock be heavier than a big one? It made no sense. Why would it become dense to the point of not being able to move, when moments earlier it was light and freely rolling? And why was it always shrinking? The throbbing in his head had already subsided and his eyelids were feeling heavy – this was all too much for him.

'Mummy and Daddy must be asleep. We need to go back to sleep too,' he whispered to Pito. He lay down and turned on one side, tucking the bed sheet between his shoulder and his neck. He then placed Pito next to his head, hoping it would act as a talisman and prevent the dream from reoccurring. A couple of minutes later he was already drifting back to sleep.

* * *

The next morning was a Saturday. When Mika got out of bed, the vibrant African sun was already shining through the shutters of his bedroom, illuminating the white walls with a series of bright rectangular shapes. A small en-suite was attached to the bedroom and after having sent the

The Man Who Kept Dying

bed sheet billowing up in the air for the sheer fun of it, he darted straight into it to relieve his bladder. After washing his hands, he walked back across his room and eased open his bedroom door, stopping to listen if his parents were already up. The unmistakable aroma of coffee and toasted bread told him they were.

He made a dash towards the kitchen, his loud steps announcing his arrival, and found his dad pouring the hot contents of a coffee pot into two cups and placing toast on a plate. The enticing smell made his stomach growl.

Mika's dad raised his head on hearing his son's bare feet pound heavily towards him, like thunder fast approaching, and welcomed his progeny with a kiss on his forehead, playfully messing his brown hair. 'How are you today, young man? Ready for breakfast?' he said with a broad smile and his usual calm energy.

'Yes,' Mika replied, eyeing the packet of cereal he loved which was standing on the worktop. He was amazed that his dad was always up and about long before he had even woken up. More amazing was that he was always showered and shaved, yet Mika never heard him getting ready.

'Excellent. Now go and say hello to your mum,' his father said with a nod in the direction of the dining room, handing him the packet of cereal. 'I'm just making some toast. It'll be ready in a couple of minutes.'

Tucking the cereal packet under his arm, Mika walked into the dining room, where his mum was standing near the dining table admiring the large hibiscus flowerbeds that were visible through the window. She loved to observe them.

'Morning, Mummy,' he said happily but with an

element of restraint, placing the cereal packet on the table and standing on his toes so that his mum wouldn't have to bend too much to give him an affectionate kiss. She was expecting and Mika knew he was going to have a little sister. The prospect excited him, for he had been an only child for many years now when most of his friends already had siblings. His parents had explained to him that his mother would be tired at times and that he needed to be calm whenever around her. All Mika had really noticed was his mother's growing tummy and that it had become difficult for her to bend and give him his usual good morning kiss.

'Good morning, you,' she replied, seemingly happy that he had made an effort to temper his usual boisterous energy. She bent as far as she could and kissed him on the top of his head, then brushed his messy hair with a soothing maternal gesture.

'I need to have a big bowl of cereal so I can keep growing fast and you won't have to bend to kiss me,' Mika said with enthusiasm, pointing his index finger up towards the ceiling. 'I will be very tall!'

'I bet your sister will arrive long before that,' his mum replied, patting her abdomen and smiling at her son's innocent comment. 'And you're already tall enough for your age, you know. Don't grow too fast,' she added with a motherly tone, placing a hand on his shoulder. 'Did you sleep well? Did you have sweet dreams?' she asked, as Mika installed himself in a chair and grabbed a bowl for his cereal.

Mika stopped in his tracks, arm outstretched, as the recurring dream with the rock and the headache it caused entered his mind. 'I need to ask you about one dream …'

he said as he placed the bowl on the table, hesitant about whether to talk about it or not.

His mum turned around to face him with a slight frown. 'Sure, what is it, darling?' she asked, her eyes soft and her voice encouraging.

'I keep having this dream ... It feels like a nightmare but it's not a nightmare,' Mika said. 'There's a very big grey rock rolling down a slope ...' He indicated the size of the rock by stretching his arms out wide. 'It's very light and it bounces around like my beach ball, but when it gets further down the slope, it becomes very tiny and very heavy ...'

Just recounting the dream was generating a mild throbbing sensation in his temples, so he cut his explanation short.

'Is that all?' his mum added. She stared at him, attentive, encouraging him to continue.

'No, it becomes so heavy that it hurts my head. I dream of it almost every night.' Mika sighed, looking down at the reflections on the shiny anthracite marble tabletop that his dad had upcycled from a broken worktop.

'What hurts your head, darling? The rock?'

'Yes, the rock. It is big and light, and then very small but so heavy it can't move anymore. This makes no sense and it hurts when I look at it and try to understand why it does that.'

'Then why don't you stop looking at it?' his mother said, a hint of concern in her voice.

Mika considered her advice for a moment and shook his head. 'But I can't. It's always the same dream and I always wake up when the rock is so heavy that it feels like my head is about to explode!' He simulated a 'boom' with both hands moving away from his head in a swift motion. 'It's like it wants to talk to me but I can't understand what it's trying to say.'

'Oh, come here, darling.' His mum opened her arms and Mika rushed to her.

'I'm so sorry this dream is bothering you,' she said, hugging him and giving him a loving kiss on the top of his head. 'But it's just a dream, remember, and you've had it so many times by now that I'm sure it will stop.'

Mika looked up at his mother. She sounded reassuring and confident, yet a small doubt persisted in the back of his mind. What if she was wrong and the rock still came back, trying to convey its incomprehensible message?

'Now let's have breakfast,' his mum said, passing her son the milk jug.

'It is Saturday today, which means that Daddy might make some pancakes tonight,' she added in an attempt to change the subject and ease her son's mind.

'Yeah, pancakes!' Mika hopped off his chair and ran back into the kitchen and pleaded with his dad to make some for dinner. He had already forgotten about the rock …

Chapter 17 – Farewell

Between life and death, unknown time

As he emerged from the visualization, the recurring dream which had troubled many of his nights as a young boy now made a lot more sense. It had been an analogy: his ultimate *Self*, which contained the wisdom of all his lives and which resided in the infinity of the spirit plane, was the large free-to-bounce rock. It then transitioned to a smaller fragment, namely himself, on the physical plane on planet Earth, which was a more limited environment. But aside from the dream itself, it was the unwelcome accompanying headache that used to disturb him the most. The message's hidden meaning had proven too much to decipher for a child who was barely ten years old.

He sensed the spirits surrounding him were anticipating his reaction, yet their postures were poised and their eyes were filled with the deepest level of compassion Mika had seen in them thus far.

He erupted with anger. 'How was I supposed to figure out the analogy?' he fumed, gesticulating. 'Do you think it's that easy to realize all this from inside a human body? No wonder humanity is in such a shambles if we spend our whole life blinded by forgetfulness. Aside from the experience, which appears to negatively affect many to the point that a specific procedure is required to reacquaint them with their non-physical nature, is there any real benefit of experiencing life on this planet? What *is* the purpose of life on this planet?' he shouted.

The revival of the dream had brought to the surface a profound resentment, which he knew was nothing more than anger at his own failure to grasp its substance. However, he needed to express his frustration at the seemingly unattainable concepts he had been presented with.

As usual, the guides didn't display any negative emotion towards him, rather they listened in silence – they had anticipated his backlash.

Hakuk, the quietest of the trio, was the first to respond, pointing one of her long fingers in his direction. 'You are a seeker, Mika, so it was only natural that these types of messages would come to you in all shapes and sizes. This was simply energy alignment in action, drawing the clues you had left for yourself closer to you. As Askayah stated before the visualization, it is only because no one around you could find a suitable explanation for this recurring dream that you abandoned your attempts at comprehending its essence. Did you ever realize that as soon as you stopped thinking about it, the dream never occurred again?'

'I didn't keep a record of all my dreams, Hakuk,' said Mika with a sigh. 'And to be honest I was just glad to be spared more of the unpleasant headaches it generated …'

Despite the non-judgemental presence of his guides, Mika sounded defeated, still frustrated by his failure to identify what now seemed obvious. But his irritation sharpened his thinking processes. One question still remained. 'Would you care to elaborate why I've been in this situation four times before and how I come to be here once more?' he asked tentatively, unsure he really wanted to hear the answer to his question.

At that comment, Adonnaï, whose joyful character dominated the group, created a puff of white smoke between her hands and let it morph into a rolled note of brown paper. She unfolded the thick parchment with great finesse, held it at arm's length like an ancient script and started reading its luminescent gold scriptures in a spoof official tone to lighten up Mika's mood. 'Let's see … a car accident at two-month's old, two back-to-back emergency surgeries at the end of your first decade, another car accident in your late teens, then a long period of time without any trouble, and now here you are again. All these events have a common purpose, Mika. You are looking to reidentify with who you really are, to remember that there is a greater you. Yet, your most successful technique to attain this is a little onerous on your physical body. You might want to revisit the method you have devised.'

'What happened during those previous occasions?' Mika replied. His anger was slowly subsiding as he acknowledged the events Adonnaï had just listed. He had indeed met with the grim reaper on several occasions and bar a few large scars across his body, he had come back unscathed from each meeting.

Askayah took over from Adonnaï, his calm energy softening Mika's visible tension. 'You had a different set of guides during those previous visits, but as your guardian angel, I was always present.' He smiled as if remembering those moments. 'As explained by Adonnaï, your aim was to reidentify with the reality of who you are, and your only way of reconnecting was to cause your own death. The other guides and I were always present to welcome you on each occasion. During your first visits, there was no need for us to hide, for you were still young enough to recognize us without any fear. Each time, we reconnected you with the truth of who you really are. Once you were reminded of your true nature, you always took the conscious decision not to cross the bridge between the physical and spirit worlds. Instead, you reintegrated your body just a moment before your death and changed the course of your life—'

'This is how miracles happen, by the way,' Hakuk piped up, edging closer to the malachite flames of the campfire. 'It simply stems from a conscious decision to continue with life under the same identity.'

'Exactly,' Askayah said. He then paused and took a long look at the beige planet behind them, as if the distant pearly sphere was conveying a message to him.

Mika had been so absorbed in the insights from his guides that he had barely taken his eyes of them and their quiet energy, but he couldn't help but notice Askayah pause.

The guardian angel continued. 'We have reached another moment of the utmost importance, Mika. There is one more step to go through, though. Please consider it a gift from us, as it is an action we have never done with you before. Once completed, you will again be in a position to make a decision about your life as Mika, that is to say to choose to resume it or to call it a day and reunite with your true *Self*. In summary, this is the crucial decision we have been preparing you for all this while.'

The Man Who Kept Dying

Mika looked thoughtful. 'It would help if I learnt of the circumstances that have led me here for the fifth time ... Besides, if we have already met on four previous occasions, why don't I remember any of our earlier encounters?'

The Native American spirit's facial expression seemed to welcome the remark. 'Because the same principle applies as when you are born. The intense focus of the experience on Earth caused you to forget.'

'How come some civilizations on other planets don't experience forgetfulness and humans do? How is this not unfair?' Anger was once more simmering in the young man's tone.

'Other planets rediscovered this truth a long time ago, but they too navigated a process of remembering and evolving. And when one leads a life with an understanding of one's true nature, it automatically becomes a more productive life,' the guardian angel explained.

As frustrating as they were to hear, Mika accepted Askayah's explanations. 'So, this procedure you've taken me through was designed to lead me to the moment of this significant decision ... which is now approaching?' Unsure about the decision itself, he sighed and looked up at the three spirits, who were all looking back at him. They appeared to display extreme pride in his handling of the situation. 'I have many more questions ...'

'We will happily go through a couple more, but you might want to save the others for the next step of your journey.' Askayah winked, once more glancing at the planet behind him.

All of a sudden, a wooden bridge appeared below the

group and the quartet found themselves sitting in the middle of it, the campfire continuing its display of various shades of green. Astonished, Mika stared at the intricate arrangement of the wooden frames. Their design was simple yet elegant: geometric patterns formed from circles and triangles, which, in turn, created additional rectangles and sinusoidal spirals. The motifs glowed with a faint golden light that gracefully complemented the mahogany brown of the wood. Instead of a handrail, the bridge had two long, flat plinths with additional patterns carved into them, delimiting their borders, and each end of the bridge appeared to reach into infinity. The magic did not stop there, however: colourful flowerbeds and sumptuous shrubs decorated each side of the platform. Their colours were particularly intense and the golden glow of the bridge slats, combined with the planets in the background, only added to the enchanting scenery. A faint, delicate scent emanated from the eye-catching flowerbeds, which probably originated from his memories rather than the surrounding blossoms themselves. The ambient energy was more peaceful than ever.

The bridge between life and death.

Mika sighed deeply. Why would anyone ever want to leave this place?

A feeling of disappointment and unease settled over him; he would soon have to part ways with his guides to conclude his journey; he would be stepping into the unknown. Yet, he had learnt that the answers to which steps he should take lay in his heart, but what surprise had his guides concocted for their special guest? He looked back at the spirits. One element had intrigued him since the visualization near the waterfall. One by one, he called them by their names. 'Askayah, Adonnaï, Hakuk. Are these names your spirit names or names taken from one of the physical lives you have elected to appear as?'

Adonnaï plucked a white flower from behind her and using levitation, sent it into the unabated flames of the campfire. The vibrant flames and glowing logs transformed into a magnificent, multicoloured bouquet. She smiled back at Mika. 'Nature. One the most beautiful creations ever. Coming back to your question, these are our spirit names. In fact, we do not possess names. Rather, all spirits have an energy signature instead of a name, but in order to be understood in terms of the human language, which uses words, we translate our energy signatures into names.'

Of course, we are conversing via telepathy. The transmission method had become so natural to him that he had forgotten the four of them were not using words in the same way as when embodied. 'And my spirit name is Milashakham?' he asked.

Hakuk grabbed his attention with a subtle movement of her right hand and confirmed his hunch.

'Milashakham,' Mika said in a soft, reverential voice. The next instant, he felt a dizzying sensation swirling within him: a whispered validation from his ultimate *Self*. A sense of sadness seeped into his mind. He was grateful for all the information he had received from his guides for it had appeesed him: all the questions that had punctuated his human life were finally answered. Whether to continue to identify as Mika or return to being Milashakham was the last one – and probably the only one that really mattered now.

'Let's all stand up and gather our energies,' Askayah

said as he extended his legs, rising in one swift movement.

One by one, the other members of the group rose and stood around the bouquet of delicate flowers. Askayah opened his arms, mirrored by Hakuk and Adonnaï. Mika joined them a moment later, extending his invisible limbs. Placing their hands on each other's shoulders, the spirits formed the beginning of a circle, of which Mika was the missing link. The spirits bowed their heads until they joined in the centre, their faces illuminated by the glow of the flowers at their feet. The young man followed suit, completing the ring. The three spirits slowly started to shift their invisible weight in one direction, then in the opposite one, keeping the clockwise and anticlockwise motion going like an invisible flow of energy, which Mika let himself be carried along with. He relaxed into the soothing, united motion as a powerful melody rose from deep within Askayah, its vibrations circulating through their extended arms, as if they were one single body. Adonnaï and Hakuk picked up the tone and when his turn arrived, Mika naturally joined in. The effect was purifying and energizing at the same time. The quartet took turns in leading the unusual singing session and after several rounds, they released their embrace and put their hands together, positioning them on the centre of their chests. They all bowed in salute of each other.

The time to say farewell had arrived.

'This practice rebalances the energy of your non-physical body so you can continue your journey and explore the spirit world on your own,' Askayah said to Mika at the conclusion of their session.

Although he was yet to recall all the elements of his

life, the chanting session had revived one particular memory. He studied the faces of his guardian angel and his guides, committing to memory as many details as possible.

Askayah turned and pointed to one end of the flowery walkway. 'This is the direction you must take. I cannot tell you what lies beyond this point because all of it will be the product of your own creation. As for your physical life, you will make it your own experience.'

'Will I see you again?' Mika said, holding the gazes of the three spirits in front of him.

Adonnaï chuckled. 'Of course! We will not let go of you that easily. Whatever your decision, we will meet again. Should you decide to reunite with your greater self, we will meet you at that moment. Conversely, if your decision is to return to your physical body, you will walk this bridge again and we will be here, waiting for you. You might stumble across us playing cards or dice to pass the time, like humans do.'

They all laughed and Mika took comfort in knowing that he would have the opportunity to meet them again. He turned to Hakuk, crossed his arms on his chest and bowed. She mirrored his actions and for the first time he detected a hint of sorrow in her usually non-emotional eyes. Adonnaï extended one hand towards him. Mika pretended to kiss it like a gentleman in an old film and she giggled – he was adamant she had experienced life on planet Earth before. Lastly, he turned to Askayah and embraced him as the elder had embraced him during the simulated ceremony near the waterfall.

Empowered by love and confidence, he took a moment and observed the planets around him. Knowing that he had once lived on one of them filled his heart with compassion for humanity and the confusion in which it lived, the same confusion he had repeatedly experienced throughout his life.

'Askayah, Adonnaï, Hakuk … so long!'

'So long, Mika,' they said as one, compassion and pride clearly visible in their eyes.

He turned and stepped onto the never-ending bridge. Less than a dozen steps in, Askayah's voice blasted into his mind, bringing him to a halt.

'Did you not forget to ask one important question?' called the Native American spirit.

The tall young man retraced his steps and said with a broad smile: 'I didn't need to, Askayah. It became evident when we were harmonizing. I forgot about the importance of self-love and simply burnt myself out. You were correct with your comment about being human. I was living in absolute ignorance of my true nature. I don't yet recall the exact circumstances in which I abandoned my physical body, but it doesn't matter for the time being, for I'm certain I will uncover them along the rest of this journey.'

'We are glad you were able to realize this, Mika,' said Askayah. 'We knew you had found the answer within you. However, it was important that you expressed it. I now deem you fully equipped for the continuation of your adventure, for it is an adventure that awaits you, believe me!' He waved his hand as did the two spirit guides.

Mika nodded, offered an appreciative smile to the group and turned round and resumed his steps. As he progressed, the presence of the guides behind him became fainter and eventually disappeared. As he continued at a light-hearted pace, the blooms bowed at his passage. It felt as if millions of invisible spirits were observing him, and with much curiosity. Whatever surprise Askayah had in store for him, Mika was certain it would not disappoint.

Chapter 18 – A new adventure

Between life and death, unknown time

Smiling from ear to ear, Mika strolled across the otherworldly bridge, welcoming the opportunity to be on his own, putting one assured foot in front of the other, or at least imagining it as he still couldn't see his physical body. Yes, finding himself again with Askayah and his guides had been unsettling news, but it had also been an insightful and surprising journey. Initially, he had felt manipulated, even afraid. So many disconcerting revelations had been disclosed that anger had replaced his usually composed demeanour; such was the nature of the revelations that he had had trouble accepting them. However, in the moments leading to his departure he had come to terms with the protocol and the greater reality from which earthlings were so far removed. What had convinced him to experience reality as a human? Although the appeal could be understood from a greater, all-encompassing, spiritual standpoint, once on Earth the experience was certainly not an enlightened or tranquil one: people were always at war with each other over the most ridiculous arguments; and they polluted the very planet that provided them with its precious resources, stripping it of its assets in the name of money, power and control. Humans with their self-proclaimed superiority were at times more animal than animals themselves – and they were slowly and irreversibly removing every single species from the planet.

What a strange reality to want to create.

Nevertheless, the most beautiful people also lived on this planet, and their dedication to arts, music, gastronomy or even problem-solving lifted the spirits of many around them. *Duality. Polarity. Separation. Dichotomy.* Earth certainly was a strange place to live; his guides had highlighted its uniqueness in that respect.

Apart from the sumptuous floral adornment, the bridge lacked any other discernible markers so Mika's sole indication of progress was the planets slowly rotating on their invisible axis around him. In the distance of the infinite starry heavens, thousands of lights floated in different directions. Were they aware of his presence among them? Mika marvelled at them for a short moment as he continued with unabated pace.

His walk took him past the yellow planet where he had, according to his guides, once lived, and closer to the pale-grey one, the very one Askayah had appeared to receive a message from. The young man stopped and scanned its rocky surface. There was no apparent atmosphere nor a single cloud, nor any other meteorological phenomenon floating above its surface. It was just pearl-grey matter with a multitude of pointy summits. He resumed his steps and after a few paces, he was surprised to discover a large gap in the flowerbeds. This was unexpected.

To his right, a large notch on the wooded plinth indicated some kind of recess. Stepping closer, he saw that the flowers around the recess formed a magnificent, ornate doorway. Beyond it was nothing but void and further afield, the grey floating sphere. Mika edged closer and came to a stop. One more step and he would plunge into the infinite void. *What do I do?*

His silent question must have been heard, as without warning a dazzling flash illuminated the heavens, disorientating him briefly.

Once he had recovered from the blinding light and his sight had readjusted, he was astonished to see a giant toboggan run made of pure white light in front of him, the large slide appearing to reach the surface of the beige planet.

'Am I really creating all this?' he asked into the void. Not anticipating a reply to his rhetorical question, he was surprised when a faint 'Yes, you are!' emanated from the pale rocky planet.

'Well, this is the moment of truth then. Apparently, I'm invited to pay you a visit, pearly planet.' Hesitation stopped him for an instant as he considered how best to use the lengthy slide. Casting his mind back to childhood trips to the swimming pool, he launched himself down the gigantic slide, flat on his back with his arms above his head.

The descent was as effortless as it was exhilarating, with the unique sensation of flying at the speed of light. Moments later, he landed with ease on a small, flat area. 'Woah! That was fast,' he exclaimed, sounding giddy. He turned to look back at the slide, but the magical toboggan run had already disappeared. Turning back around, he found himself facing the steep ridge of a lofty mountain. All other possible directions were blocked by unwelcoming, smooth vertical walls composed of a shiny, dark-grey crystal. To add to his difficulties, the ambient light was announcing the arrival of dusk – the gigantic sun he had previously observed already casting the last of its long rays behind the visible summits.

Tuning into his intuition, he opted to ascend the shiny, rocky crest. He knew that the ridge would lead to the correct destination. He also knew that at the summit of the mountain, a special presence was waiting for him – for a long overdue reunion.

The climb was slow and laborious as he imagined himself wedging his imaginary hands and feet in the cavities created by the smooth, glittering rocks. He could almost feel the invisible weight of the climbing apparatus usually required for such a climb. After a few paces, he stopped and scoured his new environment: darkness was unhurriedly taking over the clear sky to his right, a few stars already dotting its deepening navy-blue hue. To his left, the sun was reaching the horizon, creating silver reflections on the spiky pinnacles of the distant summits. Focusing back on the ascent, Mika quickly climbed to a point where the right-hand side of the mountain formed a sheer, almost polished, vertical cliff. To the left, the mountainside dropped away at a less pronounced angle, the slope punctuated by irregular formations of stones. Surprisingly, the surface of the rocks was dry and smooth and there was no sign of earth or scree; the mountain was akin to an enormous quartz with an infinity of polished facets.

As the solitary climber neared the top of the mountain, he perceived that the night was no longer announcing itself with a nuanced hue. He had to reach the summit before nightfall, but how? Of course! Surely he could simply abandon the idea of being human and let his energy form transport him to the top of the mountain, couldn't he?

The result was instantaneous. Why hadn't he thought of it sooner?

Floating above the summit, Mika looked down onto the mountainside below. A giant throne was carved into the ridge. The sharp pinnacles of the crest formed the back of the chair, and the armrests were integrated into the smoky, quartz-like rock. With its clear-cut lines, it blended into the scenery with a simple elegance. Were it not for the fact that someone was sitting on the throne, Mika would have probably not noticed it.

Lowering his altitude, he came in closer to the embedded chair which was occupied by a colossal, old man. A bright light was glowing around the imposing figure, contrasting with his tanned, wrinkled skin. His hair was long and white and he sported an equally long beard. The imposing figure, who was wearing a seamless off-white robe which covered his feet, was sitting upright with his left hand resting on the smooth, polished armrest; his right hand, in contrast, was holding the handle of a light-coloured wooden stick which seemed to have seen better days.

Whoever this spirit was, his presence was unmistakable.

Despite being the size of a fly in comparison with the serious figure facing him, Mika knew the ancient man had noticed his presence but had chosen not to acknowledge it, at least not just yet. He moved around the old man, yet the elder's stare remained fixated on the horizon.

Without batting an eyelid, the man raised his left hand

and pointed a long finger towards the horizon.

The command was implied. Mika turned and looked in the indicated direction. He immediately understood the reason behind the silence of his host: no words could have described the magnificence of the sunset that opened out before him. With the sun now below the horizon, the starry night was gradually absorbing the last pink and orange layers in the distance, like a dark-blue, velvet shade being drawn with extreme gentleness. As the different bands of colours receded one by one, the mountain peaks became alive with a multitude of reflective pigments and additional stars appeared in the sky. The silent and peaceful spectacle was exquisite.

Mika turned his attention back to the venerable man. With the sun now out of sight, the stars acted like small spotlights, providing the necessary brightness to illuminate the mountain top, its sharp features and the two presences at its highest crest.

Having observed the spectacle, the giant man smiled deeply. With his eyes still locked on the horizon, he drew a deep breath and spoke: 'Long time coming, Milashakham!'

Chapter 19 – The All

Between life and death, unknown time

Mika's jaw fell open. *Could it be?*

'Are you who I believe you are?' he murmured.

'I am indeed. Does this surprise you?' the elder replied with much amusement. He turned his head towards Mika and leaned on his left forearm. The pair of eyes gazing at him were so dark they were almost black. 'Did you enjoy the sunset? So many people do not take the time to appreciate the elegance and simplicity of a sunset …'

Almost lost for words, and still recovering from the shock of having discovered the identity of the imposing presence, Mika blurted out a reply. 'The sunset was … splendid … certainly the most beautiful I've ever seen.'

The venerable, old man raised his hand and wagged his finger from left to right. 'Tut-tut … none is more beautiful than any other when you truly appreciate the exquisite beauty of each moment.'

Mika recoiled a little. *It was the most beautiful sunset I've ever seen.*

The steady gaze of the giant man appeared to read Mika's mind. 'Please do not let my tone derail the purpose of your visit. I was merely joking. Sadly, it has long been forgotten by mankind that I possess a pronounced sense of humour.'

The Man Who Kept Dying

'Is this really *you*?' Mika asked. The answer seemed obvious, but for all he knew he could have been facing just another elder spirit.

The old man leant back in his throne, frowned and caressed his long beard. He looked up at the stars for a moment before turning back to Mika, this time smiling from ear to ear. 'My dear one, I am the Universal Force behind all there is. I am past potentials realized, the everlasting present moment and all future possibilities to come. I am everything and I am nothing at once. I am the She and the He, not to mention the It. I am the plural and the singular. I am … many other things but the list is too long to recite,' he said cheerfully with a wave of his hand, as if a long time had passed since he had last had to introduce himself.

Mika instantly relaxed. He should have anticipated this encounter would take place. 'Is it OK to admit that I'm only half surprised? I guess it is because I have often vowed that on the day I pass on, I will meet with you and ask how the Egyptian pyramids were built.'

The elder's eyes narrowed. 'Whether in physical or spirit state, you create your own reality, so it is indeed no coincidence that both of us meet at this particular moment of your journey. Isn't creation an absolute perfection once you understand its most intricate mechanisms? And yes, it is fine to admit that you are not surprised to be in my presence. Besides, I cannot be offended, so have no fear around me.' The warm and powerful voice echoed off the facets of the mountain peaks.

Mika smiled. If the ancient had come across as austere at first, his energy now only radiated positivity and playfulness. Besides, he could not have feared the encounter for the simple reason that he had never seen the entity he was facing as a person. Rather, he had always imagined it as the invisible yet cohesive driving force behind the celestial movements of planets and galaxies. But in truth, there had been times when he had wondered if there really was an underlying energy behind all the craziness around him, especially when observing the alienating behaviour of many humans. The real element of surprise, however, was that he was facing a human-like entity.

The young man was about to speak but the elder was already continuing: 'So, the pyramids … Did you know they are a model that exists on multiple planets across many galaxies? They are mighty energy conductors that can modify the energetic vibration, or frequency, of large areas. Some of their chambers were used to access higher dimensions by reproducing the effects of deep transcendental meditation. They do not really resemble their original design as they were once covered with different types of metal to better conduct energy for a variety of applications. I believe I need not explain how they were built. You once guarded one, after all.'

The image projected through Askayah's eyes of the stocky half-human, half-dog being standing in front of a pyramid flashed up in Mika's mind. 'They weren't built by humans? That explains everything.'

The ancient raised his hand and wagged his finger. 'Actually, human beings did erect these precise monuments. But humans had a very different understanding of energy and physics in those days, which happened long before ancient Egypt had risen to become

The Man Who Kept Dying

a civilization. The pyramids were never built with the intention of them becoming a burial chamber, especially when you consider the precision of their mathematical features ... Take the Great Pyramid, for example: it is the only pyramid that has eight facets. It used to be perfectly aligned to true north – now it is only a mere fraction off true north – but everything about its size, length, height, angles or the number of stones used in its construction is related in one way or another to Pi or to Phi. Several of its chambers and internal passages used to point with remarkable precision to various star systems in the cosmos, and with its metal coating, it was visible from beyond the moon when the sun's rays were upon it ... Not convinced yet? Then consider the following: despite all their analogue or digital tools, humans from your era would not be able to build it with such accuracy, for no such tools were used when it was constructed. And its assembly required little labour as the humans in that day and age had fully mastered the laws of physics and energy.'

Mika had read about such features and concluded that it had not been possible for humans to build them unless they had been assisted by more advanced beings. But to learn that they had been built before the time of ancient Egypt and by earthlings with a different degree of understanding of their environment was astonishing. *Why have we lost this knowledge?*

The elder winked. 'Isn't it funny that humans assume ancient civilizations were less evolved than they are or that evolution must be linear when it actually moves in cycles? Should you reunite with your true *Self*, you would instantly remember the details of these ancient times, for the ultimate *You* possesses all this knowledge.'

'The monumental decision ... and the very reason for my visit ...' Mika replied, gazing at the colourful, flashing stars. What a journey it had been. He had no desire to end it this soon. 'Can I ask you something?'

'Of course, anything.'

'How should I refer to you?'

The elder chuckled. 'Let me return the question. What do people call you?'

'What do people call me?' Mika repeated. He perceived a little mischief in the ancient's tone and sensed there was a lesson to come. 'It depends ... generally Mika or Mick, but also Mike or even Mickael in formal situations. Ultimately, I guess it doesn't really matter. All these names refer to me.'

The young man's host nodded his head in approval. 'Precisely! And it is no coincidence that your first name can be broken down into many variants. The same applies to me. People refer to me using a variety of names, yet all these names are referring to me.'

'Even when they assign you all sorts of disrespectful labels?' Mika wondered aloud.

'Yes, even when they do so. But truth be told, it does not matter because everyone is misinformed – I do not even have a name.' The powerful laugh that followed this most unexpected comment echoed like thunder and resonated far beyond the sky and the stars.

Time seemed to stand still for a moment as Mika weighed up the man before him. 'You really have a ... an unsettling sense of humour. I didn't expect that from you. I'm starting to think that you're an imposter.'

The venerable man paused and looked back at his

guest. His facial expression was relaxed, conveying the impression that he had fielded such a comment countless times. 'Remember, you are creating your own reality and you wished to meet with me to discuss the pyramids, which you currently are doing. But ask yourself the following question: why could I not possess humour and allow myself a level of self-mockery? But we digress. To come back to your question, call me whatever you please. I have no preference in the matter. The Universal Force, the Perpetual Energy, the Ultimate Consciousness, the All … take your pick.'

'I like the All. This sounds more … like … who you are after all,' Mika said, hesitating despite the elder's remarks. 'But, if you are the "She" and the "He", to quote you, why do you embody a lonely old man who needs a stick to walk and who sits on what seems to be quite an uncomfortable throne?'

'Because this is how you have always portrayed me, at least subconsciously,' said the ancient, his shoulders shaking with mirth. 'Even if you never imagined me as a person, the human part of you still required to see me as such. Besides, if I appeared as the sum of all energy, you would not comprehend who is talking to you. You would simply hear a voice in your head and believe that you had gone insane. Nevertheless, I can change form at will to match your creation. Would you like to see my favourite one?' the old man asked with a playful wink.

'Please!' *Who would have imagined that the All was so light-hearted and had such a sense of humour?*

The elder momentarily vanished, revealing the rudimentary appearance of the throne he had been sitting on, only to be replaced by an immense, glowing sphere.

Its centre was pure white which transitioned into a delicate gold-like colour on its surface. Strange undulating yellow, blue and red rays radiated from its core. It looked like an atypical sun – an atypical sun that could talk!

'I am love and love is the light that shines through the darkness; I am therefore the light of all lights,' it announced as an opening statement.

If conversing with his non-human life guides had been an experience, trying to have a conversation with a giant luminous orb was a whole new challenge altogether. 'Why am I not blinded?' Mika asked, staring into the incandescent sphere illuminating the mountainside as if it were daytime.

'Purely because you are looking at me through your spirit eyes and not the ones of your physical body,' the sphere replied with growing radiance.

Mika could feel the same playful energy he had sensed in the venerable man emanating from the light. 'Of course, I keep forgetting that I'm hovering between two states.'

'Not for long. You are now completing the last leg of your wonderful journey into conscious creation. However, I cannot believe that the ever-curious and playful fragment of Milashakham, which Mika is, has made all this effort to step outside its physical shell to solely enquire about the origin of the pyramids ... Go on, what else do you have for me?'

Mika looked thoughtful. Although he had anticipated that the second part of the procedure might lead to him possibly meeting the All, he remained disconcerted by its laid-back attitude. This raised many questions: in particular, he wanted to establish the missing connection between the amicable and friendly character in front of him and the old, austere figure that had initially welcomed him. Had he been subconsciously limiting his beliefs because he couldn't imagine that the Ultimate Consciousness was simply pure joy and love when he had himself sometimes struggled to display such qualities?

'Do you ever get angry?' Mika asked, staring earnestly into the brilliant white light.

The luminous sphere transformed back into the old man dressed in white, except this time his face was a lot younger and less stern. He looked intently at his guest and joined his hands in front of his beard, connecting his fingertips one by one. 'How could I?' he shrugged. 'I am pure love so why would I ever feel the need to become angry? Having said that, I do experience anger through you humans and through other life forms who express this emotion.'

Although it was easier to engage with an entity with a human appearance, rather than a spherical form, Mika was still perplexed by the reply. 'I beg your pardon?'

The ancient chuckled and raised his stick to the sky. As he waved it in various directions, animated golden letters and numbers magically formed in the air.

Mika read them in silence but was interrupted by his host's commanding voice: 'Human forgetfulness 101 – Lesson number one: Who am I?'

Chapter 20 – Who am I?

Between life and death, unknown time

The venerable man turned back to his guest, paused for effect then spoke: 'Mika, what does the Latin sentence *Cogito ergo sum* mean?'

'I do not have the foggiest idea …'

'It means "I think, therefore I am",' the elder replied, mimicking a deep-thinking pose, with his elbow bent and his thumb and index finger caressing his long beard.

'Ha! This I do know,' Mika announced proudly, still floating above the mountaintop. 'The French philosopher René Descartes stated it.'

'Correct!' The giant man leant back in his carved throne. 'A great wisdom seeker, just like you and many other humans. However, he only solved half the equation … His significant discovery was that *he was*. The question that organically stems from there is pretty simple: If I know I am, then who am I?'

The Ultimate Consciousness paused again and Mika smiled inwardly. 'Who am I?' the young man queried.

The ancient welcomed the question with a nod, pride reflecting in his eyes. 'You are *all that you are* … that is the sum of all your lifetimes as well as an individuation of me … and I am the ultimate *I Am*, that is to say the sum of all the *all that you are*. Simple!'

The Man Who Kept Dying

The elder's words sounded truthful yet remained somewhat mysterious to Mika. 'You're confusing me ... I understand the part about the *all that I am*, which is the ultimate *Me*, but an individuation of you? This part doesn't ring a bell with me,' he murmured.

The giant man nodded, seemingly expecting the remark: 'Let me offer some context; this is an important notion. You see, in the beginning of all there is, the only knowledge I possessed was that *I was*. All alone, perhaps, but I was nonetheless conscious of being. And I was content with this simple knowledge. Yet one day, as if this knowingness was seeking an answer to a question it was not yet aware of, I asked myself: If I know I am, then who am I?'

Mika listened intently. He could see the connection with the Latin sentence *cogito ergo sum*, but where would the story lead?

The All carried on. 'I rapidly figured out that finding an accurate explanation of such a notion was not going to be practical if I remained on my own, so I started to cogitate on how I could create a new experience for myself and discover who I was in ways I had never imagined possible before. I experimented with a few ideas, then one day ... I had an epiphany! It was all so simple, yet so elegant. I devised that I would divide myself into multiple fragments, an infinity of them, in fact. Each fragment would contain all my knowledge and wisdom, and although a part of me, they would all be equal to me ... for all would be me. Suddenly, the words "I Am" were taking on a whole new meaning.'

Mika nodded slowly, his eyes glued to the elder's as he absorbed his every word.

'My concept was magnificent: learn who I Am through the distinctive traits of each fragment of myself. Nevertheless, learning was not sufficient, for I already know everything ... I had to come up with a plan to give each part a different flavour, a unique perspective, a distinct signature. This is when the eureka moment occurred – I decided to *experience* who I Am.'

The giant man's eyes lit up as he started to draw diagrams in the sky to support his explanations, each magically receding as a new one was created.

'And how would I do that, you ask? By offering these fragments of myself the opportunity to live a temporary physical life in a physical world, at any level they chose – from the tiniest element to the largest ... a bacterium, a rock, a star, even a galaxy, and everything in between. Consequently, the physical world was conceived and once a fragment had experienced life there, it would return to the eternal spirit world, where we now are, to decide upon its next physical experience. I am at all times all these parts, experiencing myself as all fragments at once.'

Such was Mika's concentration that the young man felt a line appearing between his invisible, knitted brows.

'It does not end here, though. Although each fragment, or spirit, which you would refer to as a "soul" in human language, possessed all my knowledge, I decided that they should also have absolute freedom in every action they took, because I myself have no limitations. This meant that when a fragment took on a physical body, or became "incarnated" to use the human vernacular, it would temporarily forget all its knowledge and become distanced from the spirit world in order to live life to its fullest potential. In this way, I am constantly

The Man Who Kept Dying

learning about myself through every unpredictable move of every single incarnated soul in the physical world.'

As the giant man concluded his monologue, the golden diagrams faded into the night.

Mika shook his head slowly. The explanations were a real breakthrough in his understanding of the world he lived in, yet he was fuming internally. He pictured himself exhaling for a long moment as his host observed him with curiosity.

'Are you for real? Essentially, we are just a game for you … and created out of boredom at that. Great! Then why do we suffer so much? Why so much hatred, war and insecurity in the physical world? Is that part of the game you play, how you experience who you are? Does it please you that many parts of you kill each other, and sometimes in your name?' Mika seethed, lashing out at the old man, who didn't appear surprised by his guest's burst of anger.

The elder regarded the young man with a neutral look. 'Mika, do you really think that as an omniscient point of consciousness, I am not aware of the peculiar condition of mankind? Of course I am. I have bestowed upon you free will and you keep using it in an ill-informed manner,' the All answered calmly. 'The explanations I have given you are a condensed version of a much greater and more complex truth. Besides, not all forms in the physical world are equal. Some have evolved and overcome forgetfulness, while others are far more advanced from a technological standpoint than humans and yet are equally violent—'

'What is the purpose of experiencing a violent planet? What is the purpose of life itself?' Mika replied, angrily shaking an invisible arm in the air. He felt betrayed and abandoned by his own creator and consequently by himself. He was nothing but a mere pawn on the All's gigantic chessboard – which was a rather disturbing thought.

Raising a hand, the immense presence interrupted the young man's train of thought. 'You are not a mere pawn, Mika,' the elder countered, immediately addressing his guest's distress. 'Remember, you are no less than me, but you have your own unique perspective while I am the sum of all perspectives. You and I are one and the same. In fact, you are only having this conversation with yourself as much as I am only having it with myself. Because you have lived in a physical body on a planet noted for the intense experience it offers, you now believe that you and I are separate entities. But as with many, this belief system is limiting. The moment you realize that you are no less than one hundred percent of me, but with your own distinct signature, you become me and the illusion of separation ends.'

Mika frowned, restlessness overpowering his invisible core.

'To answer your question about the purpose of physical life, the ultimate *You* makes a choice about a particular lifetime as it sees an opportunity to grow through experience. Whether it is a good experience or a bad experience has no bearing on the choice taken. It is true that it sometimes chooses the more violent path to experience itself fully. How do you know that violence is not the way forward if you have not experienced it? How do you know not to plunge your hand into boiling water if you have not burnt yourself before?' said the giant man.

'Aren't our parents or educators supposed to teach us

that? And if we live several lives, why do we keep repeating the same mistakes before we learn how to overcome them? This makes no sense and your plan seems a tad precarious,' Mika said, rising above the ancient and pointing an invisible but accusatory finger at him. Although conscious he was overstepping the line addressing the immense presence with such vehemence, he was compelled to convey a message from his human viewpoint and now was his opportunity to do so.

Leaning back in his throne, the old man didn't even raise an eyebrow; rather, he smiled with contentment and once more caressed his beard, pensively. 'Your papa has a view about war, doesn't he?' He looked up, his eyes boring into an unnerved Mika.

Answering a question by asking another one was an irritating tactic. Yet Mika understood that the All was akin to a patient teacher who extracted the answers from his pupil by making him discover them for himself. He recalled the sentence once expressed by his father: 'War, when you think about it, is one of the most stupid acts ever because there always comes a moment when a few people gather around a table and agree to stop it ... so why even start it in the first place?' His thirteen-year-old self had replied that because people were prepared to lose their temper over something as futile as the branches of a neighbour's tree impinging on their property, it was hardly surprising that humans reacted on impulse before eventually realizing the stupidity of their initial argument – if they even remembered why they'd started the argument in the first place!

'Your dad is a wise spirit, and so are you,' the ancient commented as he looked beyond Mika and into the starry sky. 'You both have a very similar energy signature and have found ways to teach each other over your lifetimes. The difference in this lifetime is that you are fed up with the state of the world around you and do not relate to it anymore, whereas your dad navigates it almost effortlessly.'

'And why's that?' said Mika with a sneer, still feeling confrontational. Descending directly in front of the imposing figure, he projected himself sitting with his arms and legs crossed to demonstrate his discontentment.

'Because you live in fear and resist life. Your dad does not.'

The punchy reply took Mika aback.

'Fear is the very emotion that stops many humans from expressing their true nature, which is to express love. You see, fear was only supposed to exist for your protection in the physical world: it is a natural emotion designed to make you run faster when chased by a dangerous animal, or jump over a table when a green mamba climbs the very chair you are about to sit on.' The giant man winked. 'Nevertheless, nearly all of your societies are organized in a way that encourages fear through competition, that rewards the survival of the fittest, that only values achievements of the mind or the body and ignores the soul. Take sport, for example, isn't it one of the ultimate human paradoxes? Your sports people are the embodiment of the intense focus on body and mind in the name of competition, and in some sports they are disproportionately rewarded in monetary terms compared with the average pay cheque. Yet, you accept it. Year after year, they get paid more, damaging their bodies in the name of entertainment, until they reach the point where they have more money than they know what to do with. Yet the top sports people are venerated by those who have nothing. In another example, when club teams play against one another, supporters of one team will often hate the supporters from the other and sometimes violence will arise from what is supposed to be a game. Yet, when the national team plays, all the supporters come together in celebration, discarding their differences, only to pick them up again at the next club game … Of course, there are sports people who are exemplary, who are generous, who are inspirational, who plays sports for the absolute love of the game. And of course, not all supporters are violent. And indeed, sports are a great way in which to exert your physical energy. But this illustrates some of the many human contradictions, does it not?'

Although the content of the message was not the most pleasant to hear, the remarks had been astutely presented. Mika had never viewed sports through this lens, for he enjoyed the physical effort more than the rivalry, but it was difficult to fault the All's analysis of humanity's paradoxes. 'If fear is such an issue, what can we do to stop living in it?' he asked.

The old man waved one hand and sighed. 'Humans press me every day in their prayers and in their thoughts for an answer to that question, even when they do not believe in my existence. Every time, I send them the same reply: the miracle antidote to fear is love; reacquaint yourself with your mind-body-soul nature and notice how fear dissipates from your life, for you will remember that you are eternal and that physical life is only an experience of your own choosing. They feel this message through their emotions but think it too simplistic so they immediately dismiss it ... Earthlings prefer to believe in hardship and overcoming difficulties. Leading an uncomplicated and blissful life on Earth could not be further away from this belief system – it is all about listening to the messages expressed by your heart.'

Mika felt a sense of déjà vu. Hadn't he already been here with his guides? Hearing about concepts which were so blindingly obvious, but which in the physical world were impossible to adhere to? Placing both hands on his knees, he leaned towards the old man. He had to understand how humans could stop being led by fear, for it seemed to be the key to changing the game of life, forever. 'You said earlier that a spirit makes a conscious decision to live one type of life. Does that mean that one fragment can choose to lead a life as a dictator while millions of others elect a life of suffering under its future authoritarian regime? How does this work?'

The host's eyes moved to the nearby landscape as he appeared to reflect on the question, as if carefully choosing his next words. 'No one ever choses to be a dictator, Mika. That is the simple answer,' he said in a matter-of-fact manner as he looked back at his guest.

Mika frowned. Once again, he appeared to be missing a link. 'Then why do we have dictators, people who are attracted like magnets to power and the control of the masses? Does this stem from fear alone? Is there a darker force at play?'

'You can put it this way indeed. All spirits take on a physical form to experience their greatest potential. They choose certain life conditions to align with this potential path of greatness, such as who their parents and family will be, on which planet they will have this experience and so on ... the perfect set of circumstances or parameters, if you prefer. Once they are born, the rest of their journey stems from the choices they make, which means that they *do* or *do not* achieve what they came to experience,' the venerable man explained, displaying no emotion about the repeated failures or successes of humankind.

Although the initial joyful tone of the meeting had progressively switched to a more serious one, the All's energy had remained loving and patient as they continued to delve into the depths of life's mechanisms – some of them unnerving him. Each new revelation from his guides and the All had further deconstructed the parameters of the physical world he had been living in, constantly requiring him to rewire his mind in order to keep afloat with the continuous flow of new concepts introduced to him. But this latest one had shaken him to his energy core. 'Wait a second ... we choose our parents? What other crazy mechanisms have you come up with?'

The ancient looked at him with much compassion.

'You do indeed, prior to taking on a physical form,' the All stated as he studied Mika's mystified reaction. 'Imagine a spirit who dreams about experiencing human life as a musician. Becoming a musician is the overall desire of this experience. The how, the what or the when do not matter as much as you think they might, but the starting point is crucial. Depending on how grand it wants this experience to be, the spirit might choose to be born into a family for whom music is a way of life. Conversely, it can select a family that never listens to any music or one which even abhors it. The former path might lead to the spirit becoming a great piano player because the piano is its favourite instrument, while the latter might lead to it becoming the lead singer of a band because this happens to be the way it chooses to express its repressed musical abilities. And from singing, it then goes on to become a great composer later in life as its musical explorations continue. The beauty is that, either way, the ultimate *Self* fulfils the desire it sought to experience: it becomes a musician.'

As usual, the old man's face livened up, clearly pleased with the analogy he had used to convey the significance of the physical world. Nevertheless, Mika remained perplexed. 'That is very eloquently explained, but it doesn't explain the dictator and all the negativity. At what point does the musician lose his or her mind and opt for a symphony made of bullets and cannons?' he pointed out.

The white-bearded giant laughed. 'I dearly love humans; they are passionate yet at times possess this witty sense of humour.' He resumed drawing diagrams in the immensity of the sky. 'It is true that once on Earth, more often than not, a spirit loses sight of its goal … because of traumas, because of fears of stepping outside its comfort zone, because of the repression of natural emotions and many other psychological factors. All these reasons can lead to an individual exerting their authority over others in a controlling manner. But there is one extremely important element to consider here: it is the people around this particular individual who let him or her rise to the position of dictator. He or she can never truly achieve it by himself or herself. Why, you wonder? Because a spirit that chooses to experience negativity rarely gets to that level of complexity on its own. Indeed, it is only interested in immediate negativity. And here comes the important "how so?" factor of human group consciousness.'

The All projected more diagrams against the starry background.

'Let me illustrate this point. You, as Mika, have your own consciousness and create your own reality through your free will. And at the same time, all other humans are creating their reality on an individual basis. All humans form a group that is akin to a unified consciousness. This unified consciousness is a very powerful tool, and if all humans on Earth decided at once that war was an unnecessary experience, then war would cease to exist in your reality. Instantly! The problem is that many struggle to accept that the energetic principle behind human group consciousness is this straightforward, while many others still love the drama of participating in the battle of good versus bad.'

Looking at the fading magical diagrams, Mika slowly absorbed all the explanations. There had to be a flaw in the Perpetual Energy's architecture. If everything was designed with such perfection, why could it not apply to Earth? Unabashed, he continued his questioning. 'This explains a lot, then. But how do we steer the group consciousness? If we disagree with it, can we avoid it altogether?'

'Yes, is the short answer to your second question and I know it will please you.' The immense presence beamed. 'For example, if the unified consciousness believes that the world's population will be reduced by half as a result of a series of disasters and you do not subscribe to this belief, you will never find yourself at the location of those disasters when they occur. And they will occur because the human group consciousness has made them a reality by simply believing in or fearing such events. Yet they will be none of your concern as an individual consciousness. It really is this easy to navigate your way on Earth as a person. Influencing the collective, on the other hand, is another matter – if a plane is going to crash, it is going to crash; you will just never be on board. However, you can open up new potentials to the human group consciousness to a certain extent … We will cover this point later on, as I believe this is the reason for your presence.'

The reason for my presence? Really? This seemed difficult to believe, but if the All itself was taking the time to reacquaint him with long-lost knowledge, maybe there was a greater cause behind his unique journey. Having failed to find a flaw in the master plan, he felt his anger subside. 'Risking sounding like a broken record,' he said calmly, 'why can't humanity rise above fear, traumas or the repression of natural emotions? Is there anything that can be done to fix this?'

Under the stars, the incommensurable figure sat in silence as he considered his guest's question. The distant constellations shone brightly against the dark backdrop of the night sky. How amazing it was to visualize this spectacle without any man-made light pollution reducing its glory, Mika thought.

'I know you like your walks; they help you to structure your thoughts. Let's have a change of scenery and go for a memorable promenade, shall we?' said the ancient, cheerfully, as he rose to his feet.

Mika gasped at the towering presence before him; the

ancient was almost as tall as the mountain itself. The venerable man extended his gigantic left hand and opened it, his palm facing up towards the dark-blue atmosphere. Mika felt a strong inclination to move and place himself on the enormous hand, his infinitesimal size in comparison with the bearded man truly dawning on him.

Chapter 21 – I exist

Between life and death, unknown time

With extreme gentleness, the old man brought his fingers up into a claw around Mika and pulled him close to his chest. In one swift motion, he pushed the young man inside his heart space. The next instant, Mika was hit by an intense and radiant energy. Pure love surrounded him; pure love pulsated through him, love of a quality that mere words could never describe with accuracy. It felt so natural to be in that state he didn't want to leave it. The sensation was akin to bathing in the middle of a giant sphere of light, comprehending the immensity of the omniverse, the limitless physical and spiritual worlds. The emotions expressed by every single life form ran through Mika's energy body. It was almost too much to withstand, the infinite love and wisdom combining in a charge similar to a violent electric shock. His body shook from the intensity of the energy pounding through it. Just as he felt he was about to burst from the magnitude of the experience, the ancient delicately removed his guest from the centre of his chest, casually dropped him off on the surface of a new planet and disappeared.

Lying prone and looking up at an empty black sky, Mika remained quiet for a long moment, processing the power that had coursed through him.

The Man Who Kept Dying

The All is ... boundless!

Mentally moving himself into a sitting position, he took in his surroundings Was he in a different location on the beige planet? The grey, dusty, sandy surface was scattered with rocks of different sizes, indicating that he was at a new site. Small depressions punctured the otherwise almost flat ground. Despite the pitch-dark sky above his head, he could view his surroundings as if it was daylight.

Another mystery of the spirit plane.

Without notice, a giant face replaced the sky and Mika jumped as two immense dark eyes gazed at him.

'Ha ha! This entrance never gets old!' the giant figure laughed, a look of mischief in his eyes.

'Is this how you intend to join me for a walk?' Mika quipped, quickly recovering from the startling apparition.

The deep-set eyes stared at him, unblinking. 'Give me a moment,' the elder finally replied cheerfully and disappeared once more.

The young man smiled. He had already figured out the implied message: he should start walking and the Universal Force would continue to communicate with him, even if invisible. Mika imagined himself standing and then started to stroll towards the horizon, alone in the deserted and dust-ridden landscape.

After a few steps, he noticed he had company: a woman had materialized to his right and was walking beside him. Almost his height, she had long, shiny, dark-brown braids that curled over her left shoulder and were held back by a gold pin placed at the nape of her neck. She had a petite nose and the most radiant smile he had ever seen. The slender frame of his walking companion was draped in a long, elegant, off-white dress that complemented her smooth dark skin – the hem of the short-sleeved garment detailed with heavy embroidery. The woman looked at him; her large dark eyes were so profound they appeared to plunge into infinity. A mesmerizing beauty, she looked like a goddess from ancient times; and naturally, a white glow surrounded her.

Of course, the Ultimate Consciousness is neither male nor female – it is both!

'Do you remember the old lady you once helped down a steep flight of stairs?' the woman asked in a voice so soothing it was almost enchanting.

Mika did recall the scene she was referring to. It happened during the time he had a summer job as a park and garden officer, whose responsibilities consisted of opening and closing various parks and gardens across a large city, checking that visitors were respectful of their environment and that they abided by the rules displayed in each of the premises. It was an ideal summer job for his twenty-year-old self, as it meant he could spend all day in nature while interacting with people as and when necessary. Park officers were easily identified by the uniform they wore, which he noticed drew the admiration of children as well as an evident dislike from visitors who had no intention of abiding by the rules.

One evening, as he stood at the top of an imposing flight of stone steps, which were flanked on each side by two artificial waterfalls, a frail, old lady approached him and asked if he could lend a stable arm to help her descend the grand staircase, which led to the park's entrance. They made a sweet scene as, arm in arm, the unconventional pair slowly but surely descended the steps. The old lady didn't utter a single word until she reached the final step. She then patted his arm, thanked him and said quietly: 'You are a student and do this for the summer, don't you?' Mika nodded and she continued: 'Well, I am sure you will have exams at some point. I am a retired teacher ... I'll let you in on a secret: before your exams, repeat to yourself "Everything will be all right because I exist." For as long as you remember to say those words, they will bring you luck in your exams. Remember, "Everything will be all right because I exist."' She then smiled and walked away with small but steady steps. Mika had shrugged and tried to memorize the unchallenging sentence but had forgotten it over the days that followed. At the end of his tenure, he had recounted the story to his mother who had stopped in her tracks and said, 'You saw an angel, son, how fortunate!'

As the memory faded, he reconnected with the moon-like environment and the presence beside him.

'Have you ever wondered why you sometimes encounter people who say the strangest things to you?' the woman said with a ravishing smile.

Mika laughed as his eyes darted back to the horizon. 'You're not going to lecture me on how one aligns with energy, are you?'

'It was not my intention for you have already reconnected with this principle,' the goddess-like woman replied with poise. 'Rather, my point was to highlight how sometimes the most ordinary of people can come out with the most inspirational words. Well, guess what?'

Mika stopped and looked deep into his companion's dark eyes. 'So, you delivered me a message on that day through the old lady?'

The woman shook her head. 'I only inspired her words; she did the rest. You see, "I exist" is the most powerful sentence one can say to oneself, for it brings that person into the present moment, where the life force resides. It makes one realize that one is alive in the physical world, in the temporary possession of a physical body. It can help one survive the most difficult moments when all hope is lost. It brings clarity amid chaos. It creates a direct line to the perpetual love of the spirit world, and nothing is more powerful than someone who consciously proclaims *I exist*.'

The pair resumed their pace and skirted the rim of a giant depression, which reinforced Mika's hunch that the landscape was of a lunar nature. He looked down into the grey basin at more lifeless, shattered rocks. *Are they really lifeless?*

The woman continued her explanation. 'There was another hidden lesson in that experience: because every life form is a fragment of me, by helping this old lady you helped me and, in turn, you also helped yourself, even though you did not realize it. What goes around really does comes back around in the physical world.'

Mika stopped once more and contemplated the perfect face of the woman before him, her infinite gaze which seemed to possess the answer to every mystery. He hesitated a moment before asking: 'Did I really sign up for this? I mean, for life on this crazy planet?'

The dark-skinned lady smiled, her deep, dark irises communicating an intense level of compassion. 'Oh yes, you did, my dear one. You carefully planned your life and were so certain of your success, you knew nothing would stop you. Like many humans, the only element that has stopped you thus far is yourself.'

'Which seems to be the case for ninety-nine per cent of my fellow earthlings,' said Mika, with a shrug of his shoulders and a resigned smile. The quiet environment was having a calming effect on him. He knew he was getting closer to the important answer he sought before making his big decision. 'Can we please review how one can impact humanity in a meaningful manner?'

His companion extended a slender arm and pointed towards the horizon. 'Let's continue our walk. The view beyond this clearing is most spectacular.'

As they resumed their walk, the young man looked into the distance. *What surprises does this desert-like landscape hold?*

'Planet Earth is a unique planet, Mika,' the woman continued. 'In comparison with other planets, humans are a very young species and older civilizations would view you as toddlers. However, earthlings are very clever toddlers and you never cease to amaze many of your observers. Like toddlers, the human race does not stop to analyse and foresee the consequences of its actions before taking them. Rather, you are reactive and continue to make mistakes before learning. In summary, you need a certain amount of repetition before making up your mind about something. More evolved species would try something new, observe if it affects them in a positive or negative way, then agree that if it does not bring any improvement, they need to go back to the drawing board. Humans, on the other hand, prefer to collectively crash into a wall at full speed before acknowledging that it was not worthwhile.'

They were now halfway through the clearing, ambling

in the direction of a hill. Given their apparent location, the surface elevation could very well be the exterior aspect of a large crater.

'Is there anything we can do to change this inherent aptitude, or do we have to let time run its course and hope humanity will eventually grow into well-behaved adults?' Mika challenged. Was evolution all part of the master plan, therefore there was no need for one to attempt to influence it?

His walking companion kept looking ahead as they progressed, her serene energy contrasting with the perceived mischief of the All's previous appearance. 'You love Earth, Mika, but you are not happy with how life on it is currently structured. Yet the very fact that you ask the question means that you care more about the human condition than you think. Many other earthlings do too, but they feel trapped and unable to effect change around them. Yet, no one is ever trapped and the best action one can take is to not try to change mankind ... I appreciate it seems like counterintuitive advice, but if you first change yourself, that is, your perception of who you *really* are, the rest will follow organically. Understand that everything is energy and you decided to take on a physical form on Earth, to experience yourself as a human. There is a purpose behind your experience. Therefore, my advice to you is to stick to the statement you made prior to embodying this life and complete it. The energy generated by such an achievement is enough to change the state of your planet over time. And it does not take an enormous number of fulfilled beings to steer Earth in a new direction.'

Mika furrowed his invisible brow. 'And what was my

statement? I feel the urgent need to reconnect with it.'

The woman halted, scoured the ground and mumbled a few inaudible words as she stepped away. As the goddess-like woman reached a compact pile of large, dusty rocks, Mika watched with curiosity as she bent down smoothly and turned the heavy rocks with such ease they ought to have been hollow.

'Ha! I found it!' she said, standing up and waving a small object above her head. Her face was beaming, as if she had just uncovered a most coveted treasure. Retracing her steps, she held a small, dark, rectangular wooden box, which she opened with care, revealing a rolled parchment neatly tucked inside the thick, wooden frame.

'What is it?' Mika asked, his eyes widening as they both looked down at the mysterious paper.

'Your statement,' the goddess-like lady replied, her eyes fleetingly catching his before they went back to the box in her delicate hands. 'When you enquired about it, I asked your guide Adonnaï, via telepathy, to forward it to me and naturally, being the playful spirit that she is, she found it amusing to play hide and seek with me.'

'Is it OK to play games like this with you?' Mika asked, surprised that the All did not seem offended by Adonnaï's mischievous manners.

The woman laughed as she moved her hair back over her shoulder: 'I have already told you: nothing fazes me. Obviously, I am fully aware of the ins and outs of why you settled for an adventure on planet Earth, but I have decided that it would perhaps be better to show them to you in written format rather than simply talk about them at length.'

After securing the compact box between her left

elbow and her ribcage, the woman deftly unrolled the thick, brown paper, revealing its animated, golden content. It was rather lengthy and written in a language that Mika could not decipher. But, as if by magic, the incomprehensible shapes of the words became irrelevant as their meaning was conveyed to him.

However, the simplicity of the message filled him with unease. *Is this a joke?*

Once more, anger brewed within him, threatening the foundation of his recently rediscovered serenity. How could you remember your purpose if you had forgotten it in the first place? How could you reacquaint yourself with it if nobody had taught you that it was simply located in your heart? And how was it even possible to reacquire it when human societies were built in a way that did everything to prevent you from accessing it?'

Unable to contain himself any longer, he boiled over. 'I'm completely off course! Nothing in my current life matches my statement!' He slammed an invisible finger at the parchment. 'It is simply impossible to achieve this statement in the current state of this planet, impossible! Of all the human race, how many have actually achieved their own statements? How many? I dare you to tell me!' He screamed in anger, jabbing a finger at the thick parchment.

Mika's walking companion did not flinch. Unphased, she rolled up the scroll carefully and placed it back inside its container, which then vanished.

'Have you ever noticed that when one is angry, one is only angry at oneself,' the radiating woman replied, her enchanting smile conveying boundless empathy. 'Yet, let me tell you this,' she said, putting a feathery hand on

Mika's invisible shoulder. 'It does not matter in the slightest to me if you, or anyone, do not fulfil your purpose, for you have endless opportunities to achieve it. Nor will I ever get angry at anyone for voicing the things you have just said.' Her voice was both soothing and compassionate.

Mika sighed as his anger subsided and guilt filled his being. 'I'm sorry, I shouldn't have bawled at you. But please understand that all these discoveries are frustrating.'

'As I have just said, you have no reason to be sorry. Besides, anger is a natural emotion and it can be very therapeutic to express it. The spirit world listens and feels your pain and frustration. In a way, you are a representative of humanity and although you do not see them, many guides and spirits are listening to our conversation,' the woman said, pointing up at the pitch-black sky. As if to confirm their imperceptible presence, a legion of faint lights momentarily twinkled in the night sky before slipping back into the inky darkness.

'And you are right in saying that not many have achieved their purpose after their time on planet Earth. However, you are here with us for a specific reason and I will explain to you how you can correct your path, if that is the decision you make, of course. But first, let's walk to the end of the clearing and climb this hill. It will become clear why I have brought you here.'

The pair continued their promenade in silence towards the bottom of what Mika had earlier surmised was the exterior of a crater rather than a hill. Given the steep angle of the slope ahead, common sense would have suggested they zigzag their way to the top, but the spirit world was removed from the laws of physics. At the bottom of the slope, his walking companion offered her left hand and Mika mimicked taking it in his right. He noticed the extreme softness of her skin. The next instant, they had landed on top of an enormous crater.

The young man's jaw dropped at the view. But it was not the sheer depth and size of the crater in front of him that had taken his breath away; rather, it was the colourful planet he had glimpsed in the distance.

'Let's sit,' said the goddess-like woman. Following Mika's gaze, she added: 'Isn't she beautiful?'

Far away above the horizon line formed by the enormous natural depression, a blue, green and yellow planet, partially covered with grey and white clouds, stood out against the black backdrop. Planet Earth. All this time his intuition had been correct: he was walking on its satellite.

'Certainly is,' he said, lowering himself to a sitting position and crossing his invisible legs. 'From this vantage point, I can see why it seems such an enticing place to visit.'

The pair remained silent as they admired the place earthlings call home. He had recollected most elements of his life as Mika during his time in the spirit world, but how much time had elapsed since his arrival there? Where was his physical body? Where were his relatives? And were they aware of his current state? He pushed the questions to the back of his mind; they would have to wait until later. He needed to focus on the core meaning of his statement. 'So, my chosen purpose was that simple: to remember?'

The woman next to him nodded, one hand playing

The Man Who Kept Dying

with her shiny hair.

This was the main message he had gathered from the energy translation of the parchment. The rest of the lengthy script had concerned elements of his life, such as details of his family, ancestry patterns to be aware of, individuals he would potentially cross paths with during his lifetime as a human and which benevolent spirits could look after him from the non-physical plane.

'But what does it *really* mean to remember, if, being human beings, we forget who we are in the first place?' he asked, gesturing in the direction of Earth.

The beautiful presence flashed a ravishing smile. 'It is rather simple: to consciously be *all that you are*, in a physical world, and to live by this understanding. What does it *really* mean, you ask? It means to be in the present, where all life force resides; to be aware of your eternal nature and therefore not see death as the end but rather the continuity of life; to live each moment of your life in full cognisance of the ins and outs of the worlds that surround you and their energetic fabric; to stop sleepwalking, which in essence means to be awake. Lastly, in human terms, to be accountable for every action you take and never blame them on another person; never again consider yourself unfortunate but rather understand that you create each situation, good or bad, for your own true *Self*'s development.'

Mika absorbed each sentence. It all came flooding back now: the intuitions he could never explain but which he had experienced ever since he was a child; the profound understanding that there was something more to life but which he could never discuss without being judged or frowned upon. He remembered now. Except this time, he was not in a physical body … 'Again, this is beautifully, almost poetically, expressed, but how can humans accomplish such remembrance when they forget all these principles in the first place?' he said, his eyes challenging.

The All pulled up her knees and rested her chin on them, her eyes locked in the direction of the colourful planet. 'If it was easy, every human would do it. Remembrance is the ultimate experience on this planet; it is the experience of slowly but surely transcending the forgetfulness of your true nature. That experience will lead you to living a life in full consciousness of who you really are. From there, everything is possible. Remember, you are a fragment of me in a human body,' she said, turning her steady gaze back to Mika. 'Therefore, I announce to you that you are no less than me, in a human body. You and I are the same; you have all my wisdom and all my love. Stop listening to the whispers emanating from the ignorant or the fearful, for they instil angst in you and prevent you from moving forward with confidence. Once a spirit is awakened in physical form, its life becomes effortless, even on this young and focused planet. Your mind-body-soul connection remembers it can manifest anything into reality, it realizes that reality comes to it. You master the human body, accepting its physical limitations and yet transcending them at the same time; you go beyond your five physical senses; you retrieve access to your universal knowledge and are overjoyed to tap into it at any time. Beyond the physical experience, this is ultimately what all humans have been trying to achieve for aeons. Few have mastered it, while others try one lifetime after another as they get caught up in everyday human drama instead of focusing on their own journey.'

Despite the unemotional delivery of the monologue, Mika sensed that the All longed for more humans to reach this level of remembrance. 'So, it really doesn't matter how many attempts we make, or if ultimately we fail?'

The goddess-like woman laughed and her eyes lit up. 'Absolutely not. Because you cannot fail! It just takes longer for some than others ... And let me break the good news to you: at this precise moment on planet Earth, the situation is changing. Fast. Human group consciousness is about to reach a tipping point. You see, throughout history, spirits who had previously mastered life on Earth returned to teach these principles. Songs, poems, books, novels and film scripts containing a long-forgotten wisdom have been written. Many people heard the messages, yet they did not fully listen to them. This is about to change.'

Mika looked at the woman with surprise. Her statement was intriguing.

'Planet Earth's consciousness itself wants to evolve, for evolution is the only constant in both the spirit and physical worlds. As a result, experienced, benevolent spirits have agreed to return to Earth to awaken humanity to its ultimate reality, through their own act of remembrance. They will not try to change mankind or interfere with its different systems and structures. Rather, they understand that the simple act of remembering and living a conscious life is enough to change the energy on the planet, forever.'

The goddess-like woman looked back towards the

Earth with fondness.

'Which is what I signed up for, isn't it?' Mika said, smiling at the apparent simplicity of the challenge from a spirit viewpoint.

'You are indeed one of those experienced spirits who saw an opportunity for your own growth,' she said, nodding. Her tone was neutral despite the significance of her statement.

'Yet, here I am, reconnected to my purpose, admittedly, but half-dead, half-alive …' the young man said, his eyes fixed on the planet ahead, a hint of sadness in his voice.

'Speaking of your in-between state, I think it is high time we examine what happened to you. Do you recall the location of your physical body?' In one swift movement, the woman clapped her hands with sudden enthusiasm and rose to her feet.

Mika followed suit. The answer came to him directly – a message from his heart. 'The south of England. Do you need a postcode?' he said, laughing, enthusiastic at the prospect of discovering the exact circumstances that had led to his arrival in the spirit world.

Facing Earth, the Perpetual Energy smiled and offered her hand. The smoothness of her delicate fingers touched Mika's invisible palm.

'No, but we might need an umbrella,' she replied with a chuckle as they departed the lunar landscape.

Chapter 22 – Back home

England / between life and death, winter 2018

5.44 am

In the blink of an eye, Mika found himself standing in the familiar environment of the open-plan living and dining room of his house. The lights were on and it was dark outside, or so he guessed as the curtains were closed. Three people were in the room with him, but no one was moving, as if frozen in time: a paramedic was focused on his notetaking; his wife was aghast and in motion towards the sofa on which he, or more precisely his lifeless physical shell, was laid with one arm extended towards the coffee table.

He walked around the paramedic and his wife in an attempt to grab their attention but nothing happened. He was invisible to them. It was as if he had entered a still scene from a paused film. He looked around for the All, but she was nowhere to be seen. Crossing the living room, he approached his collapsed body and observed it. Aside from the disturbing sensation of seeing his physical self from outside his body, he concluded that this was not exactly how he had imagined he would pass away. *But do you ever get to choose the circumstances of your departure?*

'Yes, you do,' said a deep male voice.

Mika jumped and turned around. Neither the

paramedic nor his wife had moved an inch and the frozen scene remained unchanged. 'You startled me. Where are you?' Mika asked as he scanned the room in search of the Ultimate Consciousness.

'Everywhere and nowhere. I am demonstrating another aspect of myself by not being present,' the invisible presence replied.

Mika sighed gently. He was glad that communication had been re-established. 'Why is everything frozen in time? And how is it that we can choose the circumstances of our passing?'

'Because both time and death are an illusion,' the unseen voice said with much joy. 'You are now familiar with the eternal state of your spirit nature and the fact that death is just a transition from the physical to the spirit world. In the same way that you create your own reality, you can also create the circumstances of your leaving. But there are only two reasons you would depart the physical world: either you have completed what you came to experience, or the likelihood of you achieving it has become so narrow that your ultimate *Self* returns its fragment to the spirit world because completion is unlikely to occur during the physical lifetime.'

This is perplexing ... Neither option resonated with Mika. Another point troubled him. 'What about our freedom?' He leaned in for a closer look at his inanimate shell. It had to be the weirdest experience: identifying as himself yet at the same time looking at himself from a different perspective. *I do not look great.*

The invisible voice continued its explanation, its tone almost matter-of-fact, as if stating the obvious. 'Free will allows you to delay the transition for a little while, but your true *Self* knows better and although it will offer you additional time, it will ultimately recall its fragment and reunite it with its fullest aspect. This is why you should never judge the departure of someone. No matter their age or the circumstances; it is a decision of their own higher choosing.'

Mika examined his body. His eyes were wide open but lifeless, all expression absent. *I look dead yet I'm alive ...* Wearing a black bathrobe over his pyjamas, he was holding an oxygen mask in his hand, which had fallen away from his face. His other hand, which was lying on the sofa, had a needle inserted into the wrist which linked back to an IV line. The memory of the unpleasant, warm sensation of the intravenous fluid spreading through his veins flooded back to him. *I was alive at that point. What had happened next?*

'Did I subconsciously decide to leave in these circumstances?' Mika asked, with a look of concern. Thanks to his guides, he had recalled some of the events that had led him to this situation, but he still couldn't make the connection with the inert body lying on his sofa. Had he suffered a heart attack? It didn't appear so. Besides, the paramedic wouldn't look that relaxed if that was the case.

He observed his wife. His beautiful wife. His perfect soulmate for this life, which he had recognized from the moment they first talked. What had enticed him to leave her behind as a widow, especially at such a young age? Nothing made sense and from his analysis of the scene around him, it seemed his death was sudden and unexpected. Had his ultimate *Self* made the decision in his name?

'Remember, you are not yet dead ... and know that your true *Self* has not intervened in any way. This is solely the product of your own creation.' The neutral voice resonated in Mika's head.

But what does all this mean? He moved to the large armchair on the other side of the living room and imagined sitting in it. Having placed his imaginary back against the white cushion, he rested one elbow on the wooden armrest. Being back on Earth, in a familiar environment, made him realize that although he had thus far been able to see or hear, the physical senses of touch, smell and taste were different as a spirit.

'When you left your guides,' the unseen voice resumed, 'you had managed to recall that you were doing too many activities at once and that you were exhausted on a physical and emotional level ... never taking a moment to listen to yourself. Deep down, your most pressing desire was to pause your life and reconnect with your inner understanding of it. And here you are, aligning energy to serve you as you so wished, by pausing your life as Mika. What presented the opportunity for you to leave your body, you wonder? Unbeknown to you, you were living with a ticking bomb inside you, the underlying result of a poorly conducted surgery when you were quite young and underwent your back-to-back emergency operations. At the time, your body did not repair as it should have done and you were left with abdominal adhesions. In most cases, these do not cause any health issues; nonetheless, the possibility remained. Remember, you are mind, body and soul. Your mind did not know about the existing risk on a conscious level. Your body, however, was well aware of it, and you subconsciously detonated that bomb as it was the easiest trigger to pull.'

Mika recalled the ambivalent emotions that had started to creep up on him in the months leading to his predicament. He had struggled to reconcile his deeper instincts with the craziness of the world around him. The more he pushed in one direction, the more it seems he was pulled back in the other by society and people. He had taken too much on his shoulders and, unbeknown to him, he had also been living with an undiagnosed health issue ... Yet, there was an enormous difference between life forcing him to take a break and his leaving his body, subconsciously or not. 'I am adamant that I did not wish to leave my body. Could I not just have been sick and in need of rest? Why did it need to be *that* serious?' Mika said, pointing at his unconscious body.

The deep voice echoed in Mika's mind. 'Humans have a saying: "Be careful what you wish for!" As you create your own reality, this saying could not be more appropriate. One sometimes desires an outcome but does not anticipate the many paths that can lead to it. Besides, you were looking for answers about the purpose of life and seeking a reconnection with your true *Self*. Can't you see how perfect and accurate your creation actually is?' the All explained, cheerfully.

'I beg your pardon?' Mika countered, bemused at how far his creation had gone. 'How can I see perfection in leaving my body at my own wish when I'm certain I didn't desire it?'

'But you did desire it, otherwise it would simply not have happened. Stop questioning and accept the situation, my dear one. Acknowledgement is the surest way to full remembrance. In fact, there is no other route,' the voice replied, gently.

Struggling to come to terms with the All's words, Mika looked around the living room. The simple and elegant decor of the room soothed him: he and his wife had a taste for minimalism and zen. Colours were always chosen for a reason and had to blend with the different elements in the room. The living and dining space was a decent-sized room in which the furniture and decorative items complemented each other perfectly. Many small plants punctuated the blend of wood and industrial furnishings, and visitors consistently praised the atmosphere of the house as well as its thoughtful decoration. Right now, however, the energy in the room was glacial. He took a long look at the two long African masks placed on opposite walls – he had always insisted on keeping some memorabilia from his childhood. The masks faced one another. He liked to imagine they were keeping a watchful eye on the house and its inhabitants. Catching sight of the white coffee table in front of him triggered a realization: it was the last thing he had seen before finding himself in the spirit world. Beyond it, on an iron shelf, the clock on the digital weather station indicated 5.44 am.

He stood up and moved closer to the tall, black shelving unit, which covered half of the living room wall, and peered at some of the pictures on the top shelf. The wedding photographs had been taken almost a decade ago. *We were so laid-back. How times have changed.* He visualized placing both hands on his hips and sighed. *Start accepting the situation.* The words still resonated in his mind.

'So, I created my own set of circumstances to put my life on pause, but I didn't foresee that they would lead me to such a dramatic situation …' An unexpected feeling of relief surged through him as he said the words aloud, and with no hint of his feeling sorry for himself. In an instant, and to his astonishment, he had finally come to terms with the whole situation he had managed to create. Creation really operated at an instantaneous pace when in the spirit world.

Although the All was still invisible, Mika could sense it smiling back at him.

'Precisely! And your simple acceptance means that you have already worked through any guilt or shame you felt about it, which is a most crucial step in our process. Bravo!' The Ultimate Consciousness cheered. 'We have almost reached completion and the moment of your most important decision. However, there is one last topic I would like to reacquaint you with. Time.'

Mika's heart sank. *Another* otherworldly concept? 'But—'

'I know you are about to interject but bear with me. This one will literally blow your mind.'

The comment was followed by booming laughter. Given the serious tone of the conversation, Mika had missed those outbursts of laughter.

Chapter 23 – Time

England / between life and death, winter 2018

5.44 am

Standing stationary next to the shelving unit, Mika remained quiet as he waited for the All to proceed with its new topic. Having returned to the location of his lifeless body and seeing his alarmed wife had left him with complicated, unresolved questions. How would he reintegrate his physical self if he chose to do so? Where would he come back? And when? Would he have to endure the tremendous levels of pain he had already suffered? Would the detonation of his ticking health bomb require another surgery?

Caught up in his train of thought, he barely registered the invisible voice's cheerful tone. 'Time does not exist,' it explained in the background. 'It does not exist in the spirit world, nor in the physical one. It is merely an illusion permitted by what humans have labelled as the "theory of relativity".'

If the words initially failed to reach Mika, they returned with the velocity of a boomerang. 'What?' he said, his eyes widening.

The Ultimate Consciousness' laughter resonated in the room. 'I knew this would intrigue you ... "Save the best for last" as earthlings often say. As this is our final topic

The Man Who Kept Dying

and you have already reacquainted yourself with many truths from both the physical and spirit worlds, I am certain you will want me to keep it simple.'

Pretending to lean one elbow on one of the shelves of the unit, Mika nodded imperceptibly. Curiosity prevented him from commenting that 'simple' was an understatement in the journey he had so far embarked on.

The voice continued, its tone buoyant. 'In the physical realm, time is an illusion that contextualizes the notion of past-present-future, but in reality, there is only the present moment and the next possibility you choose in that moment. When you compare one action against another you have previously taken, you have one point of reference in what you call the "past" but seen from the present moment. The same applies when you envisage an action in the future: you create a point of reference ahead of you, also seen from the present moment. Conversely, there is no notion of past or future in the spirit world; the present moment is the only constant. As you have noticed on multiple occasions since your arrival, when in spirit form, every action or thought brings forth an instantaneous creation, rendering time and space inconsequential. From a spirit's perspective, a physical life is a succession of present moments with different paths to choose from, whether consciously or not.'

Mika moved into the dining area and imagined himself sitting on the walnut dinner table. He leaned back on his extended arms, letting his invisible legs dangle freely as many questions about the intriguing topic of time sprang to his mind. 'You're telling me that time doesn't exist, yet when in my body I have observed the cycles of night and day, the revolutions and rotations of the planets, the phases of the moon and their impact on tides, agriculture and many other elements …'

'Good observation, my dear one,' the All replied. 'It is because all of these elements have already been written, so to speak. You see, the secret is that the illusion of time is moving through you. Have you not noticed the elasticity of time before? When absorbed in a pleasurable activity or profound meditation and time passed faster than your usual perception of it? From your point of view, you had spent no more than fifteen minutes on your activity when in fact one full hour had elapsed. Time was simply traversing you faster. I know you have also observed that the opposite is equally true.'

Not having the benefit of the All's illustrative diagrams, Mika allowed himself a moment to absorb the mind-bending concept of time moving through him. 'This is all fascinating, if a tad complex to conceptualize and absorb. I guess it's no coincidence that you're introducing this topic in this precise location. Is the absence of time the reason why I'm able to observe this still of the paramedic, my wife and my body?'

'Absolutely!' said the Perpetual Energy, beaming. 'You are watching a frame of your timeline, a three-dimensional picture in which you have the capacity to move because you are not in your physical body. And remember, you have multiple paths in your life; hence you have the choice to return to your body even though you currently find yourself between life and death. The reason why death is reversible is because time does not exist. All it requires is for you to reintegrate your physical frame at a chosen moment prior to your death and veer onto a different track. A nanosecond is sufficient, but you can also elect to come back months or even years earlier.'

'Like a video game in which you can indefinitely replay a mission?' Mika asked.

A deep laugh reverberated in Mika's head. 'You are making quantum leaps in your understanding and are, without a shadow of a doubt, cracking the shell of the illusion …'

Mika smiled. The whole concept of time was proving even more fascinating than energy alignment or reincarnation. However, one aspect was amiss. 'But, you stated earlier that all the elements have already been written, so does it mean that my passing and my visit to the spirit world were destined to happen? Doesn't it contradict the very notion of freedom?'

'You are almost correct. It is true that all elements as well as possibilities within the physical world have already been written. But on top of that, you have the free will to navigate this infinity of scenarios through your own choosing, just as you happened to align with the particular scenario that led you to this current situation. In fact, every human has an infinite number of possibilities as a starting point. Each person sails this sea of opportunities in a unique way, based on their chosen circumstances and their understanding of their reality. The parameters that remain constant, as you pointed out earlier, are the physical planet on which you live and its associated environment. Allow me to reuse your video game analogy. As a player, you can choose from a set of existing characters in order to play the game. You can also create new characters or modify your character's appearance as well as tweak some graphic parameters in the game's environment. But the platform on which your chosen character evolves and the coding behind the game remain unchanged. And this is why you can return at a precise moment in time, which you will soon decide. In the spirit environment, contrary to the physical world, there are no pre-defined possibilities or backdrops as you can create them at will.'

Mika needed to catch an invisible breath. In his physical body, his brain would already have melted from trying to grasp the complexity of the mechanisms created by the Perpetual Energy. He sat upright. 'This is just mind-boggling … In summary, there is no linearity in the spirit world. It is our limited human perception that has led us to believe that everything follows a linear evolution,' he said as he pushed himself back onto his feet. The atmosphere in the living room was oppressive. He needed to get outside for a change of scenery. Discussing such advanced concepts with an invisible presence was simply exhausting.

'Before we go outside and to enable your complete understanding,' said the voice, 'let's hammer the final nail in the coffin of time – pun intended, of course!'

The sentence was followed by more resonating laughter. Mika mimicked rolling his eyes – he still couldn't get used to the All's witty sense of humour.

'Not only does time not exist, but you also *borrowed* Mika's body for this lifetime. You borrowed it and followed a succession of paths which have created your lifetime as Mika. But my absence of limitations means that another spirit can also choose to borrow Mika's body and pursue a rather different lifetime. This spirit might be tempted to explore music, submit Mika's body to bodybuilding or get tattoos, whatever it chooses as its journey in Mika's body ... and because time does not exist, both lives occur simultaneously without your ever being aware!'

'Hang on, you're telling me that there's a version of Mika that has big muscles, tattoos and plays guitar?' The young man chuckled at the idea. The All hadn't exaggerated in mentioning that the topic of time would blow his mind. It had!

'Correct! A version of Mika exists as such because another spirit deemed it an interesting path to follow, but it could also be another lifetime of yours,' said the voice, clearly happy to highlight this particular point.

'Another lifetime of me ... in the same body? You're stretching the boundaries of the imagination here,' Mika replied, somewhat perplexed by the boundless number of possibilities that existed in the physical world.

'I have no limitations and this makes my experience all the greater for it,' said the invisible voice with a degree of cheekiness. 'Spirits often resolve to re-experience life in the same body and explore different avenues. In doing so, they partner with other spirits who take on different roles, just to see if it leads to them achieving their purpose. The spirit who played your dad becomes your sister, your sister becomes your closest friend and so on ...'

'Woah! Careful what you're saying here,' said Mika raising an invisible hand. 'I take it then that spirits who were parents or siblings in a lifetime could become lovers or a couple in another one?' Given the absence of gender in spirits and the nature of the conversations that had just taken place, he would only be half surprised if his assumption was correct.

'Again, this is accurate,' the unseen voice replied,

quietly this time. 'And with that, I am afraid that there isn't much left to cover, my dear one.'

'Imagine telling a human that,' Mika continued – *this conversation is far from over.* 'They would hurl all sorts of abuse at you for allowing these incestuous possibilities to arise.'

'Only because they are living with the illusion of separation and do not remember their true nature,' said the Universal Force, sounding reflective. 'They might find the idea troubling or even disgusting as a human with a limited perception of reality, but once back in spirit form, there is no questioning this magnificent playground that makes up the physical life. As you previously gathered, spirits are neither male nor female energy – they are both.'

The apparent hurdles of a physical life seem almost meaningless in comparison with this rather grand master plan, Mika thought. Yet living within the limited perception of a human body feels so intense and enduring at times. *Let's move outside.*

The absence of a physical form allowed him to pass through the front door, which was standing ajar, without the need to open it. Outside, the lights of the ambulance parked in the driveway flashed bright-blue streaks across the pavement. Despite the early hour, a couple of the neighbours' lights were on. *The usual early birds. I suppose they're wondering what's happening inside the house.* He moved up the street to the nearby park. Transported by thought rather than matter, he found himself in the leafy, green surroundings in an instant. He imagined lowering himself onto a wooden bench under a lamp post and was not at all surprised when the bench started to glow and resumed their conversation.

'The illusion of time is also how spirits experience multiple lifetimes at once. You do not live one life and then return to your spirit form to take on your next exploration in the physical world. Your true *Self* is constantly exploring different paths in different lives, either with the same body or a different one, and on the same planet or another far away. As these lives stack up, you gain experience, and the progression you make in one life has immediate repercussions on all the others. Once all lives have reached their completion, the ultimate *You* retrieves all its fragments, maps new possibilities and sends its many fragments to explore brand-new possibilities.'

The glow of the bench changed intensity as the words were spoken.

'And with that, the lecture on time is finished,' the park bench stated with a bright glow.

Leaning back and extending his long arms, Mika looked straight ahead and shook his head. 'Not quite. You said that time isn't linear. So, if my understanding is correct, when one finishes a human life in 2018, let's say, could one's true *Self* decide to experience a life in say 3089 BCE or perhaps in 4016 CE?'

The bench lit up with a scintillating glow. 'The possibility exists indeed… which reminds me … you left yourself an important clue about the illusion of time,' the All added.

Mika looked down at the bench as it modified its glow. 'Are we about to have another life review?' At this point in his journey, he didn't see much value in revisiting any more elements of his life, whether from his viewpoint or that of another.

'Sorry to disappoint, unless you want to relive your birth,' the park bench quipped with a rippling glow that indicated playfulness to Mika.

The young man paused, thought about the correlation between his birth and time, and all of a sudden exclaimed: 'Of course! I was born in a leap year.'

The bench sparkled in a fashion that Mika interpreted as a 'Ta-da!'. He smiled inwardly. Despite not being fond of having to wait four years to celebrate a 'proper' birthday, he had concluded from a very young age that time was of no consequence to leap-year babies.

He looked around the different areas of the empty park. The naked branches of the tallest trees could have deceived passers-by that tall and menacing forms with far-reaching tentacles were looking down upon them. A large mansion house had once sat at the top of the park; it had later been demolished and converted into two long blocks of flats. The magnificence of the park had remained unspoiled, but Mika had often questioned whether the people living in the tall flats appreciated their grand, picturesque surroundings. He looked past the mature trees and decorative beds towards the large pond and its small natural islands on which ducks, geese and birds cohabited. Nearby, and at the centre of the park, was a fountain, which had been emptied; it would be refilled in the warmer months. It was an agreeable place to reflect, especially as he was unable to feel the cold and damp of the early January morning. He had learnt so much during his journey, yet he knew that he had just scratched the surface of the concepts that he would only truly understand were he to reunite with his ultimate *Self*.

The Man Who Kept Dying

The big decision was looming; he felt it. Should he remain here for a little longer? But there wasn't much more to learn now – was there?

'I sense your indecision,' the park bench observed. 'Which is funny because you have already made your decision. Your human habit of creating a conundrum by trying to weigh the pros and cons in a logical manner is clouding your judgement. What is your heart murmuring to you?' The bench glowed softly.

'I know, yet I have fears about it,' Mika admitted, closing his eyes to better focus on his feelings. His energy was calm but deep down, a stirring sensation was animating his inner self.

'Ah, the human fear of the unknown. Perhaps I can help you see more clearly?' said the All through the wooden bench.

Reopening his eyes, Mika was surprised to see a robin with a fluffy, puffed-up red chest and curious golden eyes standing next to him. The bird moved closer and hopped onto his invisible lap. Fixated on the gleaming eyes of the feathered creature, Mika suddenly became aware that the park around him was no more and he was standing on an unstable, shifting grey surface. With one hand he clutched a sticky yellow handrail, while the other was operating the handle of a weighty set of sliding doors …

Chapter 24 – Luis

London Underground, spring 2019

He opened the heavy metallic gate separating the two Tube carriages and stepped onto the next carriage. The warmth and distinctive smell of the Underground enveloped him as he let the sliding doors clang behind him. It was not an action one would normally perform and he instantly became the focal point of the passengers in the coach. The young man had become used to it, though. Standing at one end of the carriage, he raised his voice and started to narrate – with a pronounced Latin accent – a short story to whomever would lend an ear; the exact same story he had recounted to the commuters in the previous carriage; the exact same story he had been recounting all morning; the exact same story he had been recounting for quite a while now. The ambient noise limited the reach of his words to nearby bystanders, and aside from a group of tourists sitting right in front of him, people were quick to resume their activities and ignore his presence, instinctively.

They have probably guessed from just laying eyes on me. He tried not to feel embarrassed about the way some of the commuters had looked down on him. In a world where appearances mattered more than people were willing to admit, his dishevelled look did not do him any favours:

his previously immaculate, white trainers had turned grey from the accumulated street grime and his dirty socks protruded through the holes that had appeared between the sole and the fabric. His grey, cotton joggers bore multiple stains and his black, crew-neck sweatshirt looked tired. Just like him, they had seen better days.

Luis ruffled his long, unruly, dark hair with a hand whose skin had been darkened by life spent on the streets. Having finished the story of his current predicament, the young man took a step towards the group of tourists and presented them with a red, worn-out, cardboard cup which already contained some coins. Some gave him a compassionate look, while others averted their eyes and avoided his gaze. None showed any generosity. He had got used to the constant emotional swing between hope and disillusion. It often made him feel sad and ashamed, but he nonetheless always found the courage to keep his chin up. *If only people understood that there is no fun in doing this. It is quite the opposite.*

His expectations had not been high anyway, for it was unusual to see tourists being charitable – most of them usually counted their pennies. With a bit of luck, it might have been their last day visiting the city and they might have been happy to part with whatever small coins they had left, knowing they would be of no use to them once back in their homeland.

Luis looked ahead and moved up the carriage with heavy feet. It was around 9.30 am and it was far from being crowded, which reduced his chances of collecting much. Adding to this unproductive rush hour, the young man was already forecasting a full day of begging, hoping he would collect enough to sustain himself for another twenty-four hours. He would then grab some food and rest and find a place to sleep before starting the process all over again the following day. The repetitiveness was soul-crushing at times, and he dearly missed the familiar hue of the endless blue skies of his home country. For a short moment, he mused over the unfairness of life. *Sometimes all it takes is a few wrong turns for it to become complicated; you end up becoming a prisoner of your circumstances, unsure if tomorrow will bring an opportunity for a way out.*

As Luis focused back on the task at hand and continued to move up the carriage, four commuters ignored him. *Keep moving. People fear what they don't understand; they don't realize that by avoiding me they make me feel even more lonely and unworthy.*

He was a few steps away from the middle of the carriage when he noticed two men standing a couple of metres away from him. Both had taken note of his presence; this had to be a good omen. The closest one appeared to be in his fifties. Leaning nonchalantly against the middle doors of the coach, he was small, stocky and completely bald; dressed in a black business suit with shiny, dark-brown, leather shoes, he appeared to be very well-off. Clearly, there was no need for him to repeat his story because the man reached into the inside pocket of his jacket and extracted a thick wallet. Multiple notes were sticking out of the wallet, raising his hopes that the owner had a charitable soul. Instead, the businessman slid open a zip inside the wallet, extracted a small coin and placed it in Luis' cup.

'It is better than nothing,' Luis said to himself, recognizing a two-pound coin. He thanked the bald man with a nod and a half-embarrassed smile.

The Man Who Kept Dying

He turned to the other person, a very tall, elegant man whom Luis estimated was around his age: early to mid-thirties. The slender man was wearing light-brown business shoes, dark denim jeans and a grey patterned shirt covered by a dark-blue jacket. Standing with one hand clutching the upper rail, he appeared to be deeply absorbed in his thoughts. But Luis noticed that the tall man was fumbling in one of his jeans' pockets. Pulling his hand from his pocket, he dropped a white-and-coral-pink note in Luis' cup with a friendly smile.

Luis nodded automatically and was about to thank the man when he stopped and his jaw fell open. In disbelief, he looked at the note more closely, double-checking its value: fifty pounds! It was a rarity to experience such generosity, and the joy and happiness running though his heart confused him about whether he should express his gratitude first or cry tears of joy. Part of him felt sad that someone had clearly seen he was in a dire need of help, but the generous man didn't seem to regard him in this way, so Luis pushed away his dark thoughts of inadequacy.

Regardless of his conflicting feelings, Luis felt compelled to express his gratitude for the gesture that had totally transformed the course of his day. He grabbed the man's forearm and held it tight. The kind man turned his head and locked eyes with Luis, seemingly surprised.

'Thank ... thank you so much,' Luis said, tears welling up his dark eyes. 'You know ... this really means the world to me because ... you know ... I don't have to do this for the rest of the day,' he added as he shook his cup and gestured in the direction of the rest of the carriage.

'You're welcome. I'm happy that you can now just

enjoy your day,' the tall man replied with empathy in his voice and a broad smile.

Luis surveyed the benevolent stranger more closely: brown hair; piercing hazel-green eyes which displayed intelligence as well as curiosity; a clean, short beard; and a sincere smile. Despite the man's agreeable look, Luis was certain that he was the sort of person that could easily command attention and authority when required. Nevertheless, he sensed that he was standing in front of a humanitarian soul.

'What's your name?' he asked, realizing he was still holding the man's arm as he released his grip.

'Mika,' the man answered, still smiling.

'Where are you from? Your accent is not English,' Luis asked, his curiosity piqued by the benevolent stranger.

'I was born in France, but I've lived in many countries and in this one for quite a few years now. Can't shake off the strong French accent for some reason,' Mika said with a shrug, his tone humorous.

'My name is Luis and I'm Portuguese,' said Luis, raking a hand through his dirty dark hair. His fingernails were grimy as well. 'I came here and things didn't turn out so great for me, so it really touches my heart when someone acknowledges my situation. Thank you so much again.'

Luis' tone turned from emotional to serious. Although he would no longer have to worry about today, tomorrow was another story. He transferred all the money from the squashed cardboard cup to one of the pockets of his joggers.

'Listen, I can't do it for everyone,' the Frenchman replied, putting a large hand on Luis' shoulder. He leaned forward and murmured into the Portuguese man's ear, 'But I am a firm believer that everything happens for a reason. I also believe that things are only going to get better for you from now on.'

Luis felt Mika's words were genuine and the tone in which he delivered them empowered him, temporarily filling him with a tangible hope for better days. He had been acknowledged as a person, rather than as someone less than worthy, someone that society disapproved of because it didn't know how to deal with him. Life had a meaning again.

With his heart filled with gratitude, and sensing that he wouldn't be judged, the Portuguese man decided to open up to Mika. 'You know, this is all very embarrassing for me. People don't realize how degrading it is to have to beg for money and constantly feel like you're stealing from others or that you're a failure.' Sadness and a deep frustration coloured his voice. Nonetheless, he didn't want to complain to the man who had just made his day better than he could ever have anticipated. Destiny had placed Mika on his path but he didn't want to appear as if he was trying to obtain more from him. 'Can I give you a hug?' Luis asked, needing to thank Mika once more.

'Sure,' Mika replied, embracing Luis in his long arms and with much compassion.

The carriage shook as the train slowed to a stop at the next station. A series of beeps indicated the doors were about to open. Luis looked at the tall man, placed his hands together as if in prayer and said, 'I will pray for you, Mika.'

'Thank you. I will pray for you too,' Mika said.

Luis stepped outside the coach with his hands still held

together. The doors closed and the carriage started to move away. Still standing on the platform, Luis held the Frenchman's gaze until the train slipped away down the platform and disappeared into the tunnel.

* * *

Back in the carriage, Mika smiled. He knew he had made a positive difference to Luis' day and he felt all the more human for having parted with the fifty-pound note, which was supposed to be his taxi money for the next two days.

Isn't it interesting that those who have the least are often the kindest? The universe really works in wonderful ways. Had I not missed my train earlier, Luis and I would have never crossed paths. Especially as I rarely travel to London.

He turned and made eye contact with the businessman who had given a two-pound coin from a wallet brimming with cash. The bald man nodded and returned his look with a smile that seemed to express his respect.

You owe me. This was the only cash I had for my taxi fares for the next two days ... and there's supposed to be heavy rain. Now I'll have to walk. You seem to have plenty of notes ... You could have offered one of yours.

In spite of this he knew he wouldn't change how he had acted towards Luis. Perhaps the businessman handed out two-pound coins to different people throughout the day or the week? It would be unfair and very narrow-minded of him to judge the man solely on one action.

I'll walk back home. It's not a problem ... unless it's bucketing down. And even if it does, I can always call someone and ask for a lift.

The train arrived at Mika's station. As he stepped

outside the coach and ducked his head to avoid hitting the low door opening, a thought occurred to him, a thought that was not the product of his own mind: 'Give and you shall receive.' The message was that simple, yet it contained an undeniable and universal truth that in the act of giving, the giver always receives something back.

'Great,' the young man said with a laugh as he headed towards a nearby escalator. 'I'm going to win the lottery tonight then.'

Chapter 25 – The decision

England / between life and death, winter 2018

5.44 am

Mika stared at the icy blanket covering the grass of the deserted park. The usually vibrant green expanse looked pale, grey and still, each rigid blade awaiting the sun which would melt the frost so it could dance in the wind once more.

The visualization lingered in his mind, leaving him speechless. His journey between the physical and spirit planes had been one of intense learning, jaw-dropping discoveries and a profound reconnection with a long-lost understanding; yet, revisiting his encounter with Luis was proving complicated to process. No, complicated wasn't the correct word; it was proving *impossible* to process.

The vibrant robin hopped around him and perched on one side of the bench, tweeting brightly in the still of the morning darkness. The translation occurred instantly: 'I sense you're surprised but given what you have rediscovered about time prior to this visualization, you have no reason to be.'

'But ...' Mika said, still unable to make sense of his exchange with Luis, 'I *never* lived this moment. Nor have I ever grown a beard. I don't even own a grey patterned shirt, which I was supposedly wearing, and I've certainly never ever given such a large amount of money to a homeless person. What was this visualization all about?'

'This slice of life happens in a possible and not-so-distant future of yours,' the robin chirped with a sincerity in its tone that reassured Mika the episode had taken place – even if he had not yet consciously lived it. 'A future in which you live your life in remembrance of your true nature. You did not think twice about offering money to someone in need, nor did you pat yourself on the back for doing so. Instead, you genuinely hoped it would make a difference to Luis' life. And even if this was not the case, you knew it did not matter because you were aware that both of you had created this wonderful encounter between two embodied spirits: one experiencing generosity, the other receiving gratitude. Such moments are truly special ones in my experience through you.'

The robin became more solemn. 'Yet, you are correct in saying that you have not yet lived this moment. What you saw is a possible path you might align with if you decide to reintegrate into your physical body. Remember, time is an illusion and many potentials already exist. You borrowed Mika's body to move from one potential to the next using your free will, choosing different routes, or possibilities. The path you just visualized is one in which you have attained a high degree of reconnection with your true nature.'

Mika looked up at the cold, dark sky beyond the orange light of the lamp posts. He sighed. Normally, a small misty cloud would have formed as his warm breath condensed in the freezing temperatures – at that precise moment, he missed some of the elements of the physical world.

He turned to the robin. 'So, I might decide to grow a beard?'

'And why not?' said the red and grey bird, flapping its wings with vigour. 'On that specific path, you have come to terms with the ephemeral nature of the physical existence and rediscovered the everlasting reality of your true *Self.* You have therefore decided to be more relaxed about life, to live it in full consciousness and to experiment with it. And I haven't even told you the best part of that day. After your exchange with Luis—'

'I have yet to live this day in full, so please be my guest,' said Mika with a chuckle. Looking into the future, what a strange experience that had been. Both strange and reassuring. The knowledge that the possibility for him to be healthy existed brought him infinite peace. Many would love to have the opportunity to look into a crystal ball, and he had just had the privilege to do so.

Sensing that the young man was ready to listen again, the robin resumed its story. 'As forecasted, that particular day happened to be showery in the evening. You had been attending a two-day event where the organizers arranged to distribute virtual money to all the attendees. Much to your delight, among the items you could purchase with the virtual money were umbrellas, so you acquired one. You might have parted with the note you initially intended to spend on a faster and more comfortable ride home, but at least you were protected from the elements when walking home from the train station. You gave with an open heart, not expecting anything in return, and the energy alignment of such a gesture gave back to you almost immediately. On that day, what you experienced was the natural flow of life. Hence the choice of this particular visualization, to show you how effortless life becomes when you do not resist or fight it.'

'What happened to Luis after our encounter?' Mika asked, curious to see if his benevolent gesture had sparked positive changes in the Portuguese man's life. He projected straightening his back, pushing both hands against his invisible thighs – he could still access the memory of the physical sensation of a deep stretch between his shoulder blades and the base of his neck.

The radiant robin took to the air, flew behind him and landed on the other side of the bench.

Mika gazed with admiration at the light-red feathers of its puffed-up chest.

'All sorts of possibilities arose for him: he spent the money both wisely and unwisely; he saved it and lost it; he bought a winning lottery ticket and even died because his true *Self* had achieved the reason it came to Earth: to experience generosity. What mattered for him next was which path he decided to align with, and that path was his own creation … conscious or not. Rest assured that Luis' ultimate *Self* and yours were delighted by the experience you both created when your paths crossed as humans.'

The comment seemed matter-of-fact in contrast with the experience Mika had lived – or had the potential to live, the whole 'time does not exist' reality remaining a difficult concept for him to process.

Mika shook his head and frowned. 'So, you're telling me that the poor guy might have passed away as a result of our encounter? This is quite bleak.'

'Or won the lottery. Did you listen to what I just said?'

the bird countered with much amusement as it stretched its wings. 'Humans have a natural tendency to focus too much on the negative outcomes. But remember, never judge another spirit's choice. If your paths crossed on that day, it is because the energy match was strong enough for it to occur, otherwise it would simply not have—'

The young man buried his head in his unseeable hands. 'I'm not certain this offers much clarity as to what decision I should take.' He projected himself to standing. After drawing in a long, simulated, deep breath, he moved away from the bench down a gravel path that led to the large pond. The robin stayed by his side, keeping pace with minimal flaps of its wings.

Walking was an excellent way for him to clear his mind and he felt the urge to do so now – the important decision was no longer looming; the decisive moment had arrived. Under what circumstances would he meet his guides again? He pondered in silence as he reached the deserted road that traversed the park.

Without a word, the pair crossed the road and approached the pond. A thin layer of ice had formed on the surface of the dark water, so the ducks and geese had retreated to the trees and shrubs scattered on the small island in the middle. Despite the absence of man-made lighting under the tall trees that bordered the path circling the pond, Mika could distinguish its outline almost as if it were plain daylight. He continued onto one of the fishermen's pontoons and admired the upper part of the park from his new vantage point. Easing himself down onto the wooden platform, he could almost feel the crisp, cold air around him.

The Ultimate Consciousness, still in the form of a

robin, landed on one of the slats and looked up at him with its golden eyes.

Casting his mind back to the static scene in his house, just a couple hundred metres away, the young man simulated another deep breath and turned to the presence next to him. 'I can choose the precise moment in Mika's life I want to return to, or reintegrate my body at the moment before I left it?'

The robin flew right in front of Mika's eyes. 'Is that a rhetorical question? Of course, you can return to whatever time you so wish on the timeline of Mika's life, from the moment you were born up to a nanosecond before you departed, and you will have no memory of having ever left your body,' the robin stated with much gaiety, then returned to the platform.

Mika smiled inwardly. *Of course, the All had already covered this when explaining time ...* What a wonderful, if clearly unusual, journey he had embarked on. Yet he could not linger in this state forever.

A decision had to be made.

One of paramount importance at that.

The young man concentrated on the emotions that were running through his energy body, in particular his heart space. The promise of a reunion with his ultimate *Self* was a formidable one.

In an intense flash of clarity, his decision was made.

There was no turning back. Mika had felt it: a deep, unmistakable sensation.

'I have made up my mind,' he announced with renewed confidence. He looked in the direction of the buildings at the top the park. A couple of the windows were illuminated with a faint yellow light that contrasted with the dark-red brick of the imposing structure, the occupants behind them already awake.

Having listened to the emotions expressed by his heart centre, in the safe space of the spirit world where no one was judged, Mika felt a lingering sensation of absolute well-being – one which had arisen from finally being at peace with himself and his in-between life and death state. The absence of guilt and remorse from the self-imposed morality of never doing enough, of never being enough, had brought him to a never-attained-before level of clarity. As exacting as it had been for him to accept it, the hiatus from his physical life had been worthwhile, for he had opened himself up to lucidity.

'I do not understand this planet, and the way humanity acts is an absolute nonsense. We are blinded by the illusion of separation, ego, fearfulness that stems from almost unavoidable ordeals, not to mention a short-sightedness in most of the approaches we take ... as a result we constantly fight with each other and crush those who attempt to bring some peace to this sad place. In doing so, most avoid acknowledging their own state of ignorance and turn a blind eye on their passivity. This is no way to lead your life: sleepwalking through an entire existence, always blaming others while never taking a hard look in the mirror ... This is not how I want to live; I have always sought answers. I accept that my way of looking for them wasn't the most efficient, but I was nonetheless moving forward ...'

The Perpetual Energy remained still and listened with rapt attention.

Mika brought his gaze back to the All. 'You, Adonnaï, Hakuk and Askayah made me realize that the answers are actually simple, so simple that they are almost too good to believe. You all reminded me that this is just a game. A crazy game, but a game, nonetheless. Concept after concept, each of you revived a long-forgotten truth. Revelation after revelation, I criticized, I condemned, I denounced ... but deep down I was standing up for the human cause ... because I felt compelled to share the frustration of the many I have met with who were too afraid to speak out about the fact that *there is more to life than meets the eye.*'

'Therefore,' the young man concluded calmly, 'I will return to my body, for I have now accepted that it doesn't matter when I leave it again. I will return and I will remember my true nature. I will return to my wife, my family and all the people around me to whom my presence matters. Lastly, I will return because, although you or my guides have never mentioned it, every moment spent in your presence has made me realize that I was missing the most important aspect of being Mika: I didn't love myself as a human being. Therefore, I will return to experience the most important of all loves: the love of self.'

There was a long silence as the All observed its guest.

'These are very wise words, eloquently articulated by an equally wise spirit,' it replied after a moment, its tone delighted, almost overjoyed. 'I am glad that you have correctly listened to your heart's message. Indeed, remembrance is the first step into a new realm of being. Once rediscovered, enlightenment naturally follows when one decides to love oneself for who one really is. No more guilt or shame, you realize that you are more than just human. The moment you accept this simple fact, falling in love with yourself becomes the most natural act ever. As the Ultimate Consciousness, I can only love myself and every part of me. So, the moment you embrace self-love, you truly become me in a physical body.' The robin puffed out its chest. 'You are aware, of course, that you will not necessarily remember all these concepts once you reintegrate into Mika's physical body? In fact, you might never remember them.'

Mika stared into the golden eyes of the little bird. 'I am aware, yes. But at least I will try,' he said, his eyes filled with determination. Having made his decision, he now faced another dilemma: how far back should he retrace his steps in his current life? Going back too far in time would create a brand-new life and he might never meet his wife; but going back to just before he had left his physical body might lead to serious health issues; the possible future he had seen, in which he was healthy, was not a guarantee…

'I can once again sense your indecision. There is an avenue you might want to explore, but it is not for the faint-hearted' the All said with much excitement.

Mika visualized himself standing up. What on earth could it mean? How many more cards did the Perpetual Energy have up its sleeve?

'The only requirement is that you must reintegrate into your physical shell just *after* your physical death, otherwise it will not be possible.'

Just after? It was possible to come back after passing? And the All had waited until this moment to mention it!

'Given the circumstances of your departure, you will need to be taken to hospital because your health will be in a critical condition. Of course, the success of this unique route will be your own creation, but what I can assert is that those who have taken it have emerged forever changed by the experience ...'

As Mika leaned in closer to the small robin at his feet, eager to learn more about the novel master plan, the glow surrounding the Perpetual Energy grew and in an explosion of light, the bird vanished, only to be replaced by a familiar deep voice.

'Have you ever heard of what humans call a "near-death experience"?' said the resonant voice.

'Is it not what I am currently experiencing, being in this in-between state?' Mika asked, looking around to see if the All was about to reappear in another form.

The unseen voice continued. 'It is indeed. For once, it is an experience that has been accurately labelled by mankind: fully departing from your physical body and returning to it. Although accomplished by many, it remains a troublesome concept for earthlings' current belief systems. I know you have read about people who have died, been drawn towards a magnificent white light, experienced what humans call the "other side" and then returned to life?'

'So, this is the approach you're suggesting I should take?' Mika said. At last, a concept he was already familiar with. 'I have indeed read such stories. But are they true? Is it not solely the imagination that creates these experiences?'

'I am not suggesting anything. I am merely presenting you with options. Whether you decide to explore them or not is of your choosing. As for the truth behind the stories you have read? Good question, my dear one. Is your entire journey through the spirit world not a product of your imagination?' The All boomed with laughter.

Mika placed his hands on his hips and his head slightly tilted. A pout played on his lips which morphed into a smile. He chuckled. *You create your own reality!* It had been hammered into him so many times; surely he would at least take this concept back with him to Earth?

The invisible yet immense presence read his mind. 'It is unlikely you will recall the totality of your journey in the spirit world because it is far too complex for your brain to process; in fact, the human brain only acts as a filter of your larger reality. However, through a near-death experience, the likelihood of you remembering glimpses of your adventure is strong. What you recollect will be up to you, even if there is a risk, albeit a slim one, of you forgetting it all once back in human form.'

Absolute silence filled the air around the pond, allowing Mika to contemplate the options ahead of him.

'So, to summarize: I can either go back in time before this health incident and attempt to change the course of my life without any memory of me re-appropriating my physical body, or I can retain a glimpse of the afterlife through a near-death experience but face the prospect of what appears to be a major emergency surgery and its potential consequences …'

'Precisely!' the voice confirmed. 'What does your free will prefer to experience?'

Despite being on Earth, the peaceful atmosphere of the spirit world helped Mika connect with his heart space, allowing him to divine the path he most desired. The decision came in what would have previously been a heartbeat.

'You stated earlier that, unbeknown to me, I was living

with a ticking bomb inside my body, which was the result of a previous surgery. As this first operation took place when I was around ten years old, it means I would have to go back to my first decade on this planet to avoid living with an undiagnosed health risk. This is too far back in physical time, and I sense it would completely alter the timeline of my existence as Mika. Deep down in my heart, I am more comfortable with the near-death experience scenario, thereby aligning myself with the future you've helped me to visualize.' A sense of relief flooded through him. Just like that, the big moment had passed. He had made the oh-so-often-discussed important decision.

A moment of anticipation, which appeared to last longer than it probably did, followed.

'This is a brave decision, for one's understanding of physical life is forever altered when one reconnects with the emotions experienced during such a phenomenon. You might feel even more alienated from humanity, even more sorry for your fellow earthlings. On the other hand, you will have deep compassion for each person's journey, and you will negotiate life with full awareness and joy,' said the All with great pride.

Filled with hope, Mika relaxed. After all, was it not the fulfilment he'd been searching for all his life? And now he'd been given the opportunity to finally attain it. It had to be the most appropriate course of action. His journey was reaching its climax and all the elements were now converging towards a potentially bright future. Although it wasn't visible from his position, he looked in the direction of his house. He would soon be back there ... as a human ... as himself ... back where he had left everything that mattered to him.

However, one element still eluded him. 'One more question. Something doesn't add up. If I've visited the spirit world as Mika on multiple occasions, then why haven't I lived a near-death experience before?'

'Because you never felt the need to,' the voice said, followed by a reverberating laugh. 'As soon as you arrived, you instantly reconnected with your true nature and announced, 'Ha! I know where I am. My mistake, see you next time.' Consequently, you reintegrated into your body without any recollection of your short journeys in the spirit world. As your guides explained earlier, this occasion was different in that you had forgotten your innate connection with all that you are. It was therefore important that you unpeeled layer after layer of the larger reality in which you are now present.'

Still standing, Mika nodded and folded his imaginary arms against his equally imaginary chest. 'I fully understand now. And I am at peace with my decision.'

Looking up, he paused and allowed feelings of happiness and sadness to stir inside his energy body. Although he could not physically cry, his eyes manifested the unmistakable sensation of tears welling up. The emotions running through him were once more charged with a profound clarity. 'It's time to say goodbye, isn't it?'

'Goodbye to whom?' the All boomed, briefly illuminating the pond and its adjacent park. 'Have you already forgotten that you and I are one and the same? Besides, I am omniscient and remain present at all times for every single one of my fragments.' It added with a caring tone: 'Pay attention to your feelings, be they fleeting or persistent; the signs and synchronicities, be they subtle or plain obvious; and the words that pop into your mind or those expressed by others, be they crystal clear or mysterious. Although, between you and me, I tend to avoid the latter.'

'Because … words are limiting and you have no limitation?' Mika said with a chuckle.

'Absolutely!' A rich laughter reverberated across the surface of the pond.

As if acknowledging the completion of this particular part of Mika's journey, the Universal Force's energy then vanished, leaving the young man on his own, standing on the small platform by the frozen water.

What now? he thought, looking out across his calm surroundings. *My decision has been made. I have reached this critical moment; now, how do I proceed with the next step? My physical body is just a few hundred metres away … should I return to it and attempt to reintegrate into it on my own?*

Without warning, the world around him dematerialized and an ephemeral yet formidable energy consumed him. In a tick, he was back on the moon, sitting in the exact same spot he had left only moments earlier, the goddess-like woman sitting to his right, hugging her bent knees, her chin resting on them, her beautiful eyes pensive.

The young man turned away from her and looked back at Earth, astonished. Had the voyage to Earth been a fabrication of his imagination or had it really happened? Had the pair even left the crater they were sitting on right now?

Chapter 26 – One last piece of advice

Between life and death, unknown time

Mika looked back at the woman. She moved her hair from her shoulder and turned to him with a knowing smile. The message received was implicit; no words were required. The simple act of imagining themselves in a location had brought them to it, yet they had never left their current situation, being in two places at once. The All's words about its absence of limitations took on a brand-new meaning and Mika felt grateful to have had the opportunity to experience its limitless creation.

He felt equally grateful for the whole journey: it had offered solace in his quest to reacquaint himself with his ultimate *Self*. The spirit world was a restful place to be, where one could distance oneself from the chaotic paths of the physical world. Knowingness had brought an understanding and he was now equipped with the knowledge that resuming his life had the potential to lead to great adventures, especially if he managed to reconnect with his true nature.

The pair sat in silence, observing the blue planet. Clearly, albeit in a subconscious manner, he had elected to pause his physical life – even if the conditions in which he had done so were far from ideal. But he had created it this way, after all, and it was time to go back, to forget and possibly to remember. At least, that was the plan.

However, he had one last query for his host.

'Before we part, may I ask you one last question? It has been bothering me since I first encountered you on the mountain,' he said, his voice calm.

'Go on, my dear one,' the woman replied, already aware of Mika's question.

'You said you are the Universal Force, the Perpetual Energy, etc. Basically, everything that is ...' Mika began. 'Then, one day, in a bid to discover who you really are, you invented the physical world, a world full of experiences through which you would learn about yourself, through fragments of yourself ... And here I am, a part of this creative process ... But where do *you* come from? Who created *you*?'

The question had been on Mika's mind since the All had enlightened him about the universe's true mechanisms.

'A chicken-and-egg situation, isn't it?' the woman said with a mysterious smile. 'The answer to your question is *nothing*. Nothing created me,' she added with an uncanny serenity in her eyes.

The young man furrowed his invisible brow. 'What do you mean by *nothing*?'

Her dark eyes sparkled as they bore into him, her smile widening; she was clearly enjoying her guest's reaction. 'I always was and always will be. That is the very definition of being eternal. But at first, I was nothing,' she explained. 'I was the exact same *nothingness* you emerged into when you discovered you were outside your physical body. You knew you were conscious but all there was around you was absolute nothingness. Nothing. And you.'

Mika recalled the strange sensation of floating in the dark void.

'The more I experimented with myself, the more I started to understand that there was a simple underlying truth to the origin of nothingness: how could I be everything without first being nothing? Here lies a key concept of creation: in order to experience being something, you have to experience what it is like being nothing. Every single fragment follows this concept through its physical lifetimes. How can there be light if there is no dark? How can tall exist if small is absent? How does one know if one is old if there is no youth? In order for something to exist, a point of comparison must also exist, so that one can always situate oneself. I once was nothing and I now am everything, *and* still nothing, at once. Oh, and I, the timeless, gave myself the experience of temporality through the physical world. But none of it really matters. What matters is that you are, I am and we are all conscious of being.'

'So, no one created you?' The question was rhetorical, but Mika was somewhat relieved that there was only one Ultimate Consciousness: one central, pivotal point.

With grace, the woman rose, the delicate fabric of her dress falling perfectly into place. Mika followed suit and elevated himself to her eye level, his movement effortless. Closing the gap between them, she placed both hands on the young man's invisible shoulders, her magnificent eyes full of compassion and wisdom.

The atmosphere was solemn.

'I wish to dispense one last piece of advice to you, a musical analogy, before letting you go on your way,' she began in a soothing voice. 'Life is about the journey, not the destination. So, no matter the instrument, if you were to always play the same note, it would quickly become boring to the ear. Yet, many humans play the same note, day in and day out, without ever realizing it, always setting their sights on their destination and forgetting to enjoy the journey. When their physical life ends and the time to reflect upon it arrives, they desire to listen to the melody of their life. Imagine their disappointment when they discover they have created a dull, repetitive composition. Therefore, I encourage you to play. Play with life and enjoy the music of your creation. As soon as you notice yourself playing the same note, make adjustments and choose a different one. This does not mean that one must frenetically choose different notes to avoid moments of repetition. Rather, it implies that life's moments are to be lived at different paces, with different emotions, through different experiences. Then, when you look back at your life, the most graceful of all musical compositions will soothe the very essence of who you truly are, and you will forever feel great pride in your journey,' she concluded.

While the All was speaking, music emanated from the far reaches of the cosmos. The combined melodies, which Mika perceived were played on instruments that probably didn't exist on Earth, were enchanting.

'You are currently enjoying the symphony of the universe.' The goddess-like woman smiled as she removed her hands from Mika's shoulders. Stepping back, she turned and raised one hand towards the vast, empty, black sky. 'Each spirit is part of this universal orchestra and I am unceasingly listening to its continuous tune.'

Mika nodded. 'It is simply magnificent.' Words could

not do justice to the exquisite composition. 'Thank you. Thank you so much for the journey in the spirit world and for the enlightenment, the love and the opportunity to continue as Mika,' the young man said as feelings of empowerment ran through his energy body.

The woman turned back to him with the most ravishing smile. 'You do not need to thank me for anything. Only thank yourself. Your creation is my experience. Every lifetime is unique and allows me to experience a new possibility, and for this very reason, I am the one thanking you for continuing as Mika.' The All took her guest's hands in hers and looked deep into the young man's eyes.

Mika shivered. It was as if she was looking beyond him.

'Milashakham, you are immensely wise and the path you have chosen is one that very few dare step onto. Your greatest potential is yet to be fulfilled and your capacity to focus on a desired outcome will make the fragment that is Mika negotiate with confidence the distressing days that will follow the return to his body. I can see you have already lined up the perfect plan for him to escape unscathed, bar a couple new scars on his human shell; but if one fragment of yourself is resilient enough to endure such circumstances, it is definitely this one.'

The beautiful woman adjusted her focus back on him. 'Mika, as long as you listen to your inner voice, everything will be fine because *You exist*. Hold these words close to your heart, my dear one, and I foresee a wonderful future for you. Although there is always a possibility through freedom of choice, spirits who decide to return to their bodies rarely leave them soon afterwards. Like many others who have faced a near-death experience, you too will have a message to convey to humanity, to guide it to its greater nature. But, most importantly, you will first convey a message to yourself, to help you reunite with your ultimate *Self* while remaining in your human body. It is an adventure in human mastery that awaits you – the most transcendental and joyful one that exists.'

Infused with confidence about his return to Earth, Mika observed the All's radiant appearance and absorbed her boundless compassion.

The woman took a step back and joined her hands together in front of her chest. 'With that, it is time for you to catch up with your guides. And never, ever forget that I am always here with you; I am always here for you, for all of my fragments, because I am always here for myself. Milashakham, Mika … so long.'

The Ultimate Consciousness shapeshifted into the old, bearded giant Mika had earlier encountered on the mountain top. He looked up at the immense figure who waved goodbye, winked and disappeared, leaving on its own the exploring fragment that is Mika.

Chapter 27 – Crossing the bridge

Between life and death, unknown time

What next? the young man pondered, all alone in the lunar landscape.

His guides, whom he knew he had to meet with, came to his mind. But how would he reach them? He visualized the bridge he had crossed earlier and in the next instant he found himself standing on its wooden platform. Moving from one location to the other in the spirit world was uncomplicated and immediate, but even so, this frictionless way of moving was so unusual that it continued to baffle him.

Mika didn't have too long to contemplate the limitless motions of spirits because he was soon confronted with an unforeseen issue. Facing the wonderful arrangement of flowerbeds and their colourful blooms, he came to a standstill. He looked to his right and then to his left, then at his imaginary feet. The patterned wood lacked any indication as to which direction he should take. He proceeded to take a few steps to his right, then moved back to his starting point and took a few paces in the opposite direction before coming to a halt again. He felt no difference in either direction … Could it be that if he walked in the wrong direction, he would never meet his guides? Was it another test?

The Man Who Kept Dying

Much to his relief, the answer rapidly hit him and he laughed at himself for attempting to make his apparent choice more complicated than it was. *Of course, it makes no difference whether I go left or right. I've already decided my future and both directions will take me back to Askayah, Adonnaï and Hakuk.*

After a short amble, during which he took the time to admire the profusion of flower varieties and colours as well as the revolving planets and stars in the distance, he spied his guides. As Adonnaï had suggested, the three spirits were playing cards with much animation, and they were sitting around a new campfire, which this time burned with multicoloured flames. Approaching the group, he noticed that each card played seemed to affect the colour of the flames and this appeared to be the reason behind their lively session.

'Hello there,' Mika announced with a grin.

On hearing these words, the three spirits stopped their game by making all the cards disappear. They all rose and one by one greeted him with the broadest of smiles and a warm embrace, not in the least surprised by his unannounced arrival.

Askayah stepped forward. 'To us, you only left a moment ago, but we have followed your journey from afar with great interest. We are glad that you have come to the decision to continue your present life as Mika. What you will remember from your journey with us is what you will create during your near-death experience, but rest assured that your whole story between the physical and spirit worlds is documented within the Ultimate Consciousness Library. Perhaps one day you will be able to reconnect with all of it as Mika. We certainly wish this for you.' Askayah's tone conveyed immense pride.

'Thank you for looking after me during this extraordinary voyage of self-discovery,' Mika replied, emotion pricking his eyes. He looked at each of the three spirits. 'I admit that I've not always been the easiest one to guide, especially when I have stubbornly refused to listen to my inner intuition or to your subtle messages. I will attempt to become better at that; although I must confess that the prospect of once more forgetting leaves me unsettled. Nevertheless, deep down, I trust that the next time we meet, it will be at the end of a life lived in absolute awareness.'

Parting with the All had brought a degree of sadness, but it had been counterbalanced by a renewed optimism about his future as Mika. However, accepting that he would have to forget the bond he had created with his guides during his journey was proving harder to overcome.

Adonnaï's joyful energy caught his attention. Her belief in him radiated from her eyes, which burned brightly with happiness.

'Mika, you might only remember a brief moment of your adventure, but it makes no difference, for all beings who undergo a near-death experience are forever changed by the experience, no matter how small their recollection of the event. It is a powerful phenomenon to experience, one that emotionally transforms an individual for the rest of his or her life. Therefore, I have confidence in you. I also have no doubt that we will be in touch again, simply because you will reconnect with us in many different ways.'

The Man Who Kept Dying

'Such as?' Mika asked, putting his hands on his imaginary hips, a glint in his eye.

'Intuitions, dreams, meditations, hypnosis sessions, even talking directly to us at times. The possibilities are there, should you wish to explore them,' the tall blue spirit offered with a reassuring nod.

The young man nodded in silence. Adonnaï's comment sounded enticing.

He turned to Hakuk. Her facial expression remained the most difficult to read, but he sensed a deep compassion and fondness emanating from her petite frame.

'There is one important element we must share with you before you return to Earth as Mika,' she confided in a rather grave tone.

'This sounds serious,' the young man commented, concerned by the sudden shift in energy.

'It is,' she said, raising a long, thin finger. 'As usual, your freedom of choice will prevail, but it is possible for us to see what is most likely to happen to you in the near future, and we deem it important to share it with you.' She looked steadily at Mika as if ensuring she had his undivided attention. 'You have already gathered that you will go through a tremendous amount of physical pain. Try not to let this pain permeate your intuition. Shortly after you reconnect with your body following your near-death experience, you will be taken to hospital. A few tests and hours later, a doctor will tell you that it is likely you will need to undergo an emergency surgical procedure, and you will push the idea away. Indeed, you will be stunned by the physical origin of your problem and struggle to understand it. Later that day, a surgeon will come to your room and offer to bring you straight to the operating theatre. Unless you decide that your wish is to reunite with your ultimate *Self*, decline the offer. Your instinct will tell you that your body will not come back intact from this operation and the reason for this is simple: its physiology will be extremely unbalanced. If you want to make it unscathed, and we know you do, keep rejecting the need for surgical intervention until another surgeon becomes available a couple of days later. This doctor will be sensitive to your case and will take a considered approach. By this time, your body fluids will have re-balanced, ensuring the procedure is a success.'

The information was indeed essential. He had listened intently, already picturing the taxing journey ahead. Had he made the correct decision? Would he remember to listen to his intuition?

Hakuk continued. 'During this time, the degree of physical suffering will be off the charts, but despite the hardship, you will feel that you are not alone. This is because your body can only endure so much physical pain before your true *Self* takes a step back. During those brief moments, the pain will subside and you will sense multiple ethereal presences around you. It will be us and other spirits watching over you, assisting you. During those moments of relief, your intuition will tell you that you will make it through. Hold on to that thought and this reality will manifest before you,' she concluded. She crossed her hands on her chest and bowed.

'I am starting to believe that I might have taken the wrong decision,' Mika remarked, with a nervous laugh.

Placing a warm hand on his invisible shoulder, Askayah was prompt to reassure him. 'It might feel this

The Man Who Kept Dying

way at first, but the extreme physical pain of the experience will ensure that you will not want to repeat it ever again. You will initially curse the A&E doctor who misdiagnosed you forty-eight hours before you landed in hospital, but at the same time you will also be quick to understand that if that doctor had correctly identified your symptoms, you would have ended up in the hands of the first surgeon and this simple thought will send a chill down your spine ... You will see the perfection of the sequence of events and will never call it *chance*. Rather, you will say, "I believe I created this situation because I listened to my intuition which urged me to delay the surgery." The day you realize this will be the first time you touch upon the existence of your greater nature in a conscious manner. You might forget about it straight after, but this realization will kick-start a reconnection process that might take days, weeks, months or even years to complete. How fast this takes place is entirely dependent on your free will. Nonetheless, the cogs of that process will be set in motion and once started, they are relentless. The rest of the journey will be your creation, your history, and we will guide you through it for as long as is necessary.'

The gentleness of his guardian angel's tone comforted Mika and his confidence grew once again. 'So, there'll be a lot of physical and probably mental pain but also a realization further down the line that there is more to life than meets the eye ...' he summarized calmly.

'Exactly. As stated by the Ultimate Consciousness, it is an adventure in human mastery that awaits you,' the elder confirmed.

Mika looked at his three guides. Hesitating, he asked:

'Adonnaï … Hakuk … how long will you stay with me? Will you cease to look after me at some point?'

'Such is the existence of a guide … spirits are busy, as you now know, especially with humans,' Adonnaï said with a chuckle. 'But we will always keep an eye on you as we do with all the fragments we have helped, if less directly.'

'Is there anything else I need to learn before I leave?' As much as he yearned to resume his journey in the physical world and align with grand possibilities, he also wanted to chat a little longer with his spirit guides.

Askayah smiled at the question. 'There is nothing more to learn, Mika. You already know everything. You just need to remember that the answer to any question always lies in your heart.'

'Or the voice in your head, which is *us*,' Hakuk added, her tone light-hearted for once.

'And don't forget the one who wakes you up in the middle of the night,' Adonnaï added with another chuckle, always keen to express her playfulness.

Mika smiled and turned to the two guides. 'Thank you for showing me two non-human manifestations I never could have imagined existed. I suspect there is an infinite number of life forms that we humans have no idea about, and seeing myself embodied as one of those was quite a revelation, not to say a validation.'

Hakuk nodded in agreement while Adonnaï improvised a 'you're most welcome' dance by jumping and twirling before coming to a stop and bowing with a hand extended towards Mika. He mimicked taking it and kissing it like a gentleman, and turquoise lights beamed out of her body.

'Earlier, I guessed that you must have lived a lifetime on Earth – now I'm certain of it,' he said with a burst of laughter.

He moved closer to Hakuk and took her long fingers in his imaginary hands. As he did so, she winked at him. Mika gasped. Until now, her facial expressions had not conveyed much emotion and he had had to rely on her tone or her energy to interpret them, but she had just winked at him – and with her multiple eyelids.

'I too can perform human feats,' she replied with the faintest of smiles, clearly amused by the young man's astonishment.

Mika turned to Askayah and looked deep into his eyes, expressing his gratitude for the continuing guidance and protection the Native American spirit had provided. No words were needed. Through their silent exchange Mika understood that he had once fulfilled the same role for his elder. The nature of the Native American's smile indicated that he too remembered that Mika's ultimate *Self*, Milashakham, had once been his guardian angel.

After a moment of reflection, during which the only action came from the colourful sparks of the campfire, the young man took a deep breath and pulled his imaginary shoulders back. 'It is high time I was reborn. I am ready for a new version of Mika to be released.'

'And it will be a new Mika. That I guarantee you!' Askayah proclaimed as he warmly embraced his protégé. Adonnaï and Hakuk clapped their hands, boundless joy emanating from both guides.

The Native American spirit took a step back and asked with a grin: 'One last question, Mika. What is your favourite animal?'

'Err ... the platypus ... because it is *the* most bizarre creature on Earth ...' Mika replied, a little bemused.

'Your favourite mystical creature, to be more specific ...' Askayah added, still grinning.

Mika now understood where his guardian angel was leading him. 'Ha! The phoenix. Yes, given my numerous encounters with death, I have always joked that I have more lives than a cat and must be a phoenix hidden inside a human body.'

He paused and thought about the meaning of his own words. Stars flashed in the sky and his guides nodded in unison. A powerful sense of congruence took hold of him, as if the whole universe had just agreed to his statement.

'Wait a moment ... All this time I was this close to remembering my true nature ... The phoenix simply was an analogy for the eternal aspect of my ultimate *Self*,' he exclaimed.

At the beginning of his journey, this realization would have filled him with anger and he would have castigated the spirit world. Now, however, it amused him and he was filled with joy. Perhaps joy was not a strong enough word to define the epiphany that had just occurred. Such was his elation that the sensation of happy tears running down his cheeks manifested itself – he even felt the coolness of the lacrimal fluid trickling down his skin, his vision momentarily blurring. He felt lighter and freer. Free to move, to decide, to create and recreate. Death was just a transition and the phoenix always rose from the ashes. Far from being a mystical creature, it represented life's transformation in its grandest aspect.

Askayah's voice echoed the realization: 'It was that

simple indeed … Your affinity with this creature was far from being random: you were guided to it by us. You are now ready, Mika.'

'There is no need to wish you good luck,' Hakuk added, as poised as ever. 'It is now clear that you are resolved to depart from your old path and commence a new adventure. We cannot wait to see it unfold.'

'Hang on a second. What is the process for re-entering a body during a near-death experience?' Mika asked. In spite of his excitement, his nervousness was increasing at the thought of the great unknown he was facing.

Askayah looked amused by the query. 'You will figure it out. We cannot reveal anything to you other than it will be your entire creation. Near-death experiences are singular in the sense that you can create a short or long memory of the experience; you can take back memories from people and places you have never before imagined, see colours you have never before seen or hear music you have never before heard. Most see a bright light, others circulate freely in the room where their body is and can recall every conversation that happens during their experience. Creation is limitless and you possess a good degree of imagination, so yours will be unique and driven by your inventiveness. Simply trust that it will be what you need it to be.'

'Also, be aware that the medication you will receive in hospital can alter your memory of the experience. And your brain will attempt to "humanize" the experience as its filters struggle with the unexpected reality it has encountered,' Hakuk added as a word of caution.

'So there really is no option that will allow me to recall the totality of my journey in the spirit world?' Mika said, disappointed by the thought. Although the All had explained that the human brain would be unable to retain them all, he had secretly hoped that he would bring back many memories from his experience.

'Simply allow whatever happens to unfold. Live the experience, feel it with more than your human senses and you will inevitably remember elements of it. Even if your near-death experience is limited and you cannot recall it in its entirety, different avenues to re-explore and relive your brief journey in the afterlife exist. Trust that you will encounter them in due course. You might even be able to relive our conversations,' said Adonnaï with a calmer than usual tone.

Silent, Mika nodded. The word 'trust' was playing on a loop in his mind.

'Come, let's sit around the campfire,' said Askayah.

Multicoloured sparks flew out of the flames as the logs spat and crackled. The Native American spirit sat cross-legged opposite Mika while Hakuk positioned herself to the young man's right and Adonnaï settled on the other side. Once they were all sitting, the guardian angel extended his left arm and a large, flat shaman drum took shape in front of it. He grasped it with his left hand, positioned the frame against his chin and thigh for stability. As he opened his right hand, a drumstick appeared.

I could've anticipated this ... Askayah was once a shaman and he has chosen to keep this manifestation as a spirit.

Everyone remained silent. With a tinge of sadness, Mika guessed that the procedure was about to commence. When would he encounter his guides again? Would he ever pick up on their subtle communication and messages? Could he really trust that what he was experiencing was real and not just a long, strange dream? Would he ever remember any of it? Many questions jostled in his mind but he let them dissipate. If he had learnt one thing on his extraordinary journey, it was that there was no need to search for answers because they all resided in his heart space.

The drumstick hitting the stretched skin of the drum brought his attention back to his guardian angel. The single beat reverberated through Mika's energy body. A second one vibrated through him. The process had begun. Mika observed his guides one last time, absorbing the moment with an overwhelming feeling of deep affection.

The regular shamanic drumbeats were quick to put Mika into a deep trance, each beat sending a trembling vibration through his energy body, further disconnecting him from his immediate surroundings. Brief images of wild animals appeared before his eyes. Instinctively, he tapped the space below his imaginary clavicle, where the invisible necklace presented to him by Askayah rested.

As the drumbeats increased, his vision blurred and a soft, velvety darkness enveloped him with extreme gentleness. The powerful vibrations gradually became more distant. Mika strained to keep up with their rhythmic beat, but the more he tried to focus on them, the fainter they became, until eventually they disappeared altogether.

This was the moment.

He was ready to let go.

Between worlds, between states, he now was the sole creator of his own experience.

Vincent Ollivier

Chapter 28 – The near-death experience

England, winter 2018

5.44 am

At first, there was nothing. It felt like he was waking up from a very long sleep: his mind was numb. He tried to recollect where he had fallen asleep, but his memories escaped him, as if he was suffering a brain fog. Opening his eyes, he discovered it was pitch black all around. He strained to hear: nothing but absolute silence. Where was he? He couldn't remember nor feel anything; was he standing or was he lying down? He couldn't tell. The sensation was akin to floating in space, in a dark void.

He turned around. Staying still for a moment, he stared into the darkness absentmindedly, as if it was the most natural thing to do. The urge to move then took hold of him. He sensed he could go in any direction he desired, but he lacked a point of reference to indicate where to set himself in motion. Empowered by a sensation of lightness and freedom, he allowed himself to drift within the void, regardless of where it would take him. It felt exhilarating and frictionless, so freeing.

It wasn't long before his attention was drawn to a luminous point in the distance. Within milliseconds of noticing it, he was flying at full speed towards it. As he got closer, he slowed down, savouring the present moment. The small dot of white light gradually became larger, forming a perfect circle that glowed brightly. A playful impulse passed through his mind and he felt compelled to get closer to the luminous circle. Staring into the white light, he could make out three human-sized silhouettes standing solemnly in the middle of the bright circle. Were they in front of the intense light source or inside it or behind it? He couldn't tell for sure.

As he approached the three forms, he smiled. The warm and loving presence of the presences was unmistakable. They were there waiting, ready to welcome him back home, back to the home of the spirits, the home of all souls. He sensed their compassionate gaze upon him as he edged closer, their silhouettes morphing into figures he fondly recognized.

Then it hit him.

Wait a second – I am dying!

The thought ricocheted around his mind and he began to resist the intense pull emanating from the bright circle of light. Images of his family filled his head; he could see every member at once, either ploughing through their day or still fast asleep, depending on their location. From above, he could see his beautiful wife standing next to a paramedic in their living room. She was looking down at his body, her face filled with panic the like of which he had never seen before. She called his name, reeling in horror at his lifeless eyes.

A question from her. An absence of response from him.

He tried to answer but he wasn't in his body anymore. He was *and* he wasn't …

He observed her crouching down next to him and

The Man Who Kept Dying

shaking his shoulder. Try as he might, he couldn't feel her touch, nor could he make his body respond to it.

Another shake, stronger this time. She was now fearing the worst and was about to scream from sheer panic. He could read the successive emotions going through her mind without her having to utter a single word. The paramedic was attending to him now, a small dose of adrenaline pumping through the emergency worker's body as the word 'resuscitation' formed in his mind, his brain transmitting signals in preparation of the possible procedure.

I can't leave her! I can't leave my family! Panic consumed him.

He looked back into the white light, its inviting glow *oh-so* close to him. Staring at the stationary figures, he was overwhelmed by the purity of the love that radiated from them. A peaceful energy flowed through him, tempting him to surrender to the alluring pull. The point of no return was fast approaching.

The more you look into the light, the more you're attracted to it. No! This is not the time. The reunion will have to wait.

With incommensurable effort, he yelled, not knowing whether his voice would be heard by the figures standing within the light. 'No fucking way! I'm not going now!'

The expletive had been unintentional, but it had stemmed from pure instinct, combined with a desire to be crystal clear about his choice.

His words must have been correctly received, for he was instantaneously sucked away from the bright white light, the three figures within its perfect circle disappearing in a kaleidoscope of interlacing white and blue energy lines.

In a flash, he found himself back in familiar surroundings.

As he re-embodied, his eyes flew wide open with shock. The first sensation he felt was a violent shake of his left shoulder. Looking up, he locked eyes with his wife and noticed her dumbstruck expression. Immediately, he reached for the oxygen mask and took a deep breath. Had the gases caused him to hallucinate?

But nothing happened.

His other half appeared agitated but he had barely time to register why when a second sensation hit him harder than a hook punch. He let out a dreadful gasp as pain gripped him and his physical suffering resumed with unabated ferocity.

His wife was still looking down at him, resting a reassuring warm hand on his shoulder. She was talking to him but he wasn't listening to a word she was saying.

The paramedic loomed into view. 'You ok?' the man asked, visibly relieved that he had been wrong in anticipating a resuscitation.

What have I done? I couldn't feel any physical pain before. He winced. *Maybe I should've crossed into the light. I was pain-free out there ... they were ready to welcome me back with them, away from all this suffering ...*

But then he stared into his wife's deep, brown eyes and for a fleeting moment he saw her soul. It communicated with him that there was a reason why the two of them walked side by side through this life. Despite the gripping spasms, he managed to produce a faint smile, grateful to be back in her loving presence. After all, they still had many chapters to write together. He placed his free hand on hers and felt the needle in his wrist restricting its range of movement. Her eyes implored him for a response.

'I'm here, I'm here ...' he replied with a half-smile, half-grimace.

He had made the right decision. A decision that he knew would be the defining moment when a singular truth embedded itself forever in his mind. He might have refused to cross over into the light, but in doing so he had given himself another chance at life, and there was therefore no reason why he would not sail through this unpleasant health episode. Dying again wouldn't make any sense. Not so soon.

Although he couldn't explain it, he sensed that there were presences in the living room other than his wife and the paramedic. In spite of the exhaustion caused by the harrowing spasms in his abdomen, he silently thanked the invisible presences around him and felt they would accompany him in this upcoming chapter of his life. It would be rough at first, but Mika's heart told him that if anyone could make it through unscathed, it would be him, and that everything would be fine – because *he existed*. Unsure about the exact meaning of this last message, he nonetheless decided that he would keep these words close to his heart at all times.

Chapter 29 – A few months later

England, autumn 2018

With his laptop stabilized on a cushion that was resting comfortably on his thighs, Mika leant back in the cosy living room chair and reopened the email he had received earlier from his mum. It contained an attachment to an e-magazine that covered alternative advances in health and well-being. 'Mika, you will love one of the articles in this edition. I would be too scared to ever try it. Love, Mum.' was the simple content of the email. Although the message had piqued his curiosity, he had been at work when he received it and had decided to check it out later.

As he downloaded the attachment, he reflected on how fulfilled he felt in his new job and how much he was enjoying a slower pace of life. How his existence had changed since the harrowing health event that had taken place just seven months earlier. Following a two-and-a-half-month recuperation, during which he regained his physical strength, he had decided to take stock of his life and moving jobs had been a seamless move. Yes, the timing could not have been more perfect; his decision had been based on simply following his intuition and it had paid off nicely.

To think that the major emergency surgery had ended up being such a close shave for him … Looking back, he was glad he had stumbled across a highly experienced and pioneering surgeon. Following the surgery, the doctor had explained to him that given how young and fit a patient Mika was, he had resisted the temptation to do more than the bare minimum, and he believed he would make a speedy recovery. He had also trialled a new type of suture, which had confused many nurses when the time had come to remove them, but they had come with the benefit of leaving fewer marks on his abdomen; two additional scars were the only tell-tale sign of the grim episode, but he could live with that.

Mika doubted that the outcome would have been the same if he had agreed to go ahead with the first surgeon he had seen. 'The morbidity rate is high for this type of surgery, but I can take you to theatre right now,' was how he had introduced himself. Mika had felt a strong repulsion towards the man, and a glance at his aghast wife had confirmed his hunch. He had stared back at the surgeon and replied flatly, 'No, I'd rather try non-invasive procedures first before considering surgery.' The next day, a consultant explained that the surgery would have been a failure because Mika's fluid levels were extremely imbalanced. Two days later a new doctor arrived. Mika felt a connection with the new physician and when faced with no other option but to undergo the risky surgery, he accepted it on the condition that the second surgeon would be the one to operate on him.

Despite the positive outcome, it had certainly not been a peaceful ride: his pain levels had remained very high during the days that followed the surgery, and he had experienced extreme tiredness as a result. On top of that, he lost a lot of body mass and having lain in bed for an entire week ingesting little solid food, he discovered his muscle mass had diminished too. 'It is similar to being an astronaut in space,' the surgeon explained. 'Your muscles have not been exercised for more than a week, but you are young and fit, they will rebuild in no time. Be gentle with yourself and don't start exercising too soon, though.'

Fast forward seven months and he had regained most of the lost weight and recovered full strength and flexibility through the regular practice of yoga. With his better half, they were even planning a trip to the Alps a month later. High-altitude hiking was not yet on the cards, but the couple were banking on some gentle strolls and alpine air to rejuvenate them.

Pushing the memories away, he drew himself taller and looked back at the computer screen. He scrolled through the e-magazine's table of contents wondering which article his mum had recommended – an important detail she had forgotten to mention. He stopped at a feature highlighting new scientific findings on the link between turmeric and a reduction of inflammation in the body. *Could it be this one? There isn't much to be scared of, though.*

Further down the list, another title grabbed his attention: 'The doctor who safely lets you experience death via hypnosis.' 'That looks more like it,' Mika said in a low voice. He didn't know what the content would reveal or even why his mum had sent him this specific story, but he was intrigued. He clicked on the link and started to read about a senior anaesthetist who very early in his career had felt compelled to study the cases of patients who claimed to have had out-of-body experiences before or during surgery. Fascinated by the stories, the then young doctor had started to compile them and attempt to double-check their veracity. In most cases, it turned out that the accounts were verifiable; it was as if the person's consciousness was capable of temporarily removing itself from the body and observing the activities around its physical shell from afar, sometimes even describing activities elsewhere in the hospital or even further afield. Narratives of otherworldly experiences were equally plentiful: some individuals reported seeing a light, while others spoke of seeing deceased loved ones, spiritual teachers and more.

'How fascinating. But what if all this is just the product of the imagination and doesn't prove anything?' he said out loud.

Fast forward several decades and the doctor had partnered with a hypnotherapist to develop a brand-new hypnosis method whose purpose was to simulate a visit to the other side without the participant suffering any of the effects of an actual near-death situation. The results were convincing and the author of the article had submitted himself to one of these sessions. The writer detailed his journey and the spirits he had met during his controlled voyage to the other side. Mika stopped reading and looked beyond the screen of his laptop at the coffee table in front of him.

A recollection buried deep inside his mind was attempting to resurface. He could feel it being dragged back from the depths of his memory, like a bucket full of water being slowly winched up from the bottom of a well. The recollection remained undefined but reading this part of the article had somehow generated a strong feeling of déjà vu … yet he could not align any particular image against it.

He resumed his reading until he reached the last line of the story and paused again, laptop open on his knees. The strange sensation of déjà vu crept over him again.

Could it be?

Looking out into space, he recalled two vague feelings from his time in hospital: the first was a feeling that he was not alone. He had no rational explanation for it, but he was adamant that he was surrounded by invisible presences who were there to assist him throughout the painful moments but also to instil confidence in him, reassuring him that nothing would go wrong because they were watching over him. Who they were? He didn't know. All he knew was that the ethereal connection disappeared straight after the surgery, when he had focused on the reality of rehabilitating his body. The second feeling was that he would not die during the surgery because before being sent to the hospital, he remembered seeing a bright, white light and consciously decided not to pass through it. He had mentioned it to a couple of people following the surgery, but the anecdote had always been told as a joke because Mika believed the vision had been induced by the significant dose of drugs injected into his body and the medical gases he had inhaled at the time. One or the other had mixed the chemical components in his brain, causing him to hallucinate a very common visualization.

Yet, the article he'd just finished reading was screaming the contrary at him. An uncanny and almost impalpable sensation lodged itself deep in his heart. Was there a slim possibility that he had experienced what was described in the article? He focused his attention on the faint memory. All he could remember was seeing a bright, white light and then saying, 'No, thank you.' It had been nothing more than an hallucination.

No ...
Wait ...
There had been more!

He leant further back in the chair, closed his eyes and allowed his mind to fully immerse in the memory. There were missing elements, of that he was certain – he had only recalled a glimpse of a larger event. Breathing slowly, he calmed his brain activity, concentrating on the memory of the light, letting the images and sensations unfold before his closed eyes ... Once again, he found himself facing the light ...

It was dark all around him at first and he was floating. Then the bright, white light appeared and he moved towards it at warp speed. It was effortless ... no movement required ... his thoughts taking him from one place to another. He was making progress ... he could distinguish several people waiting within the light. He had a deep bond with those people, even though he couldn't visualize their faces. How many were they? Three? Some female presences, he sensed. Love, also. Love of a purity that he had long forgotten about. A feeling of panic filled him, panic at the idea of dying. He didn't want to go; he refused to abandon his wife, his family, his friends; he had more to achieve and he wasn't finished with life. No, he wouldn't go. In a rather impolite manner, he made his feelings clear to the beings who were waiting to welcome him. They didn't seem offended in the slightest and in the next instant he was back in his body.

His brain was quick to attempt to rationalize the memory. *Come on, Mika, it stemmed from the drugs and the pain. That is the only logical explanation.*

Yet ... deep down, this explanation wasn't satisfactory. But why? An obvious fact was emerging; some walls were being dismantled.

But then the revelation came to him: when he had moved towards the light, he had been absent of any pain, but when he opened his eyes, after integrating into his body, he had been struck by the high level of physical pain he felt, and yet he had been fully conscious of his actions throughout; they had felt more real than a dream.

He *had* been out of his body ...

The experience *had* been genuine!

He had had a near-death experience and had somehow forgotten about it.

His mind was now racing. How on Earth had he failed to remember such an extraordinary event? The reason quickly became evident: post-surgery, he had focused solely on recuperating and on coming to terms with the underlying physiological reasons that had led to his dire predicament. He had brushed the otherworldly story under the carpet, believing it had been some sort of illusion caused by the strong medication. But of course it had to resurface at some point, when he was ready for it. Given the magnitude of the experience and what it implied, how could it not?

His recollection of his near-death experience was now very clear and he was filled with incommensurable joy. Life did continue after death; this was the confirmation. What a change of perspective. Death was no longer a frightening prospect.

He placed his laptop on the coffee table, stood up and celebrated with a little dance in the middle of his living room, punching the air. He'd always believed that he'd defeated death following his successful surgery, but there had never been any combat with death ... death was just a transition.

His exhilaration of the revelation momentarily dampened as questions flooded his mind. *Why didn't I recognize the figures in the light? I'm certain I've met them before. I don't think they were deceased relatives ... I didn't sense that type of connection with them ... Was there more to the experience than I can recall?*

He grabbed his laptop and made a mental note of the name of the doctor organizing the hypnosis sessions. A quick online search threw up a website that highlighted where and when the sessions were conducted.

'Well, I'm convinced there's a lot more to uncover here ... and there is only one way to find out,' he said, laughing.

* * *

England, autumn 2019

Mika and his wife were finishing dinner with some pieces of dark chocolate and discussing, as had often been the case over the past twelve months, their new understanding of life.

Since his epiphany and the re-emergence of the memory of his near-death experience, he had engaged in much research and activities to try to unravel the mysteries of life. His journey, which had included books, videos, meditation, hypnosis sessions and even discussions with spirits through channellers had not disappointed. Although his recollection of his brief stay on the other side was limited, the young man and his spouse had immersed themselves in the journey, and both now accepted many ideas that they would have not so long ago discarded, such as seeing coincidences as their own creation or learning to listen to their inner feelings – be they a clear sentence heard in their minds or a fleeting emotion. Most importantly, they had learnt to live in the present moment and to not dwell on the past or focus too much on the future. Living moment to moment was liberating and brought more awareness to each experience; there was a palpable joy to revel in.

When Mika had divulged the details of his near-death experience to his better half, she had become pale and shaken her head. 'I saw you unconscious. I called your name and you didn't react, then I looked into your eyes and they were lifeless. This is when I shook your shoulder … twice … for a second nothing happened and I was about to scream, but you suddenly jolted and your eyes were alive once more … You looked at me as if you didn't understand where you were or who you were looking at for a few seconds. The paramedic was busy taking notes and I'm not sure he truly realized why I panicked. I never thought to mention it to you because I thought you'd just experienced a moment of absence, but your story is as creepy as it is fantastic.' Those had been her comments, but more remarkable was the fact that she had witnessed the event, validating that it had indeed taken place.

'I believe I have now completed a cycle,' Mika said quietly as he pushed his chair away from the wooden dining table.

The Man Who Kept Dying

'What do you mean?' his partner asked, imitating him. She stood up, moved around the table and straddled him, her forearms resting on his shoulders, her tender eyes scanning his.

'I'm not sure … It feels like I have remembered all that I need to remember and now I just need to live life to the full, allowing for these new parameters,' he replied as he placed his hands on the small of her back, inviting her to lean closer to him.

'And you know what?' he added with sudden playfulness. 'Remember, I always said that I would write a book about my life when I was old and had lived long enough to gather the most interesting stories?'

'Hmm, yes?' she said as she placed her slender body against his and rested her chin next to his neck.

Mika inhaled the scent of her hair and enjoyed its delicate texture brushing against his face.

'I don't need to be that old man. I already have enough grey hair and stories to tell, so why wait?' he whispered in her ear, half-joking.

His other half gave him an affectionate kiss on the neck and he felt the softness of her delicate lips on his skin.

'And what will be the title of your book, Mr I-like-to-scare-my-wife-by-dying-and-then-coming-back-to-life?' she teased.

Mika chuckled as a possible title popped into his mind. 'The Man Who Kept Dying would be a fitting title, don't you think?'

She leant backwards and locked eyes with him, pretending to be serious. 'You're irredeemable, you know that? It's not *you* who refused to go to the other side, rather *they* didn't want you over there!'

They both laughed as their foreheads touched and they lovingly kissed.

Chapter 30 – Epilogue

Spirit world, unknown time

In the golden hues of the palace's luxuriant courtyard, Askayah was waiting, radiating with happiness. Standing next to a carved, white marble bench, on which another spirit, of human appearance, was sitting in silence, the guardian angel admired the central feature of the secluded square: a magnificent, tiered stone fountain from which water cascaded from basin to basin until it tumbled into the small pool at the base, only to be drawn back up the central column to repeat its infinite motion. *Nothing is linear, everything is a perpetual and evolving cycle.* The wise Native American spirit moved towards the pool of water. Cupping his hands, he scooped up a small quantity of the crystal-clear liquid and studied its transparency against the darkness of his skin. 'It is a pity Mika did not get to experience all the tactile aspects of the spirit world,' he mused. 'The fact he remained connected to his body made the spirit environment feel like a dream to him, with limited sensations ... I am certain he will soon remember that even spirits have access to a material environment, albeit not as rigid and defined as the physical world.'

The elder spirit turned around as the discreet footsteps of Hakuk approached. She was accompanied by Adonnaï who, as usual, was floating silently. Mika's guardian angel had requested that both guides meet with him in this specific location.

As they moved down the vibrant, flower-bordered alleyway leading to the courtyard's centrepiece, the two alien-looking spirits were already aware of the purpose of the impromptu meeting: their direct assistance in helping Mika to reconnect with his true nature had been a success, which meant they would cease to watch over him for the time being. For a guide, this was a joyous and most welcome occasion, for it validated the support offered from the spirit realm. The time had now come for them to pass on the baton. But to whom?

'Adonnaï, Hakuk,' the Native American spirit announced after welcoming them, 'it is always a pleasure to be in your presence. As we have all observed with much delight, Mika has now rediscovered his true nature, at least from a conceptual viewpoint. Your involvement has been invaluable and I always knew that your expertise would be key to negotiating this crucial part of his life.'

'One always draws to them the support they require,' Hakuk said, her energy as composed as ever.

'Undeniably,' Askayah agreed. He turned towards the polished marble bench and as if the signal was implicit, the tall, dark-skinned, grey-bearded man rose to his feet. 'And this is precisely why it is my honour to introduce you to Razakiel.'

Dressed in a long, silky, crimson robe embroidered with delicate, gold, geometric patterns, the human-like spirit joined the group and, one at a time, saluted the two alien-looking guides, taking their hands in his and bowing his head. Adonnaï and Hakuk exchanged a look of understanding. Their assistance, in addition to Mika's recollection of his spirit nature, had sent the young man on a singular trajectory. Spirits like Razakiel were indeed uncommon and the energy they radiated possessed an unmistakable signature, one that set them apart from the rest of the spirit world. Without exception, they had all taken on a human form before reaching this unique state during one of their many lifetimes on Earth. The journey of these notable spirits had been far from a tranquil one and few had remained on Earth once they had achieved an unparalleled reconnection with their spirit nature – such was the contrast between their understanding of the physical world compared with their peers that they had nothing more to experience by remaining as humans. Those who had endured came to realize that humans either put them on a pedestal or, more often than not, attempted to silence them – each scenario caused by a profound lack of comprehension.

Contrary to earthlings' perception, mastery of human life had nothing to do with turning lead into gold or being reborn at will. No, it was far more subtle than that. So subtle that without a strong degree of trust and love of self, one would believe one had gone insane. Besides, most had achieved such levels of remembrance by taking on a feminine energy – another difficult admission for human societies through the ages.

Razakiel spoke his first words with a velvety softness in his tone. 'As we have all observed, Mika has now reconnected with his higher nature, but he has only reacquainted himself with abstract concepts. The next step, if he so chooses, will be to manifest these concepts within his reality and then reunite with his ultimate *Self* while being embodied as a human. It will be my role and honour to guide him on this most special path.'

Quiet until now, Adonnaï intervened with her usual buoyancy. 'His understanding of life has reached a tipping point. However, we have noticed that he possesses a tendency to get angry at the spirit world for not being clear enough and also tends to carry too much on his shoulders. He still attempts to save the world at times.'

Razakiel smiled at Adonnaï's accurate observations. 'Mika's anger is equal parts frustration and disappointment. He still holds the belief that some of the answers reside outside of him. I will guide him to the most pertinent sources to help him access his inner knowledge. His current level of recollection, coupled with his desire to comprehend the incomparable capabilities of his spirit aspect, will inevitably lead him to the most important step of this journey: the discovery of self-love, that is, the true love of self without guilt or shame. As a human, I myself embarked on and completed this most intense and extraordinary journey.'

'Mika is in pretty good hands,' Hakuk said, clearly delighted that the young man's short stop in the spirit world had resulted in such an impressive outcome.

'As we are all aware, once Mika attains this level of human-spirit connection, our assistance will cease and he will walk on Earth fully integrated with his true *Self*,' Askayah added, filled with anticipation at the prospect.

'I can foresee quite a celebration occurring on both sides,' said the ebullient Adonnaï with a chuckle.

The four spirits then exchanged various anecdotes about Mika's life and commented with much joy about memorable moments from their own physical lives, their frequent laughter echoing against the wall of the courtyard.

The ambient light was turning into a blazing tangerine hue. As the group was about to part, Razakiel turned to Adonnaï and asked with evident curiosity in his tone, 'Adonnaï, before we part, I believe you once crossed paths with Mika while on Earth. Would you mind recounting this story to us?'

'It would be my pleasure,' the tall blue guide replied with unbounded excitement. 'I am very fond of this moment we shared on that beach. I was very touched by his attitude.'

The four spirits joined hands and closed their eyes. The next instant, the visualization was unfolding from Adonnaï's viewpoint …

***

Africa, on the Atlantic coast, 1989

It was another hot day for me; the sun was casting its midday rays over the miles of uninterrupted sands and the equally long line of palm trees and lush vegetation that bordered the ocean. A few families were scattered across the fine golden sand: parents enjoying a day out with their offspring. I recognized some of the locals too, and although they wouldn't bathe at that time of the day, I did. To keep my large, barrel-shaped body cool, I spent most of my time in the water.

I happened to be an oddity in the scenery, for it was unusual to find a life form like mine paddling in the waves – by design, I am a very poor swimmer. I blame it on my short, thick legs, which require me to keep contact with the ground at all times when immersed. I can, however, spend close to five minutes holding my breath, head below the surf; but the currents in this area were strong at times, making it a rather risky activity. Even with my ton-and-a-half mass, they were as dangerous to me as I was to other species. Did passers-by know I was the third heaviest land animal on the planet? Only the wise elephant and the thick-skinned rhinoceros outweighed me.

What the humans on this beach knew, however, was that hippopotamuses could be quite aggressive creatures. 'If you see a hippo, head in the opposite direction' was a typical sentence repeated by humans. I found the words amusing upon first hearing them, for the same principle applied to many species I shared my native habitat with: elephants, rhinoceroses, snakes, lions, crocodiles … the list was long.

But I was different to the average hippo in that I did not live with other specimens of my kind, nor did I enjoy time on the luxurious savannah. Rather, I lived my life by the ocean. This had occurred by fate rather than by design: a group of humans had driven me away from my natural habitat by invading it with their machines and destroying it for the wood of its trees. One day, our group decided to escape the carnage, but I became separated from my siblings. I walked many days in search of them, until I eventually reached the stretch of beach where I had now settled. Here, the locals possessed a deeper relationship with nature and accepted me as part of the landscape. Although I was not a ferocious hippo, they never disturbed me and generally kept their distance, even when leaving food for me. Thinking about it, I was a very tranquil specimen who did not resent humankind, despite their civilization being the very reason that had led to my separation from my kind.

But back to the present day ... half immersed in the ocean, I paddled my large feet and lifted my head above the waterline like a submarine periscope. I yawned and showcased my large teeth, one of which I had the misfortune to break during my younger years. I scoured the beach ahead: there was no one in close proximity. Confident that it was safe to surface, I emerged from the water, nonchalant and cool as the water ran down my coarse-grained body. As I reached the fine blonde sands, I took a couple of paces up the beach with the intention of turning around and sitting facing the ocean. This was when I noticed a young human running towards me. I was twice his height and although I could sense he meant me no harm, his sudden, unexpected appearance made me open my mouth wide and emit a loud noise as a deterrent. When I closed my jaws, I realized that the tiny human had stopped in his tracks, a few steps away from my imposing frame. He was staring at me in awe.

We looked at each other and he smiled, evidently unimpressed by the sheer size and hostile reputation of the animal in front of him. Young humans are unlike their elders: they display no fear and therefore do not project any hostility towards the animal kingdom. Nevertheless, and having once experienced the unpredictability of human behaviour, I remained on my guard.

'Mika, don't get close to the hippo! Leave it alone!' a masculine voice shouted in the distance. A tall adult human was standing on a red and white beach towel, a large multicoloured inflatable beach ball under one arm as he frantically waved at the young boy.

'Daddy, look, it is missing a tooth,' the boy shouted with excitement, pointing at me while turning his head towards his father.

I half opened my mouth again to confirm his observation. He turned to face me and studied my broken tooth, probably wondering how I could possibly have fractured it.

'Yes, I can see that. But come back here. It can be dangerous if you get too close,' his dad replied from afar.

'How did he lose a tooth?' the young boy shouted back, not moving an inch. 'It is so big I don't understand how it could have happened?' he said gesticulating. 'Do you think hippos have a tooth fairy?'

Although I did not comprehend his last comment, the little human sounded thrilled at the idea of it.

The very young boy named Mika stood still for a moment, then said to me in a compassionate tone, 'I'd love to bathe with you, but I'm not allowed to. I hope people treat you well. Good to be here with you, Mr or Mrs Hippo. I'll do a drawing of the two of us as soon as I am back home.'

'Good to be here with you too,' I nodded as he ran back to his parents, proud and joyful that he had temporarily, and peacefully, shared a stretch of beach with the colossal and fearsome animal that I am.

Printed by Amazon Italia Logistica S.r.l.
Torrazza Piemonte (TO), Italy